SECRETS

BOOK TWO

FIERCE HEARTS

LYNN CRANDALL

SECRETS

FIERCE HEARTS, BOOK ONE

Lynn Crandall

lives—real issues people live with daily. An engaging plot made it hard to put the book down.

"There is a broadness in this book's world where emotions and awareness of life beyond the physical are acknowledged. Her characters effectively illustrate the struggles of finding balance in the battle between self-protection and reaching for help while fearing to need it. The issue of being walled off to feel safe from the danger of being open and vulnerable are a familiar human experience. I'd like to follow this cast of characters in new adventures." Lynne McLewin, Counselor and Healer // Spiritual Counselor & Healer // Non-Dual Counselor & Healer // Energy Psychology Practitioner, for *Dancing with Detective Danger*

To Mike, for everything.

ACKNOWLEDGMENTS

Thank you to the sources who willingly shared accurate information in the making of this book: my son Jamie Kurtz, technology genius; Carol Scott, drug research specialist; Lynn McLewin, counselor and healer extraordinaire; and Susan Northrup, owner of Cat Snap cat rescue. A special thanks to my family and writer friends for their support. All of the cats in the story are named after either my own cats or cats who have strayed into my yard for food and water. Thanks to the efforts of the Champaign County Humane Society, Cat Snap, and Judy Warmbier, owner of Prairieland Anti-Cruelty Program, the homeless cats received veterinary care, were spayed or neutered and placed in forever homes.

CHAPTER 1

The fall breeze whispered over Michelle Slade's bare arms, sending shivers rolling through her body. Crouched low just inside the door on her back porch, she didn't dare move. One foot twitch, one loud breath, and the scruffy gray cat in her backyard would skitter away into the morning darkness. No sweet murmurs of "kitty, kitty, it's all right," would stop the cat or bring her back any time soon.

As the owner of a cat rescue, Cats Alive, Michelle was well practiced in the routine of supporting stray cats, whether that meant simply setting out food and water or capturing them for veterinary services, then releasing them. She'd spent weeks setting a pattern with this cat. A stray cat is always looking for food, so since she first saw the cat roaming the Laurelwood neighborhood, she'd made sure food and water was available in the backyard—a patch of grass behind her apartment that was semi-private. The cat, a female she'd named Madeline after one of her favorite authors, Madeleine L'Engle, readily made the yard a regular daily stop. Twice daily, in fact. Pattern set, phase one complete, Michelle was ready for phase two. Capture.

A feral, Madeline would never let Michelle touch her, much less pick her up and put her in a cat carrier. No, get close to her and she would just as soon tear off Michelle's face. So phase two involved a humane trap. Personally, she hated the trap for the feelings of terror it evoked in cats, but in her heart she knew it was necessary if she were to have any chance of capturing them and getting them spayed or neutered and possibly homed. Madeline was just one feral cat among a sea of homeless cats, but each cat, including Madeline, would have care and support and a home, if Michelle had her way.

After she moved into her new home on the outskirts of Laurelwood, the odds of capturing Madeline would be slim because she would no longer have access to Madeline's territory.

Madeline clearly noticed the trap, but the diced chicken used as bait was too tempting for her to ignore. Michelle held her breath, her legs cramping, as the cat approached the wire cage.

Good girl. A few more steps. It's okay, little girl.

The cat's steps into the cage were cautious, but there was that delicious meat at the back of the cage. Michelle's body tensed. This was the moment she'd been leading up to. This was her last morning in her apartment, so likely her last chance to help this cat. Her nerves screamed, *Do it!*

A snap sounded in the dawn air, startling the cat, and instantly the wire mesh door dropped down. Michelle remained quiet, letting the cat do her feline freak out. She felt for her. What a terrible feeling to suddenly be trapped. Michelle couldn't help the reaction that stirred inside her, watching Madeline hiss and yowl. Futilely. It triggered such strong, visceral memories, she had to swallow down the need to vomit. She was feeling it again—the helplessness, the terror that the man who'd attacked her in her freshman year at college had left her with.

Determined to stay on task, she rolled her shoulders, hoping the knot in her stomach, the one she'd been carrying around since that awful night five years ago when she was … she trembled at the word … raped, would settle down. Three deep breaths in and out and she unfurled her body from her perch on the porch and approached the carrier, speaking the words from her heart.

"It's okay, kitty. I mean you no harm."

The cat responded with a low growl, but she stopped thrashing.

Michelle stretched tall to ease the kinks in her muscles. Mid-stretch, a glimpse of something slipping along the hedge that bordered her yard made her pause. An eerie feeling slivered down her spine as she strained to catch a better look. *Nothing. Is this vigilance ever going to stop?*

Since that horrible night five years ago, she never felt safe, always prepared for the slightest hint of something unexpected to ruin her life once again. A roll of her shoulders dismissed her fears and put her mind back on Madeline. Michelle left her sitting in the trap on the back porch and went inside to dress.

She heard her roommate, Lara Monroe, rustle in the bedroom across the hall. Quietly, she pulled on a pair of jeans and a sweater. She looked around the sparse room for her tennis shoes. All her things but a few clothes and her bed had already been moved to her new home. Even her four cats were gone, visiting with her parents across town.

Michelle was so excited to officially move to her new home later today. The house and property were perfect, and it had a special connection to her past—it was the first house her parents had bought together. Now it was the first home she owned as well. Even though it was located in an area that was now zoned for industry—the zone-change slipped in just as she was closing on the house—the lot was large and gave her the seclusion she desired.

"Did you get her?" Her roommate's voice sounded sleep-gravelly.

Michelle's tension slipped away and her heart warmed, knowing her roommate cared as much as she did about the furry little souls who had no homes. Of course she did. Lara was a veterinarian. "Yes. I'm taking her to the vet as soon as the office opens."

"Seven?" Lara yawned. "Need help?"

"No, but remember there will be people here today to move the rest of my stuff."

A low groan came from across the hall, as Michelle walked to the kitchen and poured herself a cup of coffee to take with her.

The trip to one of the vets who provided services at little or no cost for her cat rescue was peppered with Madeline's pleas for release. The pitiful meows plucked at Michelle's heart. "I know, you don't like being in the cage. But everything is going to be just fine."

The cat answered with a snarl.

"That's okay. I won't take it personally."

She stepped inside the vet's office and smiled at the receptionist. The waiting room was quiet at this hour, but that wouldn't last long. Surgeries started the day for the veterinarian, but soon enough pets and their owners would start filling the waiting room.

"Hi, Michelle. I'll take the cat right back. Dr. Baker will do the usual exam and blood test. Assuming everything is all right, he'll do the spaying and the cat will be ready by about four this afternoon, but I'll text you when we have test results." The young vet assistant grabbed the handle of the trap and disappeared into another room.

Michelle turned to the receptionist. "Put this on my bill, Molly?"

"Sure. These cats are lucky you care, Michelle."

"The stream of needy cats never stops. I wish for something better for them, but at least we can improve their lives by removing the possibility of endless litters."

Molly nodded. "Right. And fewer fights among other cats. It's amazing what eliminating the mating drive does for the overall health of the cat."

Michelle checked the clock on the wall. Just enough time to make a quick trip back to her apartment to change and grab the mail, then get to the office. The private investigator sisters she worked for, Sterling and Lacey Aegar, gave her a wide zone of tolerance, but she didn't want to take advantage of their kindness. Still, arriving late was sometimes unavoidable, thanks to Cats Alive. Though it was difficult to handle the office management work for Aegar Investigations and run her not-for-profit cat rescue, she was used to a beyond-full load— she'd gotten her bachelor's degree in three years and her MBA in two —and at twenty-three years old, both endeavors meant a lot to her. She'd worked for the sisters while going to college and they were like family. The work for them paid her bills, and her cat rescue sat firmly in the center of her heart.

She made one stop at their favorite coffee shop, then breezed into the office just thirty minutes late. "Hey, it's just me. I bring one black coffee, dark roast, and one skinny vanilla latte." No reply from the sisters' private office made her pause. The door stood open, so she poked her head in and saw that both were on the phone. They each waved a hand and smiled, beckoning for the coffee.

At her desk, Michelle sipped her black coffee, venti, sorted the office mail, checked her email inbox for both the rescue and Aegar Investigations, and answered the most pressing correspondence first.

She paused mid-sentence in an email, focusing on a glimpse in her mind. A cloudy image of a cat walking into a trap, the door snapping down, and hands reaching to pick up the cage and carry it away. Strong foreboding gripped her heart and she tried to follow the image of the cage, focusing hard. But the premonition ended just as abruptly as it had appeared, leaving her troubled.

Premonitions, vague but noticeable thoughts and blurry images of possibilities to come, were a common occurrence for her. She'd had them for as long as she could remember, but as a child they'd scared her. They'd invaded her dreams, turning them into nightmares. She'd been advised they meant nothing and she should ignore them. Her parents hadn't known any better. It worked for a long while, until as an adult, she'd opened to them again. It hadn't felt right to repress them. She'd also learned she was a member of the twenty percent of the population that carries a trait of hypersensitivity—an ability to sense others' feelings and pick up emotions from objects. Her perceptions outweighed her premonitions, but the premonitions teamed with the perceptions to enhance her awareness of life around her. It could be difficult to tease apart her own feelings from what she picked up from others and from premonitions, but she was working on it.

She filed the disturbing premonition of the cat in a corner of her mind. Nothing dire seemed to pop up regarding Madeline, but still, she couldn't help but check her cell phone for a text from the vet, just as Sterling and Lacey walked out to her desk.

"Expecting some news?" Lacey sipped her latte, then arched an eyebrow at Michelle. "Thanks for the coffee. Did you get Madeline yet?"

She nodded her head. "Yes. This morning. She's at the vet now." It didn't surprise her that the sisters knew her routine of capture, spay or neuter, and release. Though they differed in appearance and personality—Lacey, the oldest, had long, curly, copper hair and a soft center, while Sterling, a former cop, had straight, shoulder-length, mahogany hair and an edge to her—they both had hearts of gold.

Michelle admired them. They'd been through so many hard things —the Aegar Curse, they called it. First it was the loss of their father, and their mother's resulting breakdown, leaving the sisters to essentially fend for themselves at a young age. Then it was the loss of Lacey's husband Nicholas—who had been murdered by the same crime family as their father—and his return as an embodied spirit. Though Nicholas's return had forced Lacey to move on from his death, it had also given them all a special gift of opening up the world in unexpected ways, including the experience of endless love.

The Aegar Curse didn't really exist, of course, but the family blamed the curse to relieve the immense pain of their senseless reality. And each time they came out the other end stronger.

Lacey was happily re-married to Jackson now—four months ago they'd married at the Justice of the Peace— and Sterling was still going strong with her husband Ben.

Sterling reached across the desk and put a hand on Michelle's shoulder. "No news is good news, right?"

"Maybe." Anxiety swirled in Michelle's gut, even though she had a feeling Madeline was okay. She played the anxiety in her mind for more information, but it wouldn't pin down. "If there's bad news, I want to get it over with." If tests revealed Madeline had feline leukemia, feline distemper, or feline immunodeficiency virus, she would have to be euthanized.

"I understand," Lacey said while Sterling nodded in agreement, her coffee in hand. "I'm glad you do. In my three years of working with homeless cats, too many have had unhappy endings." She chuckled, her nerves getting the best of her. "You'd think I would be able to take the deaths in stride by now, but I don't. It doesn't have to be like that."

"Right. If people would care enough to spay and neuter their cats and keep them inside, the incidence of fatal diseases would decrease. If only communities would care enough to take humane action to ensure the safety and wellbeing of its homeless cats." Lacey's words carried anger and sorrow at the same time.

"You're an angel, Michelle. You make a difference, and I for one am grateful for your efforts." Sterling slanted her head and smiled at her. "Making a difference in the lives of cats is your passion. And passion gets things done."

"Thanks. You guys are the best." Michelle took another look at her cell phone, then turned her attention to her own mail. Bills, bills, junk mail... She stopped breathing. "What's this?" Her cry stopped the sisters just inside their office doorway.

"What?" they chimed in together.

"Did you hear from the vet?" Lacey knitted her brow and waited.

Michelle tore into the envelope with a return address belonging to a lawyer. She didn't have anything lawyer-worthy going on, but it scared her anyway. Her heart thumped painfully in her chest. She stared at the text, disbelieving.

"Michelle, you're scaring me. What's going on?" Sterling planted her hands on her hips and waited.

Her heart racing, Michelle scanned the letter. "There must be some mistake." She lifted her gaze to meet Sterling's and Lacey's. "It says an undisclosed party is interested in purchasing my property. It says another title search revealed a problem with my deed and therefore my property is not secured as believed."

"That's nonsense. Let me see that." Sterling grabbed the letter, her eyes moving quickly over the text. "This may be a scam of some sort. You need to call your bank." She passed the letter to Lacey.

Michelle's gut went cold watching Lacey chew at her lower lip. While premonitions and perceptions were useful, they also could be unnerving. As she drew tight focus, she closed her eyes and her sense of it clarified. The anxiety gripping her wasn't so much about Madeline as this letter. Something was wrong with her property purchase, she could feel it.

"The bank wouldn't have given you the mortgage if the property wasn't free and clear, sweetie. Don't worry. It will get worked out." Lacey laid the letter on Michelle's desk.

Michelle rolled her eyes, sinking a bit into her chair. "I'm nearly all moved in. I love it there. I've always loved it."

Lacey nodded her head. "I know."

Despite their attempts at dismissing the letter, Michelle could see it in their faces. They were worried, too. She frowned. "You don't suppose the Aegar Curse applies to me, too, do you? We are like family."

"I swear, if that's true, we need to finally call in the help of a voodoo guy, or a shaman." Sterling put on a good face for her, and the mood in the room did lift a little at her suggestion.

Michelle breathed in and out, slowly. "I like the idea. Do you suppose voodoo guys are listed in the phone book or on the Internet?"

The phone rang and Michelle let out a squeal at the same time that Lacey jumped. "Girls, if that's a voodoo doctor I'm going to faint right here." Michelle knew Sterling was only making fun of the dark mood. Sterling would never faint.

Michelle answered the phone and smiled, the result of the sound of Casey Mitchell's lively voice on the other end. Working for serious and focused Jackson Carter, Lacey's husband and the owner of another detective agency in Laurelwood, hadn't diminished Casey's propensity to see life through an upbeat lens. Sometimes he was a problem child for Jackson because of his tendency to see humor and craziness in most things, but she enjoyed his easy temperament. It was a pleasure tinged with sorrow, because she sensed he held himself apart from others.

"Is this the crazy but beautiful blond cat lady of Laurelwood?" Teasing was his solid MO.

"No. You've got the wrong number." She never considered herself less than sane and loving cats did not make her so. She giggled. "Am I speaking to the crazy lawyer turned PI of Laurelwood?"

"Oh, that hurt. Seriously, do you have a minute? I'd like to drop by your office and deliver a small donation from my parents. Something to help keep your kitty rescue going another month. I also have a delivery of cat food."

"Lovely. When do you expect to be here? I can meet you outside."

She'd met Casey four months ago at a picnic at Lacey and Jackson's house. Their paths crossed now and then because of the close relationship between the sisters' husbands and Casey. Michelle appreciated Casey's friendship, but when they'd dated briefly she'd gotten scared and told him her life was too busy to have a serious relationship. He'd been gracious, but something was always there, unspoken, between them. Though he was fun to be around, he remained a bit aloof. Which worked for her, because she needed space with nearly everyone, a buffer zone, since her rape. Boundaries surrounded her that helped her feel in control. Though it made her sad that she couldn't enjoy closeness. *Another possibility taken from me by the man on the university quad.*

But seeing Casey always managed to elevate her mood. *Waiting for news about Madeline, getting bad news about my new home ... I could use a lift.*

They made arrangements to meet in the parking lot across the street from the office so Casey could load the cat food into her cherry red Jeep.

"I'm going out for a minute. I'll be right back," she called to the sisters.

Lacey ambled out. "Why don't you take the rest of the day off? Go finish moving, take care of Madeline, and look into this stupid letter you just got." She ran her fingers through her copper waves and looked stern, for Lacey. "We can manage without you and you need to take care of things."

Resting her chin on her hands, Michelle thought for a moment. It wasn't like she couldn't handle these pressing things, she was a big girl. Still, it would ease her concentration to address them sooner rather than later. "Hmm ... I guess you're right." She grabbed her fall jacket from the back of her chair and shrugged it on as she headed out. "Thank you."

Outside, she buttoned up her coat and waited for Casey. The fall air felt crisp and clear as she breathed it in. It sharpened her thoughts.

Alone with her buzzing brain, Michelle let the possibilities of problems with her new home expand. How could anything be wrong? She'd done all the right things. It had to be a mistake. It dampened her excitement for getting settled in. The home held so many good memories of growing up and being a family—Michelle had lived there into her teens before her parents sold the house and moved into a bigger one across town. The thoughts of losing the house churned inside her gut like a bad cheeseburger from a fast-food place. It would be her haven, her safe place, a place where she could keep out the fears that had invaded her life that fateful night.

She shuddered, letting the various versions of emotions floating by from passing people pass through her. As a highly sensitive person, or HSP according to the experts on the subject, she was still learning not to let emotions of others swamp her. She could feel the anger, just know it wasn't hers to act out, her counselor told her. Funny how much the chaos of emotions floating around felt like hers. She didn't mind being abnormal, with her premonitions and high sensitivity, but it did bog her down at times.

It was one of those times, months ago, when she and Casey sat in a booth together at a fast-food restaurant and the wailing of a small boy about his food sent Michelle into a sobbing ball, that she'd told him her secret, her premonitions and sensitivities, known only by those close to her. When she'd shared it with Casey, he'd never blinked. He simply questioned about her experiences in great detail, trying to understand. His interest had warmed her heart and it had felt good to be forthright about her strangeness. A smile lifted her lips as she remembered his teasing about having to wear aluminum foil on his head around her.

"Hey, gorgeous!"

Michelle jumped, stiffened at the hand on her shoulder. It was Casey.

"Whoa there. Sorry, I didn't mean to startle you." His eyes narrowed, searching her face. "Deep thoughts?"

"I didn't hear you coming." Her private thoughts were just that, private. She shot him a smile. Heck how could she not? His face, a beautiful shade of brown framed by dark, short dreads, practically glowed with personality. "You're stealthy."

His eyes shuttered for a just a moment. "You're just distracted."

Though she felt his typical distance, kindness emanated from him. For a moment she allowed feelings for him to emerge, cautiously. "Well, hey, you know me. I get distracted easily." It felt good to smile up at him and be met with a wink. His golden brown eyes glinted back at her. She imagined how nice it would be to have that in her daily life. She naturally relaxed around him. Though she'd always sensed his reservations about sharing his private life. He was hiding something, but she never pushed him to explain and she'd never shared her dark secret about the rape.

He gave her a look, then slid a muscled arm around her shoulder and tweaked a lock of her long blond hair. "I do know you. Now, shall we load this cat food into your Jeep so you can get back to work?"

"I'm not going back to work, but yes, let's get it done so we can both get out of the cold. Be sure and thank your parents for me. You do have parents, right? Weird I've never met them."

Casey smirked. "Of course I have parents. My mom's a teacher and my dad's a dentist."

She nodded, noting the lilt of love and pride emanating from him. "So you have a good relationship with them."

"Yeah, they're all right." Suddenly his brow knitted. "Wait, it's only ten o'clock. Why aren't you going back to work?"

Michelle dropped her gaze and rubbed her toe against a crack in the sidewalk. Talking to Casey would relieve her anxiety, she knew from experience. But it wasn't his concern.

He lifted her chin to face his gaze. "C'mon. I won't tell Sterling and Lacey you want to play hooky."

"They gave me the day off." The touch of his hand made her skin warm. "I've got several things going on today, so they suggested I tie up ends."

Another smile unleashed. "Oh. I thought you might spend the day with me." He rolled his shoulders, nervously, then slanted a smile her way. "Get you more settled in at your new house. Spend some time together."

Her heart clenched. His interest in her was subtle but she felt it. It had popped up before and she'd ignored it. Ignoring was getting harder. But she just wasn't ready for more than friendship. Not yet. "Casey, I'm sorry. I can't."

He bunched his hair in both hands and slanted a somber gaze at her. "What are we talking about here? We're friends, Michelle. Can't we spend time together?" He shook his head. "I'm sorry. I know you have your reasons for needing space."

"And so do you," she whispered.

Casey flinched, as though she'd just sucker punched him. Conflicted feelings rose in him, unsettling her insides. They stood across from each other as seconds ticked by, traffic noise filling the space between them. Then, silently, he lugged several large bags of cat food to her Jeep while she watched, mesmerized by his sleek physique as much as his ability to dampen down his emotions to a place of indifference.

Check in hand and a thank you given, Michelle drove away from him as he stood beside his blue Prius. A last look in her rearview mirror caught him coaxing a brown tabby, a city stray, from behind his car and cautiously offering a bit of kibble.

* * *

"Here, little kitty. I know you're hungry. Here's some good stuff." Casey knelt and dropped a bit of cat food on the ground in front of him. The short-haired tabby shot him a saucer-eyed look and retreated.

"It's okay. You can have the food. No strings attached. How about I call you Brownie? It fits." He stood motionless, knowing the timid cat needed and wanted the food. Lucky for Brownie, he had a way with cats. Suddenly, the cat lunged and grabbed the food in her mouth, then withdrew a few feet to chomp it up. "You've made my day, Brownie. Thanks for being so brave."

When he stood the cat ran out of sight. That was to be expected. A stray in the city lived a hard life. Often city strays were kicked around in their endless search for food. He didn't blame them for being wary. It was the safe thing to do.

It was the smart thing to do. He smiled to himself, conscious of the stirring inside him of another part of him. His were-lynx self. Humans believed themselves to be the most self-aware, intelligent species on the planet, but it just wasn't so. Animals were intuitive and resourceful. Heck, were-lynxes had successfully kept their existence secret from humans for centuries. And they peacefully coexisted in colonies among humans. His colony, of which he had recently been made leader of, consisted of seven other young lynxes. There were more colonies, but they didn't interact. Each colony was unique and reflected the personalities and special abilities of its members.

On his way back to Carter, Inc., his best friend Jackson Carter's investigations business, Casey let out thoughts of Michelle. *If only I could have a way with her like I did with Brownie. Get her to trust me.*

The way Michelle had looked up into his face with those deep sapphire-blue eyes made his gut clench. Michelle was a strong woman who went after what she wanted and tackled whatever had to be done. But her gleaming golden hair gave her an ethereal sense and there also was a delicate vulnerability to her that he respected. Her heart was tender and loving, and she was full of life. But she carried a dark fear that kept her distant. Their friendship blossomed easily when they'd first met and he now struggled with a growing desire for closeness with her. Despite his need for privacy and to keep humans at a distance, Michelle had gotten to him in a way he'd really taken to. She fascinated him. And he'd begun to invite her to get closer.

Apparently keeping her distance was too important to her. Whatever drove her away, it had to be a powerful darkness, because it never left her. The days they'd spent hiking she'd let down her guard.

When the darkness in her lifted, the real Michelle came out—exuberant and confident. Then the shield would slip back into place.

The irony of her distance made him cringe. He had his secrets, clearly. And not just the really big one of his animal self. Like many young new lynxes, he'd used his inherent skills for his own benefits. He hadn't cared about consequences. He'd stolen some very nice things from the rich, but he'd gotten caught. Once. So his sentence was easy. He'd done his probation and wised up. Thanks to his father's guidance and Jackson's friendship, his brief stint as a cat burglar was behind him, never to surface again. He'd earned his law degree and worked as a specialist in medical matters. Then Jackson had convinced him to get his investigator's license and work for him. He worked among humans and socialized with humans and the members of his colony. And no human, not even Jackson, knew of his secret identity. Despite his respect for the need for secrecy, it was becoming more and more of a burden. As he'd watched Jackson struggle with his father's deceit and destructive ways, Casey's values adjusted. Needling razors cut at his life-long beliefs, demanding he make a choice. Be himself or a shadow of himself. He wanted to be himself, nothing holding back, among trustworthy humans.

With his baggage to deal with, he'd wondered at Michelle's. The evenings they'd spent together at her apartment she'd been tense. He'd never pushed for intimacy. The memory of kissing her luscious lips sent him tripping, but they'd never gone further than that one kiss.

But he still cared and though she didn't know, he did what he could to keep her safe. Whenever possible, he was never far from her, just out of sight. Whatever the darkness was, he wanted to be near if it threatened her again.

He parked and took swift steps to his office, and jumped into his work for the day. As a lawyer with a specialty in medical cases, Casey's workload was constant. This morning his inbox contained more than two hundred emails, but one in particular headed "medical device" from a client he'd helped secure a patent for grabbed his attention. He read through the email, his gut knotting, then printed the email and accompanying attachment.

"Is Jackson available?" he asked the secretary outside Jackson's office. The young woman was a pretty blond, but after the last secretary had conspired with her boyfriend to ruin Jackson's business, a thorough background check for the current secretary had been completed. Jackson had learned that education and a pretty face wasn't enough in a secretary. He needed someone who would be trustworthy.

"Yes, Casey." She twinkled an engaging smile at him. "I'll let him know you're here."

"No, I'll just go on in. Thanks, Julie."

A knock on Jackson's office door and Casey poked his head in. "Got a few minutes, boss?"

"Sure, come take a seat." Jackson sat back in his chair behind his desk and waited for him. "I'm actually just going over the guest list for the reception for Lacey and me."

Casey rolled his eyes. "I couldn't talk you two out of a tiny wedding at the courthouse, so I'm happy you're planning something big to celebrate with all your friends and family. You sure are taking your sweet time to have the reception. I can't wait for the party to begin. But meantime, there is work to take care of."

"Wow, that was quite the segue, guy. What's up?"

"This is up." Casey laid the email and the document that accompanied it in front of Jackson. "It seems the data device we helped Pretid, the developer, trademark is creating some issues."

"I see that." Jackson scoured the complaint report Pretid had shared with Casey. "The company's devices for clinical trials are selling well, but doctors are reporting patients with health problems relating to use of the data collected."

"Right. A patient in a clinical trial for an insulin pump went into insulin shock."

"Stuff happens in clinical trials, unexpected stuff. That's the reason for the trial." Jackson shook his head. "But this was a phase two for the pump. There shouldn't be this kind of incident."

"I can get a list from Pretid of all sales. See if I can narrow down a clinical research organization and location that matches the reporting issues."

Jackson ran his hand through his hair and squinted. "Can Pretid give you access to their subject database? Maybe there is a pattern there that would point to a sales batch or something."

Casey let out a long breath. The implications of a trial gone amuck were ominous. The Federal Drug Administration took great care to ensure safety in clinical trials and valid results before permitting release of a drug. However, there was a lot of money in creating new drugs, and people who wanted to corrupt the system could, as both he and Jackson knew too well. An angry man had run a fake trial last summer just to get back at Jackson's father for firing him. No one had died in the process, but a drug with bad side effects had been on its way to being released for prescription use.

"The device is solid. If trial subjects are having health issues, someone has tampered with it. I'll get right on this." Playfully, he saluted Jackson.

Jackson glared at him. "This is serious, Casey."

He shrugged. "I know. It's just been a serious morning." He wouldn't tell Jackson that he was managing so many serious things right now he needed to lighten up.

Leaving Jackson's office, Casey knew a good run tonight was in order.

CHAPTER 2

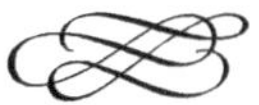

Michelle stepped through the garage entry door into her kitchen and breathed in deeply. She slowly took in the kitchen, admiring the light pine cupboards and drawers and light blue and white linoleum on the floor. She ran her hand over the butcher block countertop, then caressed the stainless steel appliances. A toasty warmth spread through her body, as she enjoyed the solid presence of her new home.

Two thumps and four unique meows announced her cats as they raced into the kitchen. "Hi, babies." Her mother had brought over the cats earlier.

She paused. Standing in the archway between the kitchen and her living room, she felt like dropping to the floor and relaxing into the thick, soft, brown carpeting, then lighting a fire in the stone fireplace and lounging there. The décor embraced her in pleasant hues of dark blue and cocoa. Everything was perfect.

She dipped her head, a heavy rock dropping hard into her stomach. Perfect except for the problems with the deed.

The weight of Madeline in the carrier Michelle carried in her left hand reminded her to take care of the cat. She headed down the carpeted hallway and into the spare room, a place Madeline could have peace and quiet from the other cats in the house. Michelle tiptoed to the doorway and closed the door behind her. Madeline stirred just a bit in her carrier, still groggy from the anesthesia she'd had today for her spaying. Tomorrow morning would be back to normal hissing and growling.

Michelle checked the kitchen clock her mother had given her. It was shaped like a large cat with a clock in its stomach and the tail ticked off the seconds, moving back and forth.

Dinner time. She hadn't given much thought to dinner. Now at six o'clock, she realized she'd forgotten to pick up some food before coming home from the vet. She stared into a cupboard, then another, both empty. The third cupboard made her smile. Her mom apparently had suspected food would be a welcome treat and stocked some snacks for her when she brought over the cats. At least she'd have crackers and popcorn to eat tonight, and tomorrow morning she would have coffee.

A knock at the kitchen door made her grab her throat. She didn't have time to recoup, because the knock was immediately followed by two people.

"Hi, Michelle." Sterling stepped through the doorway, smiling brightly.

Lacey followed. "You can't be mad that we're dropping in without calling first. We brought dinner." She held up a pizza box, smiling as though she'd brought Michelle a prized roasted turkey, complete with stuffing.

Her nerves all shot to hell, Michelle took a deep breath and tried to stop trembling. She chuckled. "I'm sorry. You startled me. You know me, easily startled. But you brought pizza. Thank you!" She turned to the cupboards and pulled out plates and glasses. Before she could turn to the table, the sisters both put their arms around her.

"We understand." Lacey rested her head on Michelle's shoulder.

Sterling slanted her head and drew Michelle closer. "We should have called first. Are you sure you're going to be okay here by yourself tonight?" Sterling bent to nuzzle Jojo, a yellow tabby who had just done a drive-by on her leg.

She dropped her gaze and shuddered. "I don't want to think about *that* again. Not on my first night in my new home. I'm not going to let him take that away from me." She shook off the dark feeling that rose in her chest so easily. She pointed at the yellow tabby. "See! I'm not alone. I'll be fine. Jojo is here, as you can see, and so are Izabelle, Munchy, and Tiger. They've already made themselves comfortable in the new home."

The pizza in the middle of her kitchen table, Michelle joined Sterling and Lacey and downed a slice quickly. "Starvation has been abated, thanks to my two amazing bosses!"

Sterling and Lacey nodded, their mouths full.

Sterling wiped her mouth. "Yes, we are amazing," she said, then ducked when Lacey swung a hand at her head.

"You nut. We're all amazing." Lacey nodded toward Michelle.

While Lacey and Sterling listed the many things that made them all amazing, Michelle listened, comfortable with the banter. The love and fun and understanding between them filled the room with a soothing sense of harmony, as though everything that had gone wrong with her day didn't stand a chance of infiltrating this space right now.

"Okay, we've waited long enough. Tell us, what happened with Madeline? Is she well and sterile now? Where is she?" Sterling took another bite of pizza and eyed her.

"Geez, Sterling. Nothing like being direct." Lacey rolled her eyes.

"I'm happy to tell you hissing Madeline is sleeping well in the back room, recuperating from her ordeal and her surgery. Tests were negative. One for the good guys, this time."

"High five!" Lacey raised her palm and Michelle and Sterling slapped it. "Tomorrow you'll release her here?"

"That's the plan. First thing tomorrow. I'm not taking her back to the apartment property. It's too dangerous, with the highway nearby. There's lots of outdoor space here for her to roam. She'll be as safe as she can be as an outside cat."

They ate in silence for a few moments. Michelle suspected the sisters had questions about the letter she'd received that morning.

Then, as though reading her thoughts, Lacey squared her with a look. "So, no news is good news?"

Michelle dropped her gaze to the table. "Not really. I talked to the loan officer this afternoon about the letter. He seemed really surprised. He left me to talk to his supervisor, and when he came back he gave a closed-off vibe. Claimed sometimes things like this happen. We left it with his promise to dig into it and get back to me as soon as he can." She looked up and met the sisters' eyes. "I don't know anything more than I did this morning, but I'm all moved in and I'm expecting to stay."

She looked away again. She didn't want to see pity in their eyes. Furry, long-haired Munchy waltzed in to the kitchen and meowed. Loudly. "Time for dinner for her, too."

"Michelle, it's hard not to know what's going to happen, but focus on being positive. I know you have premonitions, feelings, and they're valid. But nothing is in stone. Things can shift." Lacey grabbed the plates and stuck them in the sink, while Michelle scooped Munchy's kibble into a blue ceramic bowl with little white parading cats around its circumference.

Leaning against the counter, she chewed on her bottom lip. "I do have a bad feeling, but I don't actually know what that means."

Sterling frowned. "It stinks, totally stinks. But I agree with Lacey. If there is anything we can do, don't hesitate to say, Michelle. We're not just your bosses, we're friends. Friends who can investigate."

"You guys are the best. Thank you for being supportive. And thank you for the pizza. You're life-savers." Just then two more cats appeared, focusing their pointed expressions on Michelle. "I know, Izabelle, feed you. You, too, Tiger."

Their goodbyes said and Sterling and Lacey out the door, Michelle set about feeding any stray cats in the area. On the back porch, from inside a big plastic container filled with kibble, she scooped out enough to fill a small plastic bucket and carried it out to her yard. She set the bucket on the ground beside a dish of water, then lingered.

The hedges around her backyard gave her a sense of privacy and containment in the darkness of the fall night. Leaves on the four trees in her large back yard rustled. She breathed in deeply, savoring the crisp feel of air. This is what she'd wanted, the feeling of being home, enveloped by warm memories of growing up in this home with her parents and having space and privacy to do whatever she wanted.

A full moon in the starry night bathed the yard in a soft glow. She started imagining the things she could do here. Maybe even dance in the moonlight. The thought lifted her mood. *Why not?* Humming to herself, Michelle sunk into the sounds, scents, and feelings of the moment, and began moving to her inner music. She was free, alone here in her own yard. Nothing to worry about. Tension seeped away from her muscles. She slowly turned to a rhythm inside her, savoring the sense of self that rose in her, her eyes closed.

A noise from the bushes crackled, and instantly her muscles tensed. Still and on alert, Michelle peered through the darkness. It could be a stray, she thought, seeking food. If it was a homeless cat, it was too late to prevent scaring it. A movement of any sort would send it running.

So she stood still in the spot, waiting and squinting her eyes for a better look.

She held her breath, and as she did, a large figure of a furry animal slipped silently through the hedge, away from her.

Automatically, her hand slapped over her mouth. Her heart raced. Her breath came in deliberate pulls. That figure, that animal, was not at all what she'd expected to appear out of the shadows. She dropped her hand to her side and stepped cautiously toward the spot where the animal had disappeared.

The hedge bordered her half-acre backyard and split it from the rest of her property. The place in the hedge where the animal slipped through meant a short walk away from the security of her house, but she'd be damned if she was going to let that deter her from a possible identification of that animal.

She shivered in the cold air, taking measured steps to the spot, her senses perched on the edge of her nerves. She noticed a small opening in the hedge. The large animal would have had to crouch low to the ground to get through. She leaned low and tried to see through to the other side, but she saw nothing but dry weeds.

The hedge stood about to her chin, so standing on tiptoe, Michelle searched the field on the other side for another glimpse of the animal.

"Geez!" She instinctively took a step back when her gaze collided with the animal as it sat still in the field, barely visible. Inexplicably, it sat motionless, staring at her. *Can it see me?* she wondered. Her heart thumped wildly in her chest. She longed to get a better look, but she didn't dare slip through the hedge. It seemed completely at ease, sitting there staring at her through glistening eyes.

Dare she speak? Fairly mesmerized, Michelle whispered to the animal. "I mean you no harm."

She waited. Her eyes were adjusting to the darkness, so she focused them on the figure. It looked to have a large body covered with thick fur. Its head had a feline appearance and ears tipped with dark tufts of fur. *Distinctive markings of a lynx.*

Chills rolled up and down her spine. She couldn't explain why she wasn't afraid, other than the vibes she was picking up across the space between her and the animal were gentle, not threatening.

"I mean you no harm," she repeated.

The animal chuffed, then stood and began walking into the woods at the outskirts of her property. She didn't move, instead taking in its graceful walk. A few steps away, it stopped, twisted its head around to look at her, and chuffed again. A few more steps into the night and the animal was gone.

Back inside her house, Michelle ran her fingers through her hair, trying to wrap her brain around what just happened. She'd lived here all of her childhood. She'd roamed the fields that surrounded the house. The fields and the forest were her playground. Never once had she come across a large animal like she'd seen tonight. If she was right and it was a lynx, it surely was a predator of some sort, but it had made no attempt to make her its dinner.

Michelle parted her kitchen curtains and scanned the backyard. In the darkness she saw a mother cat and her kittens approach the food bucket. *Cool.* The feeling of giving these cats, who probably were homeless, a meal and a drink of water was a familiar and pleasant feeling. It was funny that the mother didn't feel protective with her kittens in an area where a big predator had just stood. She let the curtains fall back in place and turned to lean against the counter.

What an exciting first night in my new home. She checked the perky clock on the wall again to see the evening was still young, and contemplated her day. Before her thoughts got off to much of a start, a knock at her front door pulled them to an abrupt halt.

She walked into her living room to the front door and peered through the peek hole. A smile from Casey greeted her, and she opened the door to let him in.

He bowed like a goofball and presented her with a basket of fruit. "My lady, a bit of fruit?"

"You nut. Thank you, kind sir." She curtsied, laughing. "What brings you to my part of Laurelwood?"

"I'll be honest. You. Besides, I was in the area, and I wanted to make sure you're settled in and feeling secure." He cast an inquisitive glance around the living room, then headed through the hall to the kitchen.

"Go ahead, make yourself at home." She spread her arms wide and followed him. He didn't appear at all aware that he was making himself at home without asking for her consent. "I appreciate you checking, but I'm fine."

"Good." He stopped by the refrigerator. "Got anything to drink?"

"Water."

"That's not what I was thinking of, but thanks." He continued to stand in place, and she couldn't help but wonder what he was thinking. She didn't want to feel anything but her own emotions, so she closed herself to what he might bring to her.

"I saw a mother cat with three kittens walking across the street. Did they find you already?"

Despite her efforts, she felt questions roll off him, and a genuine feeling of concern. "Yes. I'm glad. There is no shortage of homeless cats in need of food and water." She pursed her lips. What did he want to know, really?

He shot a direct gaze at her, making her squirm. What was that in his eyes?

"I don't want to overstep, Michelle, I know you need your space." His eyes pinned her, asking her for something. "But I'm always going to be looking after you. I hope that is comforting to you, not threatening. I mean you no harm."

The words, words she'd just used, held so much unspoken meaning. She shifted on her feet. "You're not a stalker?"

Casey unleashed one of his amazing smiles, and it washed over her like a gentle swell in Lake Michigan. "No, not a stalker."

"Good. Because I've had one of those already." Instantly she regretted letting that piece of information escape.

"What? When? Who?" His brown eyes darkened.

"Oh, it was a long time ago. Just some guy." Michelle wrapped her arms around herself and tried to look deadpan.

Casey's smile turned sad. He rubbed his chin with his thumb, drawing her attention to his face. How could she push him away? Underneath his shirt his taut chest muscles strained the fabric, enticing her to touch. She knew from experience that delicious smooth skin the color of rich coffee wore beautifully over his firm six-pack. But despite his physical appeal, Casey's soul stood as his finest attribute.

"No. We're friends. I would never want to hurt you. But to be honest, do I want something different with you?" His gaze dropped for a brief moment, then his eyes came back to her face. "It's irrelevant. If it's meant to be, you and me, it will happen. I'm not going to push you, Michelle. I don't know what terrible thing happened to you, but I know something did. I can see it in you."

She stretched up straight, the weight of his sincerity lying like a slab of granite in her belly. Why were things always so complicated? She knew the answer. Because simplicity had been taken from her. But she could use Casey's friendship right now, as things were uncertain. "Well, we don't have to go back beyond this morning to find something potentially terrible." She pulled the letter from her purse on the counter and passed it to him.

His eyes quickly read through the letter and his mouth dropped open. "What the heck?" He read it again. "Who does this lawyer represent? What did your bank say?"

His eyes flashed at her and his voice lowered, ending in a barely audible low growl in his throat. She knitted her brow, taken aback by his intensity. "I don't know what's going on. My bank mortgage officer promised to look into it. It was an odd meeting, though."

"Odd how?" Casey stooped down to scratch the yellow tabby's ears. Jojo leaned into his hand, purring loudly.

"The loan officer at first said it was nothing to worry about, because a thorough title search had been completed, but he talked to a supervisor and came back acting all nervous. No explanation, but he said he'd check into it and get back to me." Michelle ran her fingers through her hair, then shrugged. "But I'm here now."

He stood and peered intently at her. "So, stiff upper lip and all that?"

She chuckled, her nerves jangling. "Yes. What doesn't kill you makes you stronger."

A smile spread across his face. Despite his intensity, his calm demeanor enveloped her in strength and confidence. "You sound like Sterling and Lacey. I'm sorry for this problem cropping up. How about I do a pro bono? I'll look into this, and you do me a favor, maybe find a home for a cat I might pick up from the street. Deal?"

"You call yourself a lawyer. It wouldn't be pro bono," she teased. "It would be exchanging favors. Quid pro quo."

"Details. Do we have a deal?" He slanted his head and gazed at her, emanating fondness she couldn't ignore.

She offered him her hand. "Deal."

He grabbed hers firmly and shook. "Deal." He kissed her on the forehead, lingered for the space of a breath, then paused. "Sleep well."

Michelle watched Casey climb into his Prius, smiling to herself that it fit him so well. He cared about the environment, so of course he was one of the first among her friends to buy an eco-friendly car. A sleek sports car would be a good fit with his strong, athletic build, but he wouldn't choose that over low emissions.

As he backed out of her driveway, she shut the door and stood still to savor the moment she'd had with Casey. Somehow he'd managed to cheer her up without even trying. His words assuring her he was watching out for her worked some magic, the opposite of making her feel trapped and uneasy. He had an inexplicable air of wildness to him, but it didn't scare her. It was just Casey. No, he hadn't been the problem in their relationship, that was all her. Her, and the man who hurt her years ago.

Sorrow leadened her steps down the hall to her bedroom. The work she'd done with a good counselor had helped, she knew that. So why couldn't she stand to let Casey close?

Undressed and settling into her bed, Michelle watched her family of cats join her and nestle into a comfortable place.

CASEY DROVE his car down the lane that separated Michelle's property from the grove of trees that attempted to hide a small industrial facility next door. Slowly, he drove about a block down the lane, then turned into the field beside her home and parked among the tall grasses. Quickly he pulled off his clothes, laid them on the seat beside him, and climbed out. A quick look around in the darkness told him he was alone, so without hesitation he shimmered.

He dropped down on all fours, and stretched and shook from head to toes, fully inhabiting his lynx body. He breathed deeply of the crisp air. It filled his nose and his lungs with the exhilaration of nature. Inside his head he chuckled, thinking of the television and movie versions of many were-animal transformations. All bone-bending and painful. Not true, at least not for him. Shifting from his human form to his lynx form and back again for him was as smooth and effortless as, well, a shimmer. Of course it was easy. It was a natural process for his body.

Whether he was in lynx form or in the form of a man, he had unusually keen senses of sight, smell, and hearing, in addition to an extra, special ability. All were-lynxes had keen senses as well as something special. His was the ability to see through solid objects. It was something he could turn on and off simply by concentrating, but it was limited. He could see through one solid object at a time. The heightened senses intensified experiences for him, and served as useful and pleasant traits. He raised his nose to gather a mixture of scents. None of them were threatening. Clearly, feral cats made this property a regular route on their travels in search for food and shelter. Michelle had picked a home right in their paths.

Sounds of small animals racing swiftly to safety stirred the meadow and nearby forest.

Sure, he was a predator, but any animal that got close enough to him would sense he wasn't a threat. He chose not to hunt his natural prey—rabbits—or any other kind of wildlife in favor of doing his hunting in grocery stores and eating as his human self. A good steak with roasted vegetables suited his tastes.

He took off in a brisk stroll around the perimeter of Michelle's two acres, checking for anything or anyone out of place. Relying on his keen senses felt as natural as shimmering, so he gathered scent and sound and tactile information about the property. His visual sense was especially keen, even in the dark, so he stopped in places and surveyed until he was satisfied all was well.

He headed back to his car, noticing noises coming from the industrial complex about two blocks away through the line of trees and stretch of grassy spaces. He didn't know what was produced there but he soon would. That would be another night's project.

He strode a few more spaces, then rested on his haunches, revisiting the moment in the field before Michelle caught him prowling.

The image of her dancing carefree in her yard would stay with him. She'd swayed and circled to the song insider her head, eliciting desires in him to take her in his arms and join her in that lovely dance. Had he wanted her to see him or had he just been clumsy enough to attract her attention? Either way, she'd stood there alone with him in that shared moment in the field.

The space between them stretched so far, her a human and him a lynx. His gut twisted with the knowledge that she was right, they could only be friends. But in the sacred moment when they'd stared at each other with no expectations, she'd been unafraid and kind. How could a human, a beautiful woman like that do harm to him or his species? In those moments, face to face with Michelle, the ache of deep loneliness had reached out to her for relief.

A shriek from an owl pierced the quiet, bringing Casey back to the moment, and he trotted off to his car. He stood still, taking in the full-on awareness of everything around him. He loved the damp earth beneath his paws, the mossy scent of the air, and the scriping and scraping of tree branches in the wind. He was a city were-cat, through and through, but still, the wildness of his nature took to a natural setting like the proverbial fish to water.

He opened his mind and body to the image of his human self and shimmered.

A regular shimmer and run was a necessary routine to ensure an easy transition. But beyond that, a run tended to clear his mind and set his tempo to something akin to a natural pace. It calmed his soul and assured him it was always there, running in the background, supporting his ups and downs in life.

As he drove home from Michelle's, images of her standing in her kitchen and looking out the window tonight accelerated his heartbeat. Her blond hair framed her face like an elegant drape. A chuckle burst from him at the way his mind thought of her. She was beautiful, but rarely elegant. Michelle was just as adorable in her jeans and a T-shirt, crawling on the ground to coax a stray kitten toward her, as she was dressed in a short dress that clung alluringly to her slim figure.

She was all that—beautiful, alluring, quirky, and elegant—and so much more. He tightened his grip on the steering wheel, as thoughts of her sad and frightened invaded his mind. Chaos stirred his typically calm emotional center. His brief relationship with Michelle had changed him forever. Every woman he'd ever dated had been a distraction from his loneliness, one that never lasted long. With Michelle, the connection between them had shattered any illusions that a distraction was enough. For the time they were together, he'd been gifted with a kind of intimacy he'd never had. It got into his cells and bloomed into something huge and wonderful. And when they'd broken up he was all the more lonely and alone for having had something meaningful and real, and lost it.

His parents had always preached to him to stick with his own kind. They watched and weighed in every time he'd dated a human, reminding him of the problems of keeping ancient lines healthy and sustaining the secrecy of the colony. But their words held little weight, since they had done the opposite of their advice. His mother was human and his dad was a pure were-cat.

But nature is a powerful force. And as a part of nature, love follows no lines or rules, it just is. Yet, his love and longing for Michelle with no hope of its acceptance tore up his insides.

CHAPTER 3

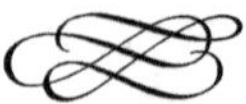

*S*till gravelly from sleep, Michelle spoke endearments to all four cats, who took turns rubbing her legs, then tiptoed into her spare room where Madeline sat in a carrier. She wanted to reassure the sweet soul that everything would be okay and that she could start a new life here on the property surrounding her new home.

Instead she said nothing, knowing the sweet nothings she wanted to say would only upset the feral cat. Best to simply put out food and release her in the backyard.

She carried the carrier to the enclosed portion of her back porch, grabbed the cat food bucket from the yard, and refilled it. *Hmm...something ate the food I put out last night.* The possibility that other ferals had already found the food was nearly as exciting as finding gold in her backyard. Her heart beating in her throat as Madeline growled, Michelle gently put down the carrier beside the food bucket and lifted the wire door. A blur of gray fur bounded through the yard and under the hedge. Sending good wishes of a healed surgical site and safe travels with the cat, Michelle took a look at her property. *My property. It's gorgeous and it's all mine.* She released a heavy breath. *At least today it is.*

She soaked in the soothing sounds and sensations of her new

home. They drifted through her body and glowed in her heart. She was home. Really home. She'd be safe here, surrounded by privacy and the memories of her childhood.

Inside, she checked the time and realized it was still early, so she sat down in front of her laptop at the kitchen table to check her emails for anything pressing with her network of cat fosters or requests for help with a cat. Jojo jumped up onto the table and rubbed his face against her typing hands. "Hey there, sweetie!" she said, nuzzling his face, then turning back to her emails.

Her inbox was full of requests for help with cats and invitations to participate in upcoming adoption events for non-profit animal care organizations. One email grabbed her attention.

"A mother cat and her two kittens were dumped in my yard. Please help me capture them and get them adopted into a good home," Michelle read out loud. Urgency spread through her body. She never got used to the cruelty people could bring to cats, but for now she had to focus on getting these cats safe.

She was in the middle of composing a response when a knock at the front door startled her. Quietly, she walked to the front door and peered through the peephole. Her former roommate's happy face, framed by short curtains of deeply dark hair, smiled at her.

She flung open the door and pulled her friend inside. "Oh, what a nice surprise, Lara.

Come in."

"I miss you already," Lara said, laughing. "I wanted to stop in for a minute. I know you have to get to work." She swiveled her head around, perusing the living room, then followed Michelle to the kitchen.

"I was just tending to Cats Alive business. Sit down. I'll make coffee."

"Thank you, but I can't stay. Just wanted to see how you were doing. Where's our girl Madeline?"

Michelle motioned to the backyard while filling the carafe from the faucet. "Out there somewhere. I released her a few minutes ago."

Lara pulled the kitchen curtains aside and surveyed the yard.

"Wow, I know I saw all this when I helped move you in, but it's so beautiful. I'm jealous. Nice house, nice yard. I love the natural setting. Probably lots of ferals around."

"I'll find out." She pursed her lips. "I saw a wild lynx last night out there."

Lara twisted a lock of her dark hair around her index finger. "Hmm...I doubt it. In North America, lynx habitat is mainly in Canada and Alaska and some northern parts of the United States. They've been reintroduced in Colorado."

"So, not an animal typically seen in the Midwest. But I know what I saw. It was very furry, had a short, bobbed tail, and dark ear tufts. It was wandering on the edge of my yard last night and into the field." Michelle's curiosity was piqued. If not a lynx, then what was the animal she'd seen? "He paused in the field and stared at me a few seconds, then paced away."

"Scary?"

"No. It was a bit eerie, but I didn't get any sense from it that it was dangerous." Michelle shivered, thinking about the lynx's eyes. "It was like he could see right through me." A short burst of laughter exploded out. "That sounds crazy even for me. But his eyes glistened in the dark so clearly. Luminous, other worldly."

"That's funny you say that. Lynx in ancient times were believed to be able to see through solid things, like the ground, walls. It was probably because of their luminous eyes, which are reflective, cat-like." Lara poured herself a mug of coffee, but began tapping her foot.

"A mystical creature, like a unicorn?" Michelle teased.

"I think you've read too many fantasy stories. Either that or your imagination is going wild."

"Kill joy."

"Sorry. Facts are facts. Lynx are typically solitary and shy around humans, but they have been known to coexist in small groups." Lara casually checked her phone. "I've got to get to the clinic. We can talk about this later, if you want. But I suspect what you saw was a big dog, maybe a coyote."

Lara gone, Michelle finished her emails. A quick shower would have to do. Beneath the spray, she went through the motions of wash-ing, as her thoughts followed a variety of pathways. Lara's suggestion that she hadn't seen a lynx just didn't track. Mentally adding doing an Internet search of lynxes to her list of to-dos for the day, she hurried to the Aegar Investigations office.

* * *

"It would be so helpful if you could take a humane trap and food to that address and stay in touch with the person who emailed me about the cat and kittens." Michelle walked through the door of the Aegar Investigations office in the middle of a phone conversation with one of her cat rescue volunteers. She nodded to the sisters at their desks, and switched hands with her phone while shrugging off her coat. "Good. I'll let her know you'll be calling. Can you handle the vet visit after we catch them? Oh good. I really appreciate it, Eduardo. Keep in touch."

Nine in the morning and already she was juggling her day's activi-ties. Hectic, yes. Did she mind? No. She was grateful for caring people and she loved her jobs, both of them.

Sterling came through the doorway to her office, a sober look on her face.

"What's up?" Michelle asked, sitting at her desk behind piles of case files for which she needed to input information and finish reports.

"When you have a minute, let's talk."

A grave feeling sunk her mood. She worked her lower lip and waited for more. "Just come in our office when you're ready."

Instantly on her feet, she followed Sterling into the sisters' private office. "What?

What's going on? You look and feel so, so—"

"We've been doing a database search on that lawyer." Sterling pointed to her computer screen. "The one who sent you the letter about your property."

Michelle started chewing at her fingernails. "Why am I scared?"

Lacey eyed her, then sighed. "It's not great news, Michelle. The first thing we did was call his office and ask who he is representing. Of course, he declined to share that bit of information. Cited client confidentiality and all."

Michelle held her breath, waiting.

"It took a bit of expertise on Sterling's part to follow the information, but she found the name of the client by, well, hacking into his corporation's server."

"You can do that? And is it even legal?" Michelle's brain was getting foggy.

Sterling slanted her head at her and smiled openly. "First of all, it's not legal. I'm careful. And I'm a cop's wife. I'm sure I have some sort of 'coply' immunity. Secondly, I have expanded my skills. Turns out technology is pretty useful when you lean in and take control."

"I'm impressed."

"Well, don't be. I have a lot to learn. But I did find out that among other high-power clients, William Carter Enterprises is represented the lawyer who sent the letter."

Michelle felt the floor move. She drew in pulls of air, trying to manage the overpowering urge to ... what? What could she do? The William Carter effect had taken a great toll on her family years ago when he took over the local daily newspaper.

Changes were put in place that her father, the executive editor, felt cheapened the newspaper. At the end of it all, her father had been fired and he'd struggled to redefine himself.

"Why would he be interested in my property?" But then she thought back to what Sterling had said—William Carter was one of this lawyer's clients, but not necessarily the one who was after Michelle's house. "Wait a minute, *is* he interested in my property?"

"Umm ... my search disclosed communications that spell out his interest and direct the lawyer to secure the property at any cost."

"I'm completely lost. My house was on the market for a month. Why didn't he just buy it? Why now?" She slumped into the couch in the room. "What am I going to do?"

Lacey spoke up. "These are all good questions, Michelle. We'll keep looking into it, get to the bottom of this development."

Her words fell flat on the floor in front of Michelle's feet. William Carter was one of the most powerful businessmen in town. No, in the world. He was the head of an extremely profitable and successful property acquisition and development company. And he was unscrupulous, deceitful, and downright mean. He'd collected power and money and left suffering in his wake. Even Lacey's husband, William's son, had felt the negative influence of his family name and vowed to make amends to the world for his father's actions. What could she possibly do to thwart William Carter?

She sat up straight. "I need a lawyer."

Sterling and Lacey mirrored her, sitting up straight in their chairs. "Yes you do," Lacey said.

"A very good lawyer, who is not afraid of a fight." Sterling pounded her fist on her desk, excited.

"Casey." He'd already offered, and she had no time to waste.

* * *

Michelle sat across the table from Casey at the deli not far from his office. The ambiance of the place felt soothing. The scent of fresh coffee and bread boosted her appetite. The background sounds of conversations around the dining room gave them some privacy.

"Thank you for meeting with me." She looked into Casey's eyes and found welcome and intense interest. His face glowed with its typical vitality. Even with his reserve, he was always all-in at the present moment. It was refreshing. "You know what we talked about last night? About a problem with my property?"

His eyes locked on hers and he nodded his head. "Of course."

She cleared her throat, a bit unnerved by his presence. "I think I need a lawyer and I was wondering if you would be that lawyer." Uneasiness tripped her heartbeat. It didn't seem right to ask for his help when she'd made a habit of late of putting him off. "Sterling and

Lacey found the lawyer's client who is potentially the interested buyer. It's really bad news."

"I know. William Carter. I did a search, too. The list of clients that lawyer represents is pretty focused."

The waitress stepped up to pour refills of their coffee. Casey smiled pleasantly up at her and the young woman reddened appreciably. Michelle waited until she'd left. "What do you mean focused?"

He looked over his right shoulder, then his left, and leaned in close. "A very elite group of business men and women make up his clientele."

She shook her head, unsure of the implication. "Do you know what that has to do with me?"

He reached across the table and took her hand in his. It sent delicious shivers through her body. Immediately, she clamped down on the feeling. It wasn't safe.

His eyes focused steadily on hers. "I don't know. Yet. But I will. Soon. I promise. We know William Carter has hurt a lot of innocent people. The other people on the list have equally bad reps. I'm going to make sure you don't become a part of the devastation."

"So you'll take my case?" Her voice sounded small to her own ears. Yes, she was worried, but mostly she was angry. Maybe underneath the anger helplessness seethed.

He squeezed her hand, gently. "Of course, Michelle. I told you I wanted to help." He held up his palms to face her. "No strings attached."

She lowered her gaze. A confusing mixture of gratitude and something close to love tightened her throat. "Thank you. When can you start?"

He laughed the easy, smooth laughter that came from his belly. "I already have. I can't wait to get in some in-his-face ass whooping. It's high time William Carter gets to know me better."

She traced a scratch on the tabletop. "I think I know why he's on my case." She held her breath, and wondered at Casey's patience. She breathed out, making a choice. "During my freshman year in college, I was raped."

Casey's posture stiffened, and he let out a quiet gasp. But he stayed silent.

"I was walking alone on the quad at night and an upperclassman, Darrel Dobosky, walked up beside me. I knew him, but not as a good friend. He was all personality and charm. He talked about the weather. Said he loved fall. Then he took hold of my shoulders and essentially shoved me behind a row of bushes that ran alongside a building. I struggled, but he pushed me to the ground. He told me to shut up and he backed up his demand by putting a knife to my throat." Her voice trembled, she heard it herself, but she didn't cry. Her words came out flat, matter of factly. A disassociated state threatened to engulf her. And Casey's eyes teared up. His anger flamed out from him but he didn't show it. He just continued to listen.

"I reported the rape to the police and went through the whole ordeal so I could do my part to stop him from hurting other women. Darrel was charged, we went to court. I even got on the witness stand and told my story again. But Darrel's father, Bruce Dobosky, is a prominent, wealthy, and influential man in this town and a friend of William Carter."

Casey nodded. "I know things about the man." He rubbed his chin thoughtfully and slitted his eyes. "Lots of publicity?"

"Yes. And a lot of what the media reported was wrong. About me, wrong. His lawyer presented me as a promiscuous flirt. Friends of his family testified that I'd been chasing after him for weeks prior to the sex. They called it sex, not rape, because he claimed it was consensual." She rubbed her arms, cold seeping throughout her body. "Darrel was acquitted. I can only guess why, but as a friend of William Carter I'm sure Darrel had some purchased friends on the jury. On his way out of court he snickered at me and mouthed … "

"Let me guess, a threat, a taunt, something disgusting." Casey balled his fists, but remained calm.

"He said he'd be watching me. I was eighteen years old. If he wanted to ruin my life, he could. I lost myself for a while. I never felt safe. I was consumed with shame, but through counseling I got a grip on my life again."

Casey moved his chair close to her. He put his arm around her and stroked her shoulder softly. "What a complete invasion of who you are, a complete tearing apart of the foundation that kept you whole."

"I saw Darrel's face everywhere I went. I tried to get a restraining order but the Carter effect prevented it."

Casey stroked her chin, soothing her deep sorrow and fear. "I'm so sorry this happened to you, Michelle."

"It was five years ago. I've told myself over and over not to surrender my life to this evil person. But it changed me. I used to think I was invincible and fearless. Ha! Not anymore. But I'm working on it, still." Tears blurred her vision, and she swiped them away. "Purchasing this house, my childhood home, was an attempt at creating a feeling of safety. I have nothing but good memories here and I thought ... " Sobs took her over, and she closed her eyes.

Casey pulled her close, stroking her hair. "You thought you'd get more pieces of your life back. And now Carter is taking it away and threatening to do more hateful things."

"You've been so considerate of my need for space, Casey. I know I've probably hurt you by not telling you it wasn't about you." She let his arms continue to encircle her, let the warmth and strength of them comfort her.

He pulled up her chin and peered into her eyes. "I appreciate you sharing this darkness with me. I know what it's like to keep secrets." He dropped his gaze and sighed heavily. "We're in this together, Michelle."

"I don't know why Carter would continue his campaign against me. The trial went Darrel's way. It was five years ago." She stared blankly ahead of her.

"You know Carter. You know he doesn't need a logical reason to do what he does. He's simply corrupt. In his mind, he probably thinks he's doing the right thing by his friend's son."

They sat in silence as minutes ticked by. Michelle breathed in and out, letting Casey's support sink in.

"What can I do for you now? Just tell me and it's done." A muscle in

Casey's cheek twitched and again Michelle thought she heard a low grumble in his throat.

She smiled. "You're doing what I need from you. You're taking my case and you're here, really here."

"Yes, I am." Casey dropped his forehead against hers, emphasizing his promise.

* * *

BACK AT HIS OFFICE, Casey resisted the urge to dig deeper into Michelle's property dispute and turned his attention to the Pretid case.

He opened his files on Pretid and began scanning the pages.

He'd helped the biotechnical company secure a patent for a state-of-the-art hand-held device and computer program that promised to increase accuracy in clinical trials and better serve the research goals. He understood the importance of accuracy during trials. The integrity of data was integral to the success of the trial. Electronic diaries gave participating patients freedom to go about their lives during the trial and enable the clinical research organization, the CRO, the ability to collect accurate data faster from the device by simply downloading to the program. Uploaded to a secure system, the data could be accessed and shared across trials.

Pretid planned to tailor devices and data collection programs for specific diseases, but this particular trial involved insulin pumps. Now in stage two, the trial's use of the electronic diary was in testing efficacy and delivery of the dosage used in the pump.

Though not the first electronic diary on the market, it presently was expected to be at the top of the market when released for public use.

He'd requested information from Pretid about trial locations and where the problems were occurring. He checked his mail and his email, but found nothing new from Pretid. Frustration crept up his neck and tightened his throat.

Casey leaned back in his chair and stretched his arms above his head. He turned to look out the expansive windows that lined one exterior wall and breathed in and out to clear his mind.

His thoughts drifted to last summer, when Jackson's company became implicated in a drug trial that was falsifying data. It was not typical to find a completely falsified trial.

The FDA and the professionals involved in the pharmaceutical research field worked hard to ensure protocols were safe for patients and trial results were accurate. Lives were at stake.

He absentmindedly rubbed his chin, his gut twitching. The drug business was a highly competitive and lucrative field. Things could go wrong. What went wrong with this trial wasn't even irregular. Patients in trials understand that there are unknowns. But people behind the scenes who invest in the development of new drugs and new devices sometimes don't see clearly. They choose to ignore symptoms, even things such as hallucinations and heart palpations, and categorize them under *insignificant* because they want the study to go forward. That's why sometimes drugs were recalled, even after they'd been approved.

But he didn't like it when things went wrong. A trial subject with the disease, in this case diabetes, should not encounter life-threatening situations.

He drew his fingers through his hair and took in the information on his computer screen. Someone in his town was corrupting his client's good work. It had to stop.

He lifted his eyes to the wall between his office and Jackson's and saw a fuzzy image of his boss and friend staring out the window in his spacious office. Jackson was a great guy with a lot of smarts and a lot of heart. He had a lot on his mind. He'd worked for his father for a few years after getting his law license. It was during that time that he'd learned his father's ways were toxic, for him and the world. He'd admired his father very much for his successes. But what he'd believed about his family couldn't stand up to his first-hand scrutiny. The knowledge hit him hard and he'd made a deliberate decision to leave his father's work and strike out on his own with a business that could help right wrongs of his family. Jackson hadn't actually been the one to cut off his father from his life with Lacey and her son Tyler—he'd left it up to his father to make the choice.

Appreciate new lawful and humane tactics in business and be in his life, or continue in his old ways, without his son around. William had chosen wrong. It'd been hard for Jackson to hold his ground against one of the most powerful men in the world, but he'd done it. Afterward, William became even more harsh and ruthless. It was a burden on Jackson's soul, but with Lacey and Sterling and Ben as his anchor, he'd managed to make a good life and head a prosperous business.

Casey closed his sight to the other office and leaned his head back again.

Casey knew the ways of humans pretty well. He loved humans, and Jackson was one of the finest humans he'd come across. But even though times change and everything evolves, humans could produce amazing beauty and fruits of love but still thrive on the lowest level of existence. Selfishness and greed. And unfortunately, Jackson's father, infamous William Carter, remained one of the most selfish, greedy, and downright evil humans he'd ever known. His attempt to steal Michelle's rightful property was just an example of that greed and malice. Casey's blood boiled at the thought of William's debauchery hitting so close to the humans he loved. He didn't even try to suppress a low growl in his throat. He would put a stop to William, one way or the other.

His cell phone vibrated on his desk and he saw on the screen that Lara Monroe had texted. She wanted a meeting of the colony tonight. He texted her back he'd be there. On top of his work at Carter, Inc. and his search into Michelle's mortgage issue and safety, Casey always had colony management to contend with. Just something to take in stride. His leadership meant a lot to him. His colony of were-cats was made up of both "pures," were-cats who were direct descendants of two were-cat parents, and "moggies," were- cats who had human and were-cat parents. As the first moggy to hold the position of leadership of his colony, he intended to equalize the population of his kind. Parents and older were-cats remained members of the colony, but were inactive in colony activities. It was probably the youth of his colony members that had given him an edge in being chosen as leader. The younger members were more open to evolving. He considered it his job to lead the group in assessing what the shape of changes would be, including revising ancient rules. Fortunately, his second in command, Lara, believed as he did that change was due.

* * *

THE HEADLIGHTS from Casey's Prius shone into the dark, lighting his way through the forest on the winding road that led back to his parents' house. His parents' home had been home base for his colony for as long as he could remember. His father, Larry, kept things close to his vest and his mother, Camille, supported him. His mother was a human who carried a recessive gene for were-cat traits and his father was a pure, born from two pures. In his experience he'd found that pures expect to run things, including deeming a moggy's home unfit for colony concerns. But somehow his father had made it so.

His father had been a colony leader. He preferred to follow. He'd said it made life simpler for him. Casey thought of his father as quietly subversive, but his father would never agree to that description. How else could his life be explained? He didn't like to rock the boat, yet he'd married a human. The stories Casey's mother had told of the arguments about the marriage between his father and his grandfather made his father sound brave and strong and his grandfather ferocious. His parents' marriage had caused a split in the colony of the time. Some followed his father as the new leader and adopted his father's house as base, and some chose to go a separate way.

It was convenient that the meetings typically were held here, because he could see his parents and his colony cats in one visit. Efficient. Plus there was the added benefit of his mother's cooking. She often cooked a meal for them all and it was always delicious.

He parked and stood outside, taking in the comfortable sense of being at his haven. It had been the place he could escape to and be himself after days at school being human. Luckily for everyone involved, were-cat children didn't transition to full were-cat ability until eighteen years old, after high school graduation, so designated colony mentors could help them make the changes by keeping them at home. Casey chuckled, remembering his transition. It was a bit rough. Since each were-cat retains their human personality, in his case he resisted his mentor's attempts to "tame" him or advise him to stick close to home while his shimmering was random and out of control. He'd wanted to be free to be himself, lynx and all, and felt unnatural at pretending.

Things were different for him now. He carried a sense of being comfortable in his lynx skin and his human skin, so he didn't need to act out or have the security he'd grown up with here in this grand home.

Secluded among large oak trees, his parents' home was more than one hundred years old. It stood tall at four stories high and was lined with large windows inset into the brick. Without moving he could summon an image of the gardens in the back that his mother kept green and healthy. As a child he used to play around the tall hedges that enclosed the gardens of rose bushes and simpler flowers, including daisies, hydrangeas, and peonies. In the warm months it made a plush and inviting spot, but now, with fall in the air, it would be dying down for the cold months.

He lifted his nose to catch the scents of his home and got whiffs of a range of smells, familiar scents of his fellow colony cats: Asia Blue, Lara Monroe and her brother Asher, Elizabeth Sands—Tizzy for short—Conrad Pike, Quinn Arons, and Booker Chase. Booker's wife, Shaun, was human, and she rarely attended colony meetings.

Casey took the four steps up the stairs, through the front door, and into the entryway, then felt rather than saw his friend Tizzy barrel into him, her slim arms wrapping tightly around him.

"Hey, Casey!"

He hugged her hard. "Hi, Tizzy. You about knocked me over."

She laughed heartily. "If I had wanted to knock you over you would now be sitting on the floor." The young woman sparkled up at him, her brown eyes the warm color of cognac, pinning him. In her were-cat form she was a beige-white lynx with the ability to leap higher than any of the rest of them. In her human form she stood a mere five feet, two inches and had the energy of a spring. "You're late. We've been waiting for you to show up so we could eat dinner."

"I know better than that. Since when do any of you have the grace to wait for me or anyone else?" He rubbed her head of cropped blond hair.

"Funny. We're not that wild." Tizzy winked up at him.

Casey chuckled. "Yes you are. So, is everyone here?"

"Not everyone, but those who are you'll find waiting in the other room." She pointed to a room down the hall.

In the den, Casey kissed his mother and hugged his dad. Conversations floated around the large room and bounced off the deep mahogany wood paneling. Groups of overstuffed upholstered chairs and a matching sofa made for comfortable seating in front of the large, limestone fireplace, now crackling with a small fire.

Lara, the pure cat who had called the meeting, stood from her spot across the room. "Dinner will be ready soon, so shall we begin the meeting?" Lara was a sweet bobcat and a skillful vet with powers to heal.

A roomful of nods and grunts answered her, and Lara began.

She scanned the room for attention and shoved a shoulder-length twist of her dark hair behind one ear. Her dark, nut-brown eyes glistened in the light of the fire. "We have just one item to discuss, but it's of great concern. At my vet office I've been getting calls from worried cat owners whose indoor-outdoor cats have disappeared. These are healthy cats who are regular patients in my clinic." She cleared her throat and glanced around again.

"How many?" Asia Blue, a sassy moggy with hazel eyes that sparked confidence pursed her lips. Her telepathic powers with other animals offered great insights into many issues, but it also gave her a direct link to an animal's frantic or desperate moments. She had honed the skill of maintaining calm within her own boundaries.

"I've heard from four owners. It's been happening for about two weeks." Lara sighed and her shoulders slumped. "Look, I know outdoor cats run into trouble all the time. Their lives are at risk when they run around outside. But these cats have homes where they have established patterns of always returning to. I'm concerned something foul is going on."

Asher Monroe, also a pure and also a bobcat—as well as Lara's brother—sat up straight on the couch. "Have any returned since they went missing? Are there any particular locations we're talking about from which these cats have disappeared? If there is a pattern, that would be something to investigate."

Quinn Arons, a moggy and a lynx, stretched his arms over his head and yawned. "Yeah, that would be a place to start. Some of us could track."

Lara nodded. "I haven't found a pattern, but I know the locations of where each cat resides. I'll email you each the home territories for the missing cats. Those who can track can let the colony know where and when. We don't all need to track together, but the sooner we get results the better. Put this on the top of your to-do lists." She dropped her gaze to the floor. It didn't take a telepath to pick up the severity of emotions in the room, and Lara's concern was palpable. "This is urgent. We all know the cruelty that humans can inflict. I don't want this disappearing act to go on. I'll email Conrad and Booker to get them up to speed. Thanks, guys."

Asher leaped to his feet. "Does that mean it's dinner time?" He laughed heartily and grabbed Asia around the waist. "I think this cat could use a bit more meat on her bones."

Strong and lithe, Asia smoothly slipped out of his hold and beat him to the dining room, Asher steps behind.

Casey smiled to himself. Even in their human form, Casey saw his colony cats in their were-cat forms. Their temperaments were such an integral part of them, no matter what form they were in.

As Lara stepped up beside him, he sobered up. Her expression was still somber, so he waited in place while the others gathered around the table and helped themselves to dinner. "There's more, isn't there."

Lara chewed on her bottom lip and stared into his face, searching. "I know what you've been doing at night. You've been shimmering and watching Michelle."

He nodded, knowing there was more coming.

"If the others found out you're putting us all in such jeopardy, your authority may be questioned. You may even be ousted. This is serious, Casey."

He rubbed his thumb against the stubble on his chin. "Serious how? I'm careful. Why do people keep suggesting I'm not serious about serious stuff?"

A whisper of a growl rumbled in Lara's throat. "We all take chances when we shimmer into our cat form. But you engaged Michelle as a lynx. She may try to find out more about this phantom lynx that is not afraid of humans. She's already asked me what I know about lynxes."

Casey shook his head, annoyed. "I am well aware of the colony's need for secrecy. Just as everyone was aware when my parents married and when Booker married Shaun. I know the rules. I don't believe the colony has anything to fear from Michelle. I don't like you reprimanding me like I'm a new shifter."

"I know you—"

"You know as well as I do that Michelle needs protection and someone with my heightened strength, agility, and sight can make sure she's safe." The annoyance began blistering into outright anger.

Lara slanted her eyes at him. "And someone like you who cares personally about Michelle may let those feelings sway your good judgment. Your responsibility is to the colony, especially as its leader."

Casey took his turn to rumble a low growl, a warning to Lara that she was overstepping. "I appreciate your input, Lara, but I am doing what is right. There are factors to consider that you're not aware of. That's where you must trust your leader or advocate for a new one."

Lara bent her head. "No, I think you're the best leader we could have. I'm just concerned, and if I am, soon others will be, too. I don't want trouble in the colony." She dropped her hands onto her hips. "I care about Michelle, too. You know that."

Casey flashed her a smile, signifying the topic was closed. "Let's get in there before they've eaten all the food. Then later maybe a good run would ground your anxiety."

Lara dropped her head onto his shoulder, then looked up with nervous eyes. "That would do me good."

CHAPTER 4

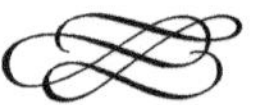

A colony run suggestion fell flat at the dinner table. Other commitments took priority, so at the door, Casey, the last one remaining, told his parents good night and stepped into the quiet of the forest that surrounded his parents' home.

Temptation to run alone pulled at him. The keen senses of sight, scent, hearing, and touch reached out for the richness of the forest, just a shimmer away.

Not tonight. Tonight he would use those keen senses to enter the world of one William Carter with one purpose in mind. To expose his motives for going after Michelle's property.

On his drive to William Carter Enterprises' administrative campus, Casey's thoughts entertained the idea that maybe Lara had a point. It was important to keep the presence of his colony secret. Lynxes were not native inhabitants of the Midwest. Other colonies lived in other parts of the United States and in Europe. Casey's colony had little contact with them, but Lara managed a database of other were-cats and a history of his colony.

But his colony of were-cats lived wherever they chose. There were no boundaries and they could survive in any setting habitable for humans. Still, humans' reactions to sightings of wild animals, native or not, leaned toward securing their own habitat. Elimination of the threat. So he and his colony cats lived as were-cats in secrecy. He had no problem with that. It was the way things stood.

When it came to Michelle, everything got scrambled. Keeping parts of him secret came at a price. Loneliness, deep and heavy, colored his every day. It was a price paid by all part-human, part-nonhuman beings, especially for those living in an urban environment among humans.

He parked under a large tree down the street from the William Carter, Enterprises campus and turned off the car. He sat in the dark, desperation warring with detachment.

When Michelle broke off with him, the loneliness didn't simply return, it nearly took him over. It shouted in his head, brutal thoughts of getting what he deserved for letting her get close. It tainted his dreams with endless dark hunts searching for her in nameless and unfamiliar forests.

Casey shrugged off the clamor of loneliness, and focused his vision on the building down the street. It was his prey tonight.

He put on his mask, made sure his bulletproof vest was on securely, and checked his gear one more time, then slipped out of the car and crouched low to the ground, moving slowly, one cautious step at a time until he reached an employee entrance.

He eyed the keypad for a quick second, then did his magic and hooked up a tool that cracked passcodes. Inside, he didn't expect much more in the way of obstacles. Hundreds of people worked in the building and went in and out this door and others like it every day. It didn't call for lasers and such.

Security guards were expected, though, and he kept his senses aware for one's approach. He didn't need night vision glasses. His vision was made for darkness. Lynxes were nocturnal by nature and hunted prey in the dark.

Moving swiftly, Casey bounded down the stairs to the records room. He'd done his homework and knew his way around. His eyes peered through the walls of the room, checking for workers or guards. Lines of computers stretched across the large room.

Destination one.

He made short work of the locked door. Tonight, his former cat burglar skills resurrected with ease. Something like riding a bicycle?

It didn't matter which computer he hacked, so he just picked one and sat down to get to work. Hacking was not his strong suit, but he could manage with the help of his electronic tools.

"In. Good girl." The mask he wore muffled his whispered words. Flipping through folders and subfolders led Casey on a chase. He checked his cellphone for the time, urgency pushing his breathing. Too much was at stake to blow this opportunity. Time passed so quickly and there were so many places to look.

A window popped up requiring another password. *This might be a different level of security.* He keyed his electronics to run through password possibilities. The speed of the search was fast, but the waiting made him squirm in his seat. He beat out the seconds with his gloved finger on the top of the desk.

He jerked his attention to a sound he heard from somewhere close. Peering through the walls into the hallway, he caught the light of a flashlight bobbing a few doors away and the guard carrying it.

Time to jumpstart this project. An alert prompt on the screen made him sigh. *Finally. I'm in deeper.*

And then he had it. Legal communications between William and his lawyer. *Correction. Sleazy lawyer.*

All the while listening to advancing footsteps, Casey ripped through a list of dated emails and documents until he found several that referred to property acquisition. Namely, a directive to acquire Michelle's property at any cost, and quickly. And more. Specific details of plans related to her property.

He grabbed his cell phone and snapped pics of the documents. *Bingo!*

Again, he peered through the wall. This time no security guard. *Probably checking out another room.*

He slowly twisted the doorknob and pulled the door open a sliver. Now was his chance to exit. Adrenaline rushed through him, tightening his muscles and readying him for swift escape.

Silently he ran up the four flights of stairs to the Big Guy's office. Being a were-cat again paid off with superior agility and endurance, but he stood catching his breath for seconds, before slipping into the dark hall and sprinting to the door with the nameplate that read *William Carter, CEO.* Casey smirked. *He left off King of the World and other such superlatives.*

Again, unlocking the doors—outer and inner—was quick work. *Destination two.*

He knew he was pushing his time envelope and went right to Carter's file drawers. He was betting that William was computer savvy enough, but preferred hands on and hard copies of his documents. The first drawer he tried was locked, but Casey didn't miss a beat. He slipped his fingers along the top of the cabinet and found the latch that would release all four drawers. A quick jimmy, and he continued his search. He bet the contents of the top drawer would give him what he wanted. Files named "case studies" and "research projects to-date" stood out to him and he quickly scanned the contents.

His heartbeat pounding loudly in his ears, he began putting together a loose outline of William's intentions. A low growl rumbled quietly in his throat. He snapped photos with his cell phone of specific pages, then continued his search. He backtracked through the files to make sure he hadn't missed anything important, but when he saw "Pretid" and "property acquisitions," he suspected he'd found invaluable information for his client and Michelle's problem. The cell phone couldn't click fast enough as he photographed each page in the files, his ears attentive to any possible intrusion. He scanned the receptionist's office on the other side of the wall. Only darkness. Quietly, he slipped through Carter's office into the adjoining secretary's office, then slanted open the door and scanned the hallway. Dark and empty. He crept swiftly down the hall to the stairway, then stopped.

Nearby, the sound of an elevator door opening sent him sprinting down another hall.

"Wait there. You. Stop!" Another security guard stood in the second hall.

Casey instantly pivoted and headed for a wall of windows as two guards raced toward him.

"I said stop!" ordered one.

The guard brought up his gun and took his stance. Casey brushed a look in his direction, then checked to confirm that his tools and his phone were safely stowed inside his pockets. He leaped with his shoulder toward the window, but the pop of a gun, followed by a powerful thud in his side sent him sprawling clumsily out the window.

His feet slammed onto the pavement and he struggled for balance. One last glance up at the guards standing menacingly at the window and he faded into the shadows. He trotted to his car, dragging in breaths as best he could. "Way to go, Case," he muttered to himself. "Way to wake up the neighborhood."

He rested against his car for a split second, then pulled off his mask, tore at his clothing, and ripped off the Kevlar vest under his shirt. He breathed in deep breaths of the night air, regaining his strength.

Disgust filtered through as he drove home, mixing with the pain the bullet had inflicted. As intrusions and data searches went, his visit to Carter's place had gone very well. He'd gotten what he wanted. But he'd botched it. Now things would get more complicated. Now the police would be called and an investigation would ensue. It was hard to shrug off his mistakes, but he knew he'd done a good job of covering his tracks. He'd done what he had to do. He just hoped it didn't turn around and bite him, or more importantly, Michelle.

MICHELLE FINGERED a button on her shirt, listening to one of her fosters reporting that the kittens he'd been caring for were ready for adoption.

"Thanks, Jamal. I'm trying to find them a permanent home. Do you think you could participate in an adoption event that's coming up? You could bring the mom cat and her kittens."

"Of course. Just send me details and I'll be there with the little family." His voice was pleasant, optimistic. It was honey for her heart.

"Will do." Her phone beeped. "Oh, I've got another call I should take. Thanks, Jamal! You're the best."

The name on her phone was that of a board member for Cats Alive. Michelle pulled up her composure and clicked on answer. "Hi, Jackson. What's up? Are you calling as a friend or a board member?"

"Hey, Michelle. Does it matter?" He chuckled into the phone.

"No, I just need to know what hat to put on." Lacey's husband offered much to Cats Alive. He had business savvy and a big heart. Like him, everyone on her board was a friend. But doing business meant adopting a professional attitude. It helped her keep her bearings.

"Okay, then, put on your non-profit owner hat. I've been looking over the quarterly tax information. It looks like you've done a good job of crossing your Ts and dotting your Is."

"Thanks! Why do I feel that's the compliment before the criticism?"

"I don't want to be critical. I do want what's best for you and Cats Alive. We're running on fumes, it looks like. I wonder about a fundraiser. And maybe we need an actual accountant. Someone who would remove any possibility of popping a red flag with the IRS."

"That would be excellent. I've tackled the taxes for several years because someone had to do it. An expert would be great. But you just said we have little operating funds."

"And you don't think a fundraiser would enable us to hire someone?"

"I can always hope," Michelle said. "But you know me, I'm willing to take on anything that will help us take care of more cats and get them homed. If it means doing paperwork myself, so be it. If you have another way, spill."

Jackson laughed again. "I don't have many thoughts, but how about we talk about fundraiser ideas at the next board meeting. We haven't done one in a while. I'll table the accountant idea until we improve our bank account."

"Sounds like a plan. Jackson, do you know what I dream of? A large facility for Cats Alive that offers comprehensive services, in a cage-free sanctuary for all cats, regardless of their adoptability. We would offer a permanent comfortable home with access to outdoor enclosures and veterinarian care, as well as adoption services. Do you think we can improve our bank account enough to do that?"

Silence stretched between them. "I think it's a grand plan, Michelle, one I could certainly get behind. I don't mean to sound an alarm. I appreciate your skills and willingness to do what needs to be done. I'm probably overreacting."

"Thanks. We'll brainstorm at the meeting."

The phone call ended, Michelle tapped her pencil against the table. Jackson's concern about the IRS was a worthy concern, but she didn't know any other way than what she'd been doing.

Although Jackson's suggestion needled her insides, Michelle moved on to her next project, that of the return of one of her rescues. It saddened her heart. But she blamed herself. Over the course of running Cats Alive she'd come to understand the importance of following her gut. Every time she overrode her instincts and believed in the adopter in question, the cat was returned. The reasons didn't matter. It amounted to the same thing. The cat had a home and then had it ripped away.

In this case, a perfectly lovable and adorable gray shorthaired named Ally was again unwanted, all because the college guy Michelle had believed in didn't actually have what it took to provide a permanent home. If she'd listened to her gut, she wouldn't have homed a cat with the guy. He'd seemed like a very reliable and likable young man, but she'd sensed he wasn't ready for responsibility.

Thoughts rammed through her head. She wanted to stick her finger in his face and remind him that he came to her. He'd begged for a cat. She'd told him the cat deserved a permanent commitment. He agreed.

But it was her fault. She'd hoped so hard for Ally that she let hope distort her instincts. When she'd taken her back, all she'd told the kid was she wanted what was best for the cat and for him. Clearly it wasn't a good fit. And she'd smiled at him.

Of course it was true that she wanted the best for Ally. So was the fact that people could be so shallow, so unwilling to stick with a commitment, even one so meaningful to a gray, furry soul.

She checked her clock. Eight o'clock. Still early enough to call a foster for Ally, now lying in her lap. Michelle rubbed a hand along the sleeping cat's back and Ally responded with a gentle purr. "I love you," Michelle murmured.

Forty-five minutes later fosters George and Jane Pribbles carried Ally, carrier, blanket, and all, out to their car. Michelle frowned as their car backed out into the lane. It wasn't fair that the cat was in transition again.

She put out food and water for ferals, pausing to ground herself with the brisk breeze and sounds of dried leaves rustling. Still for several minutes, she couldn't stop herself. She squinted out into the field beyond the hedge, hoping to catch a glimpse of the lynx again. It was silly to think it might visit again. It was a wild animal. Even so, she stood waiting and hoping. Listening for a sound in the darkness that could be the lynx walking close.

As minutes passed, Michelle remembered the reason she'd come outside and realized her presence here would deter hungry cats and kittens. With one last look around, she walked inside.

Jojo jumped into a kitchen chair, meowing, while Tiger stared at Michelle. "Hi, guys." At the sound of the kibble pouring, Izabelle and Munchy joined the gathering. Taking care of her own cats wouldn't make the transition for Ally any easier, but it did relieve the scrambling helplessness in her body. She knew some of that fear belonged to Ally. But she also knew it sent her own fears up an octave, as well.

Suddenly she was there again. The scent of the college man's cologne in her head. Trembling, shaking, as she did that night on the quad in her freshman year when the son of a well-known and prosperous local businessman pushed her to a secluded spot and forced her to the ground. Helpless, she'd tried to scream, but he'd covered her mouth and threatened to kill her with the knife in his other hand.

She'd tried to scramble away, kicked and shoved. That knife came close to her throat and she'd gone limp.

Panic bloomed in her chest as she stood in her kitchen, reliving the moment. He'd taken so much from her that night. And then the trial had taken what was left— all her sense of herself, her confidence, her pleasure in relationships, her security—and replaced it all with shame and fear. Her counselor had told her those feelings were normal responses for rape victims. *At least I'm normal,* she thought wryly.

Her only choice was to move on despite his acquittal and live as though injustice didn't matter. Every thought of the grin on his face when he walked out of the courtroom stabbed her like knives. The memory pulled at her arms to circle her body.

She shook her head. *No. I will not do this.*

She reached for salvation from a window, pushing it up and grabbing the cool air from outside to fill her lungs. Another shake of her long hair—an attempt to bring herself to the present moment—and the impressions from the past began to fade. She gripped the windowsill, willing for a complete return to the now. Her eyes adjusted to the dark and she held her breath. Something large, something furry, something gorgeous slipped through the hedge and stopped in the middle of the yard. The lynx sat, his eyes luminous, and cocked his head one way and then the other. He emanated peace and serenity. She allowed it in and she soaked in it, completely silent. She didn't need to say a word. His confidence spoke for her. He didn't need assurances, but he gave them to her, miraculously.

Without fear, she smiled at him. The animal chuffed, once, twice. Then he trotted off, turning back once, then slipping through the hedge and into the night. Was the lynx limping? The thought of an injury made her scowl. She wanted to help, but of course that wouldn't be possible. She walked outside anyway.

Seconds later, a loud yelping cry from the field prickled her skin. More wild yowl than growl, the sound echoed loudly, profoundly. Goosebumps prickled her skin. She crouched under the hedge and walked a few steps into the field, her eyes peering into the darkness for the lynx, just to make sure the animal wasn't hurt. But if he was out there among the grasses and trees, he was well camouflaged and she couldn't see him.

Curious thoughts skipped through her mind. His presence was illogical, and yet he had visited again. His behavior wasn't normal, and yet it seemed deliberate. The moment settled inside her, strange, warm, and comfortable.

Too early and too awake for her to even think of sleeping, Michelle grabbed her laptop and walked to her bedroom. She carefully plopped down onto her bed and let her cats find places to settle in while she clicked on her search engine and typed in "Lynx." Scanning the list of search results, she chose one with images and information from a wildlife refuge.

When the image of a lynx opened, she sat straight. "That's the animal I've seen," she proclaimed to her cat audience, who were each too busy grooming to pay attention.

Delighted with her find, she perused information, filling her head with text about habitat, different species of lynxes, behavior, and even mythology.

She didn't know the bobcat was a species of lynx. She didn't know that today's lynxes were ancestors of lynxes who were around in Europe and Africa during the last Pliocene period. And she didn't know that ancient people believed the animal manifested as a shape shifter with exceptional strength, keen hearing, and dexterity and agility. In addition to the myth Lara had told her about, that lynxes could see through solid objects, according to the mythology the animal had the ability to heal quickly and draw insights from their keen senses. Of course, some religions believed were-cats, cat shifters, were actually witches or demons, and hunted them to kill.

Settling back against her pillow, Michelle turned what she'd read around and around in her mind. She didn't believe in malevolent species of animals. No, the malevolent types were humans who didn't understand nature and were afraid.

I'm not one of those. I don't know what's going on, but I do know that animal is beautiful.

She set her laptop on her nightstand, turned off the light, and nestled under the covers.

Delicious wonder and peace filled her as she let herself drift off.

CHAPTER 5

$\mathcal{C}$asey sat up in bed, the dream he'd been having still alive in his head. He rubbed his hand through his hair. Sweat beaded on his forehead. "Oh, my God." His heart thudded hard and fast in his chest. He glanced at the clock on his nightstand, sucking in deep breaths of air. *Four in the morning.* Loneliness lay heavy in his heart.

The dream had been so real, so terrifying. So unusual.

He set his feet on the cold wood floor and sat still on the side of the bed. He took in the room, his room in his house, and sorted through the images in his dream as his body reactions calmed.

He was accustomed to dreaming as his lynx form. Dreams of running through fields with the speed and exhilaration of freedom made frequent nighttime appearances. But this dream made him shiver. He dropped his head in his hands and lived through it again.

He saw himself standing in his human form with Michelle in her backyard. Darkness enveloped them comfortably and a starry moonless sky contained their moments of shared solitude. He'd brought her warm hand to his lips, the scent of her skin heady and alluring. She'd laughed, delighted when he pretended to take a delicate nibble of her skin.

Casey balled his hands. The moment of togetherness in the dream thundered through him as he revisited what happened next.

He'd lost control. He'd done the unthinkable. He'd shimmered, right in front of Michelle, into his lynx form. Horrified, he'd stood there as his purest self and her screams echoed fiercely against his heart.

Nearly staggering with despair, he stood and walked across his room and leaned his arms against the window. The quietness and stillness outside stood in stark contrast to his inner turmoil. He stood in the dark, naked, and let the reality of his dream enter his waking moment.

He knew all his life, before his first shimmer at eighteen years old, that he could never share his secret with any human. He'd always accepted that. It made sense. It was different for his parents. His mother had known of were-lynxes' existence through stories passed down in her family of ancient relatives biting human mates, transmitting lynx blood, and introducing the lynx gene into the family line. But that didn't change the rules. He believed if humans discovered the truth, his life and his colony would be in grave danger. At the most positive end of likely possibilities, he and his fellow were-cats would be made lab animals in some government facility. At the other end of possibilities, they'd be slaughtered as abnormal animals that threatened what humans considered normal.

He pounded his fists against the wall, frustration and loneliness crashing through him. How could he ever entertain the idea of a relationship with Michelle? Why did his subconscious think he could? He couldn't put her at risk or his colony. And he wouldn't allow himself to try for a relationship when it would require secrecy, even though he clearly longed for complete honesty with her and a closeness and acceptance he'd never had.

While watching Michelle last night, that knowledge of never being real with her had nearly torn him apart. The feeling roared up from his gut and rushed out into the world in an anguished yowl.

He twisted his neck and rolled his shoulders. A run would settle his nerves, but better use of his time right now would be to take the energy running through him to his office at work, where he could put it to use for Michelle and for Jackson's business.

A heavy sigh escaped him as he stepped under the warm spray in his shower. The water poured over his face, down his body, and into the drain, where he hoped it carried the longing and yearning for more. He'd always believed in the timing of things and the organic move of nature left to its natural action. But this move toward a relationship with Michelle was out of step. The time would never emerge naturally for a coming together in the way his heart craved.

An abrupt shift took him to a place inside that wanted to tackle his problems. Casey dressed and jumped behind the wheel of his car and drove to work, the information he'd gathered last night in a bag on the seat.

A quick stop at the coffee shop to pick up a breakfast sandwich and extremely large black coffee first—thankful they opened early—then he made the short trip to the office, pulled into his parking spot, and shifted fully into work mode.

He unlocked the front door and winced as he pulled. "Oww." His shoulder objected to the heavy door. The dream and his attention on work had pushed the pain to the back of his mind. Besides, by mid-morning the sore area would be healed, thanks to his were-cat blood.

He took the stairs to his office two at a time and set his laptop on his desk. While it booted up, he downed his sandwich and savored the bold taste of his coffee, immersing himself in the rich silence around him.

No guilt prickled his insides. Technically, he had stolen information and Jackson wouldn't like that. But when it came to William Carter, all bets were off. The man's methods were brutal. He took what he wanted when he wanted and left scorched earth behind. Remorseless.

Casey wiped off his fingers, took another gulp of coffee, and jumped in. First up, loading the files and images of documents he'd acquired at Carter Enterprises. He saved the files in a secured area of his laptop that required another password, one he changed every day.

He rubbed his chin, focusing hard on the pages. His muscles tightened, as the implications bloomed larger and larger.

Carter Enterprises wanted Michelle's property because it sat next to a research and development company with an undisclosed objective. That benign looking facility two blocks from Michelle's home belonged to a shell of Carter Enterprises. Casey clenched his fists, realization of the close proximity of danger to Michelle sending fiery bursts raging through him. Something rang familiar. Something about the facility. He cross referenced the materials Pretid had sent him and stopped when he found the list of CROs conducting trials of Pretid's device. The location of each site was listed. The facilities' locations were spread across the Midwest. One stood out to him, making his stomach clench. Only one facility reported problems to the Institutional Review Board that monitored drug research, and that had been by an unnamed member of the team. Casey sucked in his breath as he stared at the location of that problem facility. It not only belonged to Carter Enterprises, it was located two blocks from Michelle's home.

Holy shit! He shook his head, trying to contain the magnitude of Carter's plans and the simplicity of his motive. The project was already underway and massive problems seemed to dictate enlarging the facility and the buffer zone between it and the outside world. That's where Michelle's property—rural and secluded—came to Carter's attention.

Words such as "immediate correction of unforeseen side effects," "collateral damage," and "remove threat of discovery" went right to his gut. Even under normal circumstances under the guidance of a company with morals and ethics, these kinds of situations would raise huge red flags and prompt control measures that would not endanger others. But Carter Enterprises had no such morals or ethics. Michelle's property was already under siege and Carter's lawyers clearly were paying all the right people to ignore her rights and create an illusion of impropriety at the bank.

Reading on, Casey's breath froze in his lungs. He fisted his hands and slammed them against the desk. It couldn't be! His father's name popped up on the page with a list of Carter's projects. His father. The land grab and undisclosed project involved his own father, Larry Mitchell. How? Casey had no knowledge of his father even being acquainted with Carter.

He read further, his anger and dismay swirling together in his body. He couldn't deny what the paper said. It included Larry Mitchell in the list of investors in Pretid's device trial.

Cold fingers of disgust twisted around his throat at the same time his world crumbled like dry bread.

His father and William Carter, Jackson's father, were working together, using Pretid's device to corrupt yet another drug trial. The end game was hidden somewhere, and this tampering with the device was only the top of the pile of shit they were building.

Anger and confusion mixed with urgency and frustration drove him to his feet. He glanced at his clock on the wall. Six-thirty in the morning. He'd been reading through his find for two hours. It still wasn't even morning for people going to work today. He pressed print for the most telling pages. His steps against the carpeted floor marked off the room, back and forth.

Outside, the morning sun was just rising. Through the wall of windows he could see the pinks, oranges, and yellows color the sky. But while the dawn of the day offered a soothing palette, it contrasted painfully with the ragged dawning in him that Michelle could lose her home. She could be haunted forever by the malevolent danger of William Carter. This game of torturing Michelle could end with her death, he feared, and his world thundered bleakly in his body. He wanted to throw off his clothes and run and run in lynx form for as long as he had strength in his muscles and breath in his lungs.

He gulped in deep breaths, steadying his emotions. He couldn't run; he had to talk to Jackson. It wouldn't wait another minute.

He shrugged on his jacket over his sore shoulder and strode out of the building. Climbing in his car, he heard his cell phone ringing and glanced at the number. Dread sank like a soggy sponge in his gut. It was William Carter, and Casey suspected he wanted to talk about the break in, whether he had any actual knowledge about it or not. He clicked on the ignore button and focused on driving to Jackson's house as quickly as possible. His laptop on the seat beside him shouted at him to hurry, but he should at least let Jackson know he was about to be invaded at the crack of dawn.

Then his phone chirped, a sign he was receiving a text. One look at the screen and he saw Lara wanted to talk. He pushed the button for activating his onboard hands-free phone and said, "Call." He waited for the phone's voice to verify, then he spoke her name. Seconds later Lara picked up.

"Good morning, Casey. Sorry to bother you so early." Her smooth voice's friendliness held a tone of concern.

"Not a problem. What's up?" Casey pulled over to the curb so that he could concentrate.

"I have specific locations where the four cats I mentioned at the meeting live. Doesn't mean that whatever happened occurred in those places. Free-roam cats are known to range territories of thousands of acres."

"Sure. But those locations are a starting place. Have you organized anything yet?" He rubbed his chin in thought. What he needed to share with Jackson weighed urgently on his shoulders, but early morning gave his colony a window to search for the missing cats before their day's activities took over their time. "Why don't you let everyone know the coordinates and we'll team up in the four locations."

"Are you available now?" Her voice lilted.

"Yup. Organize it and send assignments as soon as you can. I've got pressing matters but these cats need to be protected. Let's see what we can find this morning."

"Consider it done." She hung up and before he'd pulled away from the curb Lara sent the list of locations and he had the coordinates to a home in rural Laurelwood. "Looks like I'm teamed up with Asia." He shook his head, hoping Asia could stay on task for once.

He slipped across town, determination boiling in his body. He didn't know yet what had happened to the cats, but he had a gut feeling it wasn't benign. Free-roaming cats could get into all sorts of trouble all on their own. A lot of threats in the environment could be lethal. The sooner the colony had answers, the better for the cats, assuming they were still alive.

The idea lumped in his throat. He knew very well that death was a part of life, but it never set well with him when innocent and somewhat helpless animals became victims of human activities.

He checked his GPS and made a turn down a country lane. The sunrise stained the sky with pinks and oranges, though the sun wasn't completely up yet. Casey didn't need streetlights to see beyond his headlights. The farther he drove up the lane the more overgrown it got. When he spotted Asia in the dry, tall grasses that surrounded the small house on the property, he pulled to a stop. He nodded to her and she nodded back, before slipping off her clothes just inside her car door while he did the same. He opened to his lynx form and let exhilaration of his shimmer take him over.

Standing on all fours, he waited for Asia to walk over, letting the lynx form settle solidly. His keen senses of his lynx nature never left, but in this state they intensified, becoming wild and raw.

In afterthought, Casey realized it might have been a good idea to first talk with Asia, because in lynx form they couldn't speak. *Oh, well.* Her telepathy would come in handy and she at least would know what he was thinking. He slanted his head at her and she nodded. It was time to get down to tracking.

Asia's medium-brown fur spotted with dark brown framed her white chest and belly. Powerful, high-spirited, and telepathic with animals, she was a formidable creature. A reporter who covered the police beat, she had no trouble managing the cops or the sleazebags she wrote stories about for the local daily.

Casey motioned to Asia that he would take scents at the house and she joined him.

Better that they both know the cat's scent. It was far better than a description for accuracy.

Fortunately the small, one-story house was dark. He imagined a retired couple living here, enjoying a simple life. The lawn was covered with dropped leaves from the maple trees that stood stately around the house. He trotted up close to the house, his nose to the ground, searching, while Asia disappeared around the back. Casey took a few steps onto the covered front porch and caught a prominent whiff of cat food. A dish filled with canned cat food sat on one end of the wooden porch. According to Lara, this cat had gone missing two days ago, so the owners apparently had hope still for its return.

Casey turned his face up. The sun was weak behind clouds, but it was up. He chuffed at Asia. *We need to hurry this up.* A low growl sounded as she rounded the corner of the house. She'd picked up a scent. Together they followed it to the edge of the yard and into the field. The only sound in the morning was that of their paws crackling twigs and plodding through dry leaves. The scents stirred with their footsteps, but Casey's sense of smell hung hard to the scent of cat.

Asia broke to the side, swiftly tracking a new scent. He could tell it was new because she'd shook her head and pawed delicately at the ground when she'd first nosed it.

When the scent of the cat suddenly disappeared, the lump in Casey's throat dropped to his gut. He scanned the field for broken branches or scraps of fur. A burst of a cry from Asia alerted him to run to her now. Bracing himself for cat remains, he sprinted to her find—human footprints. About four. A rectangular impression in the dried weeds confirmed what they feared. This cat, and probably the other missing cats, had been trapped and taken somewhere.

Anger burning in his chest drove him. He trotted around the space for more evidence, something to lead them to the cat. Wheel tracks that led through the field and back out onto the lane made fury rise into his chest and up through his throat. A piercing yowl echoed through the field.

This cat had been stolen.

Asia padded up to him, chuffing. She laid her head on his shoulder and stayed there for minutes. Casey drew in desperate breaths. If it turned out that the other free-roamers were stolen, too, then someone was deliberately collecting cats. He rolled the muscles in his shoulder, easing the tension in his body. It was a short distance between stolen and the realization that something nefarious was at work. If not, why the secrecy? Why thievery?

Casey directed Asia back to the cars, where they shimmered and dressed. He quickly checked a text from Lara and called out to Asia. "The others are done tracking, too. We're meeting at Lara's apartment. I'll see you there."

She ran her hands through her short bobbed hair and gave him a subdued look with her hazel eyes. "At least we didn't find a carcass." She shoved her hands into her skinny jeans pockets and gave the property one last scan. "I'll see you at Lara's."

Casey sat in his car watchfully as Asia climbed into her car and drove out to the lane, heading to town. She was a member of his colony, his responsibility. More than that, Asia was his friend. He wanted her safe.

Twenty minutes passed as he followed Asia's car to Lara's home. Parked on the street in front of her apartment and staring at the privacy fence surrounding Lara's backyard, Casey heard activity that could only mean his colony cats were in lynx form. He walked to the front door and checked the doorknob. The door was unlocked. He pushed it open and walked into the kitchen where clothes were piled and draped around the room. He took the few steps to the bathroom and stripped, then dropped to all fours.

In the kitchen he found the back door conveniently open and pushed through to sit on the grass just down from the porch, where he could observe his colony.

Asher, a lean, dark-spotted tawny bobcat, walked past Tizzy, a beautiful beige lynx who taught school, and gave her a hard nudge with his head. It nearly knocked her off her feet, prompting Tizzy-like playful sparring. In the city setting it was important not to scare the neighbors with eerie yowls, but that didn't stop the two from wrestling, with a few chuffs here and there.

Conrad stretched lazily along the fence at the back of the small space, his golden fur dotted with dark brown gleaming in the sunlight. By his relaxed presentation, it would be hard to deduce that this lynx was an intense investment banker and a bad-boy with women, whom he dated with fervor. But his unguarded rest was cut short, when Quinn, a russet lynx dotted in the typical dark brown spots, aimed his equally russet-colored eyes at Conrad and leaped on top of him. No surprise, Conrad grabbed a mouthful of Quinn and pulled him to the ground, which was a major feat. Quinn was strong and agile, as were all lynx, but his work as a construction contractor kept him exceptionally powerful. His construction work made a good fit with his superior spatial sense.

Not to be left out of the fun, Asia jumped on top of the nearby picnic table, then landed with a plunk on the lynx rolling on the ground. It was all in good fun, but that didn't mean the wrestling was gentle. Low growls issued playful warnings, but no one backed down.

Leave it to Booker, a brown lynx with glimmering topaz eyes, to call time out with a series of chuffs. The others ignored him. He shook his head and padded over to the picnic table, where Lara now sprawled, and watched the tussle. Like the lynx in the group, bobcats Asher and Lara sported large, furry paws, a short stubby tail, tufted ears, and facial fur that made them easily identifiable.

This relaxing moment gave them all an outlet from the stress of learning that something malevolent was going on with stray and roaming house cats. That they couldn't talk to one another didn't matter in these moments. They related to each other, silently speaking just as articulately as they would with words.

Casey's muscles were weary with tension. He had a lot on his mind to deal with and it all hammered at him. But as the colony leader, he knew this downtime was essential to their wellbeing. And he sure as hell didn't want to sit on the sidelines.

He stretched his front legs, then his back legs, and yawned. A burst of adrenaline lit up his muscles, and he sprinted around the perimeter of the enclosed yard. *That got their attention.* Lara leaped off the picnic table, Asher not a split second behind, and led a chase that the others quickly joined in. When he completed his circle, Casey leapt to the top of the table and stood still, all four legs planted solidly in challenge. All seven cats circled slowly around the table, intent on Casey's every move. He swayed back and forth, taunting. A sort of laughter bubbled in his body, lifting his spirit. He couldn't laugh but he could chuff. The others offered up chuffs, as well. A chorus of quiet chuffs resounded in the air.

Now I have them. He pulled back on his back legs, then sailed over the others, and landed on the grass behind them.

They came for him, but he tested their reflexes, swaying from left, then right, then dashing through the open door to the kitchen. His feet slipped on the tiled floor, but he was still able to run toward the bathroom. He shoved the door behind him and quickly, effortlessly shimmered.

He heard paws running toward his door. "I'm naked!" he warned, and heard their retreat. They all were accustomed to nudity among the colony members, but his feeble attempt to deter them had worked anyway.

CHAPTER 6

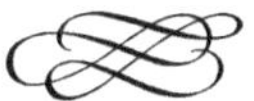

Casey walked into the kitchen and took a seat at the kitchen table. Others emerged dressed from various rooms in the house and joined those already there, munching on muffins Lara had set out. The mood floated like heavy fog in the room.

He put on his leader face and stood to address his colony. He first looked at Tizzy and Asher. "Did you find the missing cat's scent in your location?"

Tizzy spoke up first, rolling her big cognac-brown eyes. "Sure we found the scent, tracked it all the way to where it stopped."

Draped against Lara's corner couch, Asher frowned. "She's right. It was as if the ground has swallowed up the cat."

Booker spoke for his tracking mate, Lara. "It was the same story for us. The home sits on a cul de sac. The cat's scent is all over that area, but the scent was old." He squinted, and aimed his topaz eyes at Casey. "We did find tire tracks. They looked like they were from an SUV. My guess is the cat went with whoever was in that vehicle. They could have tranqued it, though it's not feral so the cat might have walked right up to them, especially if they offered some really yummy food."

Everyone's eyes turned to Conrad and Quinn. "Go ahead, give the news." Quinn motioned to Conrad.

"Like you all, we found the cat's scent, tracked it into a nearby empty lot, then we lost it." Conrad's honey brown eyes narrowed. "There were signs of an SUV in the mud. I think they trapped the cat not far from the house, then took it."

Lara dropped her gaze. "It doesn't sound like a healthy situation for the cats. What do we do about it?"

Quinton swallowed a swig of juice to wash down his muffin. "What can we do? We need to know where these thieves are taking the cats."

Casey rubbed his eyes. His disrupted sleep was catching up with him. "I agree. I'll triangulate the home bases of free-roamers and see if that leads to anything." He slapped the side of his thigh. "Now I have to get to work. Thanks everyone for putting in the time."

He waited to leave until only Lara remained. He wrapped an arm around her shoulders. "We'll get ahead of this thing, whatever it is, Lara. I'll be in touch soon. Don't get too down. That won't help anything."

She sighed heavily. "I know, I know. But it's hard. If these cats are in danger, everything inside of me is eager to storm the castle, bring them back to their owners."

"Yes, I feel the same way. I just believe our colony can kick butt rather effectively and quickly." He gave her a smile, then rubbed her hair playfully until she returned one of her own. "Go take care of the animals you can help at your office."

"You're right." She gave him a little punch to his gut. "Enough with the pep talk. Get out of here so I can get to work."

"Magic hands saving lives." He winked, and walked out the door.

The open window next to him blew chilly air into his Prius and out the other window. Casey saw the traffic around him, the stop-lights, and the road, but thoughts plagued him. Thoughts of Michelle, a target for William Carter's menace. He knew his focus on Michelle's property was personal. And that sent mounting rage pounding through his body.

The morning's revelations stacked up like boulders blocking his view. That was something he wasn't accustomed to. He'd have to get closer to the snake himself, see what he saw.

By now Jackson—or Jake, as Casey sometimes called him—would be at the office, but Casey needed to make another stop first. He had to see Michelle, confirm that she was safe. Even warn her if he could do so subtly.

Despite his concern, a smile slanted across his face. No way. Michelle's perceptions were too keen and her intellect too high to miss anything. He'd just have to try harder. After all, he'd managed to keep his biggest secret, his identity as a lynx, from her detection.

He slid his car into a street-side parking space, practically on autopilot, and strode to her office building. The man walking toward him barely pierced his radar until the man stopped in front of him, flashing a smile.

"Excuse me, I need you to come with me." The smile vanished and the man opened his jacket a bit to reveal a gun clipped to his waistband.

Casey's muscles tensed. "I think there's some mistake, fella." Maybe he could talk his way out of a confrontation. He really didn't have the time for it and he suspected he knew what this was about. "I don't want any trouble."

The beefy man smirked. "No trouble. William Carter just wants a word with you. In fact, he wants a word with you and that bitch you've been following around. Not even out of your way, right? Just head upstairs."

He wanted to tear out the thug's eyes. He could do it, but he wouldn't. Not right now.

Not when Carter was showing signs of being poked, and that could be advantageous if Casey managed the moment correctly. "Like I said, I don't want any trouble. Lead on."

"Upstairs." The man nudged Casey through the door and up the stairs to Aegar Investigations. At the third floor, the elevator opened and a cocky William Carter stepped off and into the hallway.

"Bring him inside," Carter ordered.

"Oh, I'm disappointed," Casey cooed. "Where's hello, how are you today? You get up on the wrong side of the bed this morning, Carter? Haven't ruined anyone's life yet today?"

Carter rolled his eyes and waltzed into the Aegar sisters' office.

Casey's heart clenched. Michelle was sitting at her desk. Her eyes went wide at the sight of Carter.

"Hi, Michelle, look who I brought with me. The big bad wolf." He gave her a grin, then turned to Carter's bodyguard. "Thanks for the escort, but the gun was a little much, big guy. I was coming here anyway, right?"

The bodyguard stood silent, a soldier dedicated to his boss's evil cause.

Carter shifted to one foot. The smile he wore did nothing for his stone face. "Good morning, Miss Slade. Are you alone in the office?" He didn't wait for her answer. He sauntered to the sisters' private office and opened the door. "Yoohoo. Anyone home?"

Casey winked at Michelle. He could see her hands trembling. But she didn't hesitate. Quickly, she stepped to the office door, cut in front of Carter, and closed it behind her. "Yes, I'm alone this morning. Can I help you?"

Carter stepped back and surveyed Michelle. "Nice of you to ask, Miss Slade. But really, I've already secured what I want."

"Then why are you here?" She stood straight, holding back her shoulders. Casey admired her attempts to stand her ground, but Carter's smug attitude burned in him like strong medicine.

Carter ignored her question, turned to him, and smiled ... again. He put his hand to Casey's shoulder and squeezed, hard. "I'm sorry I missed the niceties, my boy. How are you today?"

Casey gritted his teeth. The pain in his shoulder from the last night's bullet stung just enough to let him know it was there. He didn't miss the subtle point—Carter thought he knew Casey was the masked burglar who no doubt showed up on security footage. He shrugged. "Like Michelle asked, what do you want? I know you're not here to talk to the investigators. You probably knew they weren't here."

William's eyes narrowed and his smile dropped. "I thought I'd kill two birds with one stone since you so obligingly showed up just at the moment I arrived to talk to Ms. Slade."

Casey slammed his fist on the desk. "Enough. No more glib remarks to entertain your sorry self. What. Do. You. Want?"

"I want you to stay out of my business." He held Casey's look for a long moment, then turned to Michelle. "And I wanted to hand deliver this notice, Ms. Slade. You can read it for yourself, but essentially you have thirty days to move out of my house."

Michelle took the letter, her eyes blank. "Your house? I'm not in your house."

"Oh yes you are. I signed the papers yesterday at the bank, taking over the mortgage. It's all in the notice. It turns out the mortgage banker you worked with didn't work with an ethical title company. The deed you were given is null and void."

Casey watched, helpless, as William Carter stole Michelle's life. There was no question now that the man was targeting her.

Michelle dropped the notice onto her desk and pursed her lips. The room emptied of air. "That's all? You simply wanted to deliver this notice? Surely you don't expect me to take this at face value." Michelle's eyes flamed with anger. "And surely you don't believe I'm unaware of your motive."

"My motive?"

She came from her desk and stood staring up at Carter. "You don't like losing. This is your way of putting me in my place, letting me know you're not happy that I fingered the rapist, your buddy's son. It's not enough that your friend's son was acquitted. You have to step on me, take away my home, and who knows what else you have planned for me?"

Carter twisted a grin. "Oh, that motive. Maybe this time you'll learn. I can do anything to you I want."

Casey leaped at Carter, swiftly circling his neck in a headlock. "That sounds like a threat." He gritted his teeth and glared at the bodyguard. "Put away that gun or your boss is going to get what he deserves." His fury gritted his teeth and he had to stomp on a growl rumbling in his chest.

Michelle marched to the bodyguard and demanded the gun. Casey stopped breathing, seeing her face down the gun.

"Give the girl the gun," William managed to say.

She stuck out her hand and the bodyguard surrendered it.

Casey let go of Carter and shoved him toward the door. "Now, both you get out. And don't ever go near her again."

Carter collected himself, adjusting the collar on his dress shirt and running a hand through his hair. "See that you stay away from my business, Casey, or I'll notify the police."

Casey shook his head. "I know you have the cops in your pocket, but I'm making you my personal business. Be sure of it."

Carter headed toward the door, but turned back to glare at Michelle. "Ms. Slade, I expect you out of my house. I'll be watching you."

Casey slammed the door closed as William and his bodyguard barely got through the doorway. Immediately, he spun on his heels and went to Michelle. He so wanted to wrap her in his arms, make all the pain go away.

Instead, he stood in front of her, waiting for a cue. Her eyes glazed, she drew in rapid breaths as she stood still in the same spot.

She set down the gun, then turned her beautiful blue eyes up at him. Pain and sorrow and fear all combined to release one tear, then another. But she didn't reach out to him.

"What can I do?" His voice soft, pleaded to let him in.

Trembling, she fingered the envelope from Carter. "I don't understand. Why is this happening, why is he happening?"

She started to melt to the floor, shaking badly. Casey gently put his arms around her, lowering to the floor with her. He guided her head to rest on his shoulder, taking in the shaking rippling through her. "I'll find out, Michelle. I promise."

"It's never going to stop. Not ever."

Casey rubbed her cheek, trying to soothe her senses. "It feels like it now, I know. But it will end."

He could feel her coming back. Her breaths became even and her trembling stopped. She aimed clear eyes at him. His words were sinking in. He was in this with her. "I don't want you to be alone. I'm taking you home and I'm staying with you."

She nodded her head without objecting. Suddenly, a subtle shift in Michelle's expression glazed her face. He knew better than to interfere. She was getting a premonition. The premonitions didn't take her over completely, but he knew from experience that if he didn't distract her she'd get a more thorough glimpse.

"I've seen this premonition before. Just like the first one, I see a cat." Her eyes remained directed in front of her. "The cat is walking into a trap, then the trap is picked up." She breathed in and let it out slowly. "That's it." She hunched her shoulders and pursed her lips.

"The premonition troubles you?"

"Yes. There is fear and confusion in the cat. I feel danger." Michelle shivered. "I wish I would get more of the picture."

Casey's heart stuttered in his chest. First she shared the terrible experience of her rape, then a disturbing premonition. It would be a lot for anyone to deal with. Admiration and acknowledgement of her strength expanded inside of him.

"Why are you looking at me like that, all googly-eyed?" Michelle fidgeted with a beaded bracelet on her arm.

Casey smiled. "Because you're amazing. Your premonition is spot on. Stray cats are coming up missing. Lara and I and some friends have been trying to figure out what's going on with the missing cats." Fire lit in her eyes, and he shot her a sheepish smile.

"And you didn't tell me?" She leaned in and pointed to herself. "I'm a cat person. I own a cat rescue. You didn't think about including me in this investigation?"

"You're right. I should have." Casey rubbed his forehead and stared at the floor. He knew why he hadn't included her. It instantly would have become complicated. Once again, his secrets made demands and he'd complied. He ran his fingers through his hair, his mind warring with his beliefs and his heart.

Michelle cleared her throat. "Okay, as long as you understand I need to know about it and I want to be involved."

She took in another heavy breath and slumped in the chair, as though all her energy had been drained.

"I think it's been difficult for both of us to reveal everything. We're letting out private stuff piece at a time." He studied her sensuous lips, the rise of her cheekbones, and wanted to take away all the missteps he'd made since they met.

Her lips lifted and she aimed her misty eyes at him. "I know I'm guilty of holding back. How many people do you know who have premonitions and can feel other people's emotions? That's some seriously flaky stuff. But you've never made me feel odd."

Guilt traveled up and down his spine. The air in his lungs got stuck in his throat. *You have no idea about my secrets.* "See, we're good for each other."

She chuckled. It came out weak and breathless. "You're tired. Let's get out of here."

His brain made an abrupt shift as he slipped the envelope holding the notice into his pocket and drew her to her feet. As she gathered her belongings, Casey marveled at the change of things in just a few days. He'd been on his way to talk with her and the sisters about what he'd found out about Carter's plans, but he'd never suspected it would go down this way, with Carter revealing himself so blatantly. Bad for Michelle's emotions but good for him to witness and have more pieces to put together.

* * *

MICHELLE'S SHAKES settled down in Casey's car on the ride to her house. There wasn't much conversation. She didn't have much to say, other than to let Casey know Sterling and Lacey were out of town on business. She just didn't have much starch in her body and her mind had gone numb. Sunk into the car cushions with her thoughts shut down seemed like as good a place to be as any right now.

When they pulled up into her drive and she got out, the walk to her door felt stiff, her legs heavy. In the kitchen, she noted it was lunchtime, but her appetite lacked any enthusiasm for food.

"Here, let's sit in the living room." Casey guided her to the couch.

"I don't feel like talking." Michelle slumped into the couch and rested her head against the back.

Casey scratched his chin, eyeing her, but she couldn't pick up any sense of his feelings. She was too closed down.

"I know you don't feel like talking, or anything else, for that matter. But I think you have to." He took a seat in the upholstered chair across the room. He propped his elbow on his knee, then rested his chin on his hand, his expression soft and at the same time firm.

Something in her rose to meet the solid feel of his presence. With her world swiftly falling away, he felt safe and of good substance. Blood warmed in her body. Her breaths opened up to fill her lungs.

"You didn't need to bring me home and you certainly don't need to stay the night with me."

He nodded. "Yes, I do."

She tapped her fingers on the arm of the couch. It would be so easy to go toward him.

He'd been nothing but kind and gentle and protective since she'd first met him. But thinking of it sent her heart racing. And if he hurt her, what would it mean?

"No you don't. I am fine."

Casey threw up his hands. "I know you can take care of yourself, Michelle. I know you're fine. But I'm not leaving you here alone, not when William Carter has declared his malicious intentions. I know he's a bad son of bitch."

She let out a deep sigh, and watched as the rigid carriage of his shoulders softened. His beautiful golden eyes, gentle and kind, pleaded with her to trust him. Fears predicted hurt and rejection and betrayal, making it impossible for her to get any valid premonitions, so screw premonitions. All she had was right now.

The understanding and love emanating from him softened the hard edges of fear and sorrow. Maybe it was time for her to come out of the darkness and live as she'd dreamed of before that dreadful night on the quad.

Tentatively, Michelle fingered a black dreadlock that fell between his eyes. He shifted his gaze to capture hers. His eyes glistened, the way they so often did, and he gently traced the outline of her lips.

She nuzzled his cheek, savoring the scent of him. It soothed her nerves. It drew her in, promising places of peace and security.

Her eyes returned to his, finding intense arousal in them. She dropped a delicate kiss to his cheek, another to his bottom lip. His taut muscles flexed against her and his breathing came faster—just as hers did.

"Michelle, are you sure?" He placed his question quietly at the outer edge of her ear, his breath whispering on her skin.

She responded by seeking his delicious lips and melting into a lingering kiss. When she pulled back about a millimeter, her lips still against his, she answered. "I haven't been with a man since that day in the quad, which I don't count. With you, in this moment, I'm very sure."

He lifted her in his arms while she rested her head against his firm chest, and carried her to her bedroom and set her on the edge of her bed. Reverently, he tugged at her sweater, lifting it over her head, then removed her bra. Her insides tingled so vibrantly, she thought she might explode. He took her breasts, one at a time, into his hands, staring at them, caressing them. When she thought she couldn't take it any longer, he kissed one nipple, then the other, driving her further into the stratosphere.

While she tore his shirt off, he moaned a heady, dusky groan. Michelle's hand roved over his back, fingering the dimensions of his muscles, then bent to kiss his hard chest, while unzipping his pants.

He kicked off his remaining clothes, then tugged off her pants and underwear so swiftly he nearly knocked her over. She stretched out on the bed, making room for him next to her.

Lying beside him on the bed, Michelle's protective walls dropped like they hadn't in years. Pressed dark skin to pale skin with Casey, she closed her eyes and lived the moment. He dove for her mouth, all the while caressing her shoulders, her breasts, her arms. Her mouth danced with his, their tongues tangled. Her heart sang to the crazy beat of his against her chest.

When he trailed kisses over her breasts again, she grabbed his back, losing track of everything but Casey's flesh. When he continued to drop kisses to her stomach, her thighs, then her moist center, she arched to him without holding back.

She pulled at him, coaxing him up, and pushed him on his back so she could pleasure him. Her mouth did to him things she didn't know she knew. A moan escaped from his lips, and she thought she heard a low rumble in his chest. It sounded primal and uncensored, and something in her responded, wanting more of him, wanting all of him.

Directing steamy eyes at her, Casey pulled her face to his and placed a sensuous kiss to her lips, while he flipped her onto her back. "I love you, Michelle." His voice came out gravelly and gruff. "I know I'm not supposed to but I do."

Michelle stared up into his face with tear-blurred eyes. His tender words drifted to her and filled her heart with joy.

She had to have him, now. She whimpered, "Please."

He paused for protection, but Michelle's yearning for him intensified. "Casey."

Instantly, Casey filled her longing, aching center. A gasp escaped her lips and she loved him right back with all of her body, all of her being. They rocked together, her heart beating with the pulse of life, as she let ecstasy wrap around her and sparkle through her. When she climaxed, he came with her, and she understood why people called out to God during these moments of bliss.

Exhausted and euphoric, Michelle watched him move off her and snuggle up close.

Almost in synchrony, their breathing slowed as they relaxed side by side. She traced the lines of his muscles. His arms, his chest, while he shined adoring eyes at her.

Michelle couldn't help herself. Laughter effervesced out of her, unbidden. "Hey, what's so funny?" Casey shoved her playfully.

"Nothing, actually. I'm just so happy." She leaned toward him and placed one, soft kiss to his chest.

Casey kissed the top of her head and sighed. "Thank you. For sharing with me." "Sharing with you?"

He tweaked a lock of her hair. "Yes. You know what I mean." A soft smile came to her lips. She did know.

CHAPTER 7

Michelle offered to make lunch, but Casey got up from her bed with a thrumming in his gut. He needed to square away her safety, then talk to Jackson.

He lingered as long as he could at her door as they lavished each other with kisses. He didn't want to leave her. Being close to Michelle, tasting of her and expressing his feelings, lingered inside him in a very pleasant way. He stood close to her, close enough to enjoy the soothing blue of her eyes, and stroked her sweet lips.

"Do you really have to go?" Her sweet breath wafted over his skin and incited a riot of clearly inappropriate thoughts.

"I do." He pulled her close, so close her heartbeat drummed intoxicating beats against his chest. More than wanting to be around her for the pleasure of it, he didn't want her to be alone. She wasn't safe. And she'd just shared with him her dark secret as well as herself. It hadn't escaped his notice that she'd failed to return his spoken love for her. But what she'd done was a huge step and he didn't want to leave her alone in that. He had to pull everything together to make sure Carter would never bother Michelle again, and he needed to do that now. "Promise you'll stay inside. I'll be back, but in the meantime, stay inside, please. Don't leave for anything or anyone."

She promised him she'd stay home and before he drove away he instructed Quinn to keep watch at her home during the rest of the day. As a contractor, Quinn could leave a jobsite whenever he chose and his workers would keep working, so Casey didn't feel too guilty about giving him the protection duty for the day. Tonight would be something to deal with later.

Traffic on his way to his office slowed him enough to make his muscles tense. He was used to juggling multiple projects, but Michelle was no mere project. Her position in William Carter's crosshairs put her at the top of his list of priorities. Trouble was, the threads of the Pretid case and Michelle's problems with her home and Carter all twisted together. He had to push himself to his limits to get each element under the microscope before any more drug trial participants were hurt and Michelle came to real harm. Just thinking of all the harm already done to her by Carter and the Doboskies pushed his pulse higher.

But first he had to quiet his growling stomach. It'd been too many hours since his early breakfast. He needed to eat. He pulled into a parking space outside of a small coffee shop and rushed inside to grab a chicken sandwich with coffee. On the way out his eyes locked with what looked like a businessman—short haircut, trench coat, and underneath, a suit—sitting near the door. The look the man gave him made Casey's gut clench. He breezed past and out the door, hoping his instincts were wrong.

A few steps to his car, Casey saw a reflection of the man in his car window. Annoyance creeping up his neck, he turned to face him. "Can I help you, sir?"

The man walked closer, stopping an arm's length away. "Beautiful afternoon, isn't?" The man glanced at the sky, then landed a penetrating gaze on Casey.

"Excuse me, I don't know you, and I'll have to beg off. I'm in a hurry." Casey stepped away and headed to the driver's side of his car, the man right behind him. "Look, I asked you if I could help you. I don't want to discuss the weather. If you've got something to say, spill it or walk away." His demand elicited a sweaty scent from the other man, but he didn't move away.

"My name is Agent Doug Callahan. I do need to talk to you, Mr. Mitchell. It's urgent." With that declaration he opened his jacket just enough to reveal a badge attached to his belt. "Could you take your food across the street to that plaza? You can eat while I tell you what I want." The man looked over his left shoulder, then his right, then back at Casey.

The man gave Casey an agitated, scratchy sense of ill ease, but it seemed he had no choice but to hear him out. *What could the FBI possibly want with me?*

He took a seat on a stone bench in the city plaza and bit into his sandwich. He never felt an awkward silence when conversations went nowhere, but if there were to be a time when the phrase would fit, this was it. Casey had downed some coffee and half of his sandwich before Callahan finally spoke.

"Mr. Mitchell, I believe you've put yourself right smack dab in the middle of a very sticky situation."

Casey knitted his brow. "Sticky situation? I assume you've done your homework, Agent Callahan, and know I'm a PI. Sticky situations are common for my line of work. Get to the point." He drew in deep breaths to quiet the unease filtering through his body, putting him on edge, like a cat preparing to pounce.

Callahan shrugged his shoulders and squinted. "A bottom line man, huh?"

Swallowing his last bit of sandwich, Casey just stared at the man. *Do you have a point, man?*

"You are in a particularly advantageous position to do your country a solid good deed."

"Oh, not so much a sticky situation as a good position for you to use me, right?" As a lynx, Casey's perspective often stood a good distance from what normal humans considered an opportunity.

The man shoved a hand in his pocket and pulled out a cigarette package. He drew out a lighter from the other pocket and lit up his cigarette. A pull in and blow out and Casey felt sick to his stomach. "Do you mind putting that out? I'm allergic to toxins."

A frown deepened the lines on Callahan's face, but he dropped it and rubbed it out with his foot. "Listen, you're right. The request I'm making is right up your area of expertise. I need you to get in good with William Carter. The FBI has been investigating his various businesses for months, heck, probably years. There's something big going on and we don't know what it is. I need you to find out. Since you've already taken on a client who has grabbed Carter's attention, you're the man for the job."

Casey lowered his head and stared at him with his best menacing look. "Carter is involved with lots of people. Why me? What is my expertise you're referring to?"

Callahan leaned close, too close, considering the lingering stench of cigarette and fear on him. "You have a record, Mr. Mitchell. I know all about your skills set."

A lump, large and hard, filled Casey's throat. "You mean my cat burglar skills. My former penchant for jewels and other expensive things."

Callahan smiled, showing an uneven row of stained teeth. "Other people's jewels. You never did any time for those incidents of breaking and entering or thefts. But now is a good time to serve your country and help put a stop to Carter's criminal activity."

"Whatever it is, because you don't know." Why were his teeth grinding? This annoying man or the predicament he was proposing? "I think I'll pass."

Callahan squared him with a glare. "I'm not asking. But all I need from you right now is reconnaissance."

"You mean you want me to be stealthy, break into William Carter's company, and find out what's going on that's 'really big.' That about right?"

"Exactly."

"Or what?"

"Excuse me?" Callahan coughed, a very heavy, very wet cough.

"What happens if I decline?" Casey crossed his arms over his chest, still holding his coffee.

"I revisit that record."

"You can't just lock me in jail. I did my probation." This guy was really making his gut burn.

"The FBI can make you do whatever we want. Don't you know that? Now, do the work, and report to me by calling this number." He gave Casey a card with a name and number on it. "Then we'll go from there."

Casey didn't like the never-ending sound of that. He shoved the card in a pocket, then headed across the street to his car.

Mid-way to his car, Callahan called to him. "Chilly out today." He pulled his coat closed and waved to Casey.

"Yes, it's turned cold, all right," he muttered to himself, and pulled into the street.

He clocked off in his mind the things required for him to comply with Callahan. The idea of being coerced to help the FBI tasted bad in his mouth. It wasn't that he was opposed to helping nail Carter, it was the principal of limiting his freedom of choice. He rolled his shoulders and contemplated the best way to handle this new situation with Jackson. Tell or not tell?

He pulled into his parking space at work and ambled inside to his office, still not knowing.

Casey printed the various documents he'd collected from Carter and laid them on his desk. Pretid. Carter. His own father. Expansion. Research. He stood above them, willing his mind to pull in all the unknown bits of information and build a complete picture. One he could judiciously act on, without causing harm with unexpected consequences.

"You look serious." It was Jackson, standing in the doorway.

Casey didn't bother to cover up the information on his desk. A heavy sense of sorrow slowed his movements, as though he were walking in water over his head. He shot a glance at Jackson, wishing he didn't have to deliver the news. Jackson had already suffered too much hurt by his father.

"Come on in." Casey beckoned him and pointed to a chair, as he closed the door. Jackson knitted his brow. "What's up, Case?"

He sank into the chair at his desk and gathered his thoughts. "I've got information about the Pretid case." He cleared his throat. "I've acquired documents from Carter Enterprises that tell a large part of the story."

Jackson frowned. "You acquired?"

Casey stared at his questioning look. "Don't ask if you don't want to know the truth, boss."

A little muscle in Jackson's cheek twitched. "Go on."

"Unbeknownst to Pretid, Carter Enterprises has tampered with the electronic diary we helped them patent and are using the device to corrupt a trial of an insulin pump."

Jackson dropped his head against the back of the chair, sighing heavily. "Do you know why?"

"Not yet. I think it's only the most noticeable part of your father's current plans."

His eyes piercing Casey's, Jackson shook his head. "What else do you know?"

Casey shuffled the documents and pulled up the one about expansion and research, handing them across his desk to Jackson. "It appears that your father's research company is using the device in some kind of project. I don't know what that is, not yet. But something about the study has gone wrong. Notice on the page you're holding the words 'unexpected side effects,' 'collateral damage,' and 'property acquisition.' That research facility is being run by a shell company for Carter Enterprises. It is located a few blocks from Michelle's property. I'm only speculating, but I think whatever research is being pursued there has dangerous elements. The swift zone change, Michelle's deed problems, and the Pretid device malfunctions are all a part of a big plan. I think the plan includes hurting Michelle, specifically, but not as a primary goal, just a plus for your father. He's using the need for more room and more privacy as a way to exact revenge on Michelle. She was raped by one of his cronies' sons and Michelle pressed charges. The rapist was acquitted but apparently Carter is still angry at Michelle's audacity for accusing the young man."

Jackson leaped to his feet. "Will it never end?" He paced from one side of Casey's office to the other, back and forth.

"There's one more thing, Jake.'

Jackson stopped midstep and turned a glare on him.

"Don't hate the messenger, man," Casey said.

A deep sigh escaped from Jackson. "Sorry. What more?"

"I've been recruited by the FBI to get close enough to your father to get information that would give them something to charge him with. The agent, who not-so-nicely engaged my services, said there's something big in the works and I'm to find out what. Apparently your father's been in the FBI's scrutiny for years, but they've never been able to get anything of substance on him."

"You said recruited." Jackson rubbed his chin. "Have your breaking and entering skills come to their attention? Let me guess, probation be damned, they're putting the screws to you."

"It's not funny."

"I know, I know. Thank you for telling me, Casey. I'd hate to learn you've jumped ship and joined my father's business."

Casey walked to the window, taking in the afternoon ambiance of nature. It did little to lift his soul.

Behind him, Jackson's footsteps stopped. He had to tell him the rest, no matter how much it hurt.

He turned to Jackson and dipped his head. "I'm sorry to have to tell you this about your father. But—"

"Damn it. It's my father. Always my evil father, behind all things bad."

"I know. I know it hurts."

"No you don't. Your father, as you've pointed out, is a dentist. He's always been there for you. He's a good man. You don't know what it feels like."

Casey's heart imploded. "I do." He shook his head. "If you'd read all the papers, you would have found my father's name."

"What do you mean?"

"My father is working with your father in this mess. I know exactly how much it hurts. It's as though an atom bomb just flattened my entire life."

Jackson put a hand his shoulder. The place on his shoulder where the bullet grazed him didn't hurt anymore, but his heart sure did.

"I'm sorry, Case. There's got to be an explanation, one that puts some sense into this, one that absolves your dad. One thing's for sure, we're in this together. And if we have to, we'll get Lacey and Sterling to help investigate."

"Thanks. I'm on it. It's my case to work. I just needed to tell you what's going on and what I've discovered. Of course, the FBI thing rubs me wrong, but I didn't want to keep that secret from you. I can deal with it. But just so you know, I do plan to work undercover at the research facility. I'm going to ask Carter for a job."

Jackson nodded. "When you go for something you really reach. Okay. Keep me in the loop. Be safe."

Casey watched him leave, closing the door behind him. Time to think, time to puzzle out mounds of divergent bits of information and put them in their place.

But foremost in his thoughts stood Michelle. He knew when he gave an order his colony cats would obey. That included Quinn, so Michelle was covered for the day.

Then why was helplessness climbing up his spine and spreading throughout his body, taking all the starch out of his muscles? He looked at his arms and flexed his biceps. His strengths were more than physical. His ability to shimmer into a powerful animal gave him an edge. But he was helpless to his feelings for Michelle, a human. He knew the rules of secrecy and he would never put his colony or his species at risk. Still, his love for Michelle had been ignited. There was no going back. There was only living with that love in secrecy and separation or taking a risk that none of his colony members would support. No one but maybe Booker and his wife Shaun.

* * *

MICHELLE RUBBED her hand across Jojo's back, putting her attention on his soft yellow fur. He purred loudly, and turned to climb close to her face. She rubbed the sides of his head and watched him close his eyes while purring like a motorboat. The sound of it soothed her confusion. She sat on the living room floor with him and let his soft pawing on her lap quiet her anger.

There was nothing left to do but start packing. After Casey left, she had called her mortgage broker, hoping he'd clarify her right to ownership of her dear little house. He wouldn't take her phone calls.

The letter from the lawyer that Carter had dropped in her lap had been sent to her bank as well. She'd talked to the manager and been given her the standard "It's out of our hands" blow off. No one in this town could stand up to William Carter.

She hadn't had the heart yet to call her parents. The purchase of their former home by one devious William Carter would potentially drive them to do something rash. One did not do rash with Carter and get away clean.

But she had thirty days. She was not lying down and letting Carter walk over her. Things were different now. She'd vowed already not to let the rape determine how she would live. Now, resolve thrummed steady throughout her body. She'd taken a big step toward completely reclaiming her life when she dared to let Casey close. Revealing her secret to him had given her strength. By God, this was her life and she'd live it how she pleased.

Jojo looked toward the backyard window, then jumped off her lap. She heard the meowing, too, and went to the window to look out with Jojo. Her heart leapt. Madeline stood outside. Her presence was a good sign. She was coming back here for food.

Michelle gave a quick, dismissive thought to the memory of Casey's directive to stay inside, then crept to the back porch. She filled the bucket with cat kibble, trying very hard to be invisible and silent, then slowly stepped into the lawn. Madeline eyed her, a low growl grumbling in her throat.

"I mean you no harm, kitty, kitty," Michelle cooed, then placed the bucket a few feet from the cat. *So far, so good.* Madeline kept grumbling, but didn't blast out of the yard. Michelle took shallow breaths and carefully walked backward toward the porch, her fingers crossed.

If anyone was watching, she knew they would probably laugh at her antics. But Madeline's well-being was important. If food was unavailable here in her yard, Madeline would stop visiting, maybe even starve eventually.

One more step and Michelle was on the back porch. She leaned close to the corner wall where she was almost half hidden. Madeline's head went into the bucket and she warily took bites. Michelle's heart glowed, watching.

Suddenly Madeline popped up her head and tentatively scanned the yard. Michelle's breath caught. A small cracking sound had interrupted the cat's eating, but it hadn't scared her into running away. After a moment's pause, she ducked her head back into the bucket and resumed eating.

Another crackling whispered through the air, sending a shiver stuttering through Michelle's body. She got no sense of foreboding or fear, but something was out there in her field. Maybe it was the lynx. She willed it to come through the hedge. The lynx had given her a solid feeling of protection at earlier sightings. She could use some of that right now.

The sound didn't bother Madeline, probably because it wasn't from an approaching predator. Moments passed and Michelle's body stiffened, frozen in place so as not to intrude on Madeline or the lynx that possibly lurked nearby.

Madeline raised her head and licked her lips, then dipped her head into the water bucket Michelle kept filled and waiting. Except for the wind tossing the branches into creaking sways, she didn't hear any more extraneous sounds. Madeline finished her drink and sauntered off toward the field at the back of Michelle's property. Michelle let out a sigh and stretched her limbs. Curiosity burbled inside her. She hesitantly walked toward the side hedge. That's where she'd seen the lynx before. Maybe she'd get lucky and see him again.

She dared to peek over the hedge and began scanning the field. The dried weeds and grasses would provide camouflage, but not a lot since the fall season was taking its toll. Just about to give up, Michelle caught a flicker in the corner of her left eye. She turned quickly, just in time to get a glimpse of a large animal. Her heart raced at the sight of a lynx. But not her lynx. This lynx had russet fur, dotted in brown. As quickly as it passed through her attention, it was gone. It could have been the trees teasing her imagination.

But no. There was no mistaking the characteristic markings and tufted facial fur and ears.

Thoughts whirled in her head, distracting her as she walked back to her house. Two lynxes in the area were startling.

The crunch of a car on her driveway grabbed her attention. She didn't know whether to run inside and lock all the doors or see who had just pulled up. This fear, this confusion, felt all too familiar. It was a state of living she'd planned to leave behind here in her house as she made a new life.

So she didn't do anything. She just stood at the porch, torn between the fear and the power to take control of her life.

She closed her eyes and tried to settle her warring parts.

"Hey, what are you doing out here?"

At the sound of his voice, Michelle opened her eyes and let relief blanket her. "Casey."

He eyed her quizzically, then pulled her close. "What's going on? Didn't I ask you to stay inside?" He tossed glances around the property, but never let go.

She rested her head against his solid chest and breathed in his musky scent. It calmed her and strength and resolve trickled briskly throughout her body. She pulled back and offered a contrite grin. "There's nothing going on. It's just me. Me and my hypervigilance."

He nuzzled her neck, sweeping kisses up to her cheeks, her forehead. "Something triggered your attention, Michelle."

"My imagination. I came outside to feed Madeline—"

His eyes flashed, happiness glistening in the piercing hazel irises. "Madeline found her way back here? Of course you'd ignore my request to feed her. Encouraging her to come here for food is the right thing to do."

Self-confidence and determination swelled in her chest. He understood and supported her choices. "Yes. It's important to establish a new pattern for her. And then I saw a lynx."

Casey's pleasure dropped from his face. "Really? Where?"

Michelle pointed to the field. "Right out there. It was just a glimpse and it happened so fast that I could have mistaken it."

"But you don't think so." He crossed his arms and nodded his head. "Could you describe it?"

"What I saw was a large animal in the brush. It was russet color."

"And you're sure it was a lynx?" The wind tossed his hair in his face and he shoved it behind his ears, his gaze steady on her.

"No. It had the right physical characteristics. I've seen a lynx here before." He froze. "You have."

It wasn't a question. Michelle picked up thundering fear rolling around Casey. It made her gasp.

He opened his mouth to talk, then closed it. His eyes searched her face. Gut-aching misery came next, triggering her own fears. The minutes stretched and Casey just stood there, helplessness dripping from him.

"Casey? Did I say something wrong?"

He looked wistfully at her and he slanted a weary smile. "No. Not you." Casey wrapped an arm around her shoulders. "Let's go inside."

Inside, Casey guided her to the kitchen table, where he pulled out a chair for her and sat across the table. She'd rather snuggle up under his embrace, but she understood his reserve. That was his way, but she'd also made it difficult for him to get close without unintentionally raising her walls. It would take time.

"So it was the lynx that scared you out there?" He rubbed his thumb across his chin, and the scratchy sound of his stubble raised goose bumps on her skin.

"No." She dropped her head and measured her words. "It was you driving in my driveway. I heard the sound of the car and I just froze."

He reached across the table and took her hand in his. "I'm sorry for startling you, Michelle. Tell me how I can do better?"

A pleasurable sensation of power and tenderness rolled off him, the fear gone. Slowly, she drew her eyes up to meet his. "It's not you. It's me. I've been working very hard to just put the fear behind me. I think I'm doing the right things to reclaim my life finally, but now … "

He brought her hand up to his lips and kissed it gently. "You don't have to explain. I understand. This new threat from Carter is putting the pressure on your wounds. It's inevitable, Michelle. You've been through hell and your instincts are programmed to take care of you. They're what have kept you sane these years since your assault. But you're making great progress. Your triggers are rapid fire, and in the past I'm sure you didn't get a choice, they just happened. You can't fault yourself for your simply brilliant defenses."

The earthy tenor of his voice and the words he'd spoken filtered through her body and lit up her heart. "I like the way you think. In fact, I think I got a moment or so to decide what to do, flight or fight. I froze mid-decision, but it's a step in the right direction, ya think?" She flashed him a smile and got one beautiful Casey smile right back.

"That's a positive way to look at it."

The moment shifted, inexplicably. His enthusiasm for her healing process remained noticeable, but something else troubled him. He drew in a deep breath and she could sense his indecision.

He chewed on his lower lip and avoided her eyes. He pulled in another breath, then directed his gaze on her. "I have more information about your property, Michelle."

Her breath hitched as she waited for the bomb to drop.

"I have more to investigate, but so far it looks like plans for purchasing your property have been fast-tracked because a William Carter project has gone awry. He wants to put the problems behind him and move fast into the next stage."

"What does my property have to do with William Carter's project?" Casey steadily stroked her hand and she matched her breathing to it.

"I don't have all the details yet. But it's serious, the project, I mean, and his intention to take over your property. I don't want to scare you but he owns the facility down the street and that is where the project is taking place." He twisted in his seat, still holding her hand. His facial expression was sober, but impatience twitched in his muscles.

She pursed her lips and contemplated the spot she was in. "So I guess I start packing."

"No. This is your home and I intend to make sure it stays your home."

Not an ounce of doubt colored his statement. She took hold of his assuredness and determined to stand in it with him. "What can I do? I'm not going to just cower here day by day."

He walked to her side and gave her a tug up. He put his hands on her hips, sending warmth swirling throughout her. "You take care of your cats. You run Cats Alive, and you go to work. You live your life and let me take care of the investigation, and when I need your help, I'll ask. Oh, and I'll have someone keeping an eye on you and your property at all times when I'm unavailable."

"I don't want to impose on your life and it's unnecessary for others to take time away from their lives to protect me."

He gave her a smirk and shook his head and she knew she wasn't winning this one. But she couldn't deny the relief filtering through her, knowing she wouldn't be alone and vulnerable.

"Then that's settled," Casey said. "We're going to do what it takes to thwart William Carter and we're not giving up."

"I don't want to give up. It just all seems so complex and daunting. But I'm glad you're here with me."

"Always, babe." He pulled her chin up and met her lips with his, softly, tenderly.

The feel of his body pressed to hers and the taste of his lips sent heat cascading through her. Michelle pulled back and met his eyes, steamy and glazed. "You're so perfect," she murmured.

Instantly his mouth devoured hers, his tongue darting and dancing with hers. Cravings for more deepened her breaths.

Breathless, Casey took her face in his two hands and pierced her with his luminous eyes. "Are you sure about this?"

She answered by nuzzling in close, and kissing a spot just under his ear.

Her heart thumped loudly in her ears and she knew it wasn't a warning triggered by fear. Oh, the defenses tingled throughout her, but she was getting used to letting them go silent under the sweetness of Casey's tenderness.

He returned her favor by brushing a hot kiss to the similar spot under her ear, then her cheek. Delicious sensations fluttered through her, lighting a flame deep inside her.

"Damn it!" Casey pulled away to answer his vibrating phone in his pocket. He checked the screen, then frowned. "I have to take this, Michelle. I'm sorry."

Still breathless, Michelle nodded her head. She pointed to her bedroom and mouthed, "You can have some privacy."

CHAPTER 8

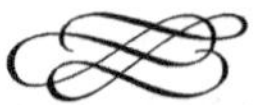

"What's up, Lara?" Casey shoved down the effects of kissing Michelle, clenching his teeth and letting out a strained sigh.

"I need to talk. Do you have a minute?" Her voice carried concern laced with tension. Casey scratched his head. "No, not really. But go ahead, what's on your mind?"

Lara cleared her thought. "You assigned Quinn to watch Michelle's house this afternoon." She paused, a heavy pause.

"Yes. Is there a problem?" He kept his voice low, so that Michelle wouldn't hear. He knew there was a problem but he wanted to hear from Lara first.

"Well, he did his job. He didn't see any problems." Again she cleared her throat. "Spit it out, Lara." He tapped his foot on the carpeted bedroom floor, waiting. "Is he here now?"

"No, he left. Right after he saw you pull in. And give Michelle a hug."

"Ah, I see. Did he also tell you that Michelle saw him in her field?"

Her voice dropped low. "No, he didn't mention that."

Casey knew how the colony felt about interspecies relationships, but he was the leader. He was charged with leading his life in such a way that he would keep the colony safe, doing things that were right. And the colony cats were to respect his decisions. "No, all he thought of reporting was that everything is okay … except the leader. The moggy leader, who hugged Michelle. He didn't feel the need to report that Michelle saw him." Casey rubbed his eyes, trying to sort out the implications of, well, hell, the entire day here at Michelle's house.

"You knew this wouldn't be easy. You and Michelle. It's not automatically a moggy versus pure situation." Her voice was still low, but the tension was gone and Lara's tone sounded kind, but businesslike.

His thoughts whirred in his brain, taking him to a variety of places, and none of them involved sitting here in Michelle's bedroom, taking in Lara's words. "Thank you for giving me a heads-up. I'll have to give it all some thought."

"I know you will. Meanwhile, I'll let Quinn know he messed up."

"No, I'll talk to him. If he brings up the topic, just tell him I'll be in touch."

He hung up, dropping his head into his hands. *How could I have been so stupid?* He'd been so careless about allowing himself as a lynx to be seen. By Michelle. All he'd thought—no, felt—at the encounters was the longing spearing his heart over and over. He'd worn the loneliness for so long. Desert dryness filled his soul. He ached for true connection, engagement at the soul level. And it was Michelle who'd intensified his need. He'd lost his mind and ventured to connect without any thought of consequences. Just a bit ago the moment had presented itself for him to tell the truth and he'd let it pass by. He had a choice to make and then an afterwards to live with the consequences.

He drew in a deep breath and went in search of Michelle. All he had to do was follow the small cat parade down the hall. He laughed out loud. "Michelle? I think it's dinner time."

She met him at the doorway to her bedroom. It lit up his heart to hear her laughter, bubbly and delighted. "Hey guys." She gave Jojo, Izabelle, and Munchie a rub to their heads. "Tiger is sitting on my bed, but he won't be far behind the parade when I get out the cat food."

"Just let me get out of the way!" He followed last in line to the kitchen, where Michelle made quick work of feeding her cats.

Casey peered out the kitchen window, his keen vision taking in much more than Michelle would see. It was still early, about five o'clock, but dusk had already settled into darkness. Still, he could see through the night that nothing looked amiss around her yard and field right now.

"Are you on duty, Casey?" She came up behind him and wrapped her arms around his waist. It ignited the intense longing for intimacy. *More than lovemaking, though that would certainly be nice.* It was a longing for connecting at a level of holding nothing back. Nothing.

"Um ... yes, I'm on duty." His thoughts remained stuck on the possibilities before him. His belief that everything is evolving.

"See anything out there? Maybe a stray cat or a lynx?" Michelle let go and stood beside him, peering outside.

"Nothing noteworthy. No ferals and no lynxes." He touched her nose and gazed at her sweet face. "You're so beautiful."

A twinkling chuckle escaped her throat. "You're full of shit." She turned toward her fridge and started pulling out fruits and vegetables. "You don't have to compliment me to get me to make dinner. I'm happy to feed you."

The smile she shot him registered somewhere in the area of his heart.

He had to be truthful with her. Honest and totally himself. He had to lay it all out there, take the risk that could lead him to perfect joy or utter rejection.

Michelle paused, holding the knife she was using to chop vegetables. "You're quiet. Why are you staring at me like that?"

Casey angled his head and kept his eyes on her. She put the knife down and knitted her brow. He rubbed his hand across his mouth, nerves jangling mercilessly. "I ... "

"What is it, Casey? You can tell me anything." The soft flow of her words poured throughout him, lulling him.

"Can we sit down in the living room?"

"Of course." She took his hand and led him to the living room. She sat on the couch and gestured for him to sit beside her.

"There are things I want you to know. Things about me and my life." He dropped his gaze to the floor, suddenly questioning his decision. Something very much like paralyzing fear rolled around in his gut. This awful sensation was new to him. Fear was usually something to manage and move past. This was different. "But what I want to tell you could change everything. I'm afraid of scaring you."

"Scaring me? How? With the truth? Even when it's hard, the truth is always better than a façade or a lie, Casey. I know you well enough to understand that you believe that, too."

She pulled his face up to meet her eyes. The clarity of her sapphire blue eyes urged him to continue. "I've made a decision to show you my reality. In doing so, I could put myself and others at risk, but I trust you. I just don't know if I should do that to you."

"Stop talking in code and tell me or don't tell me." She drew in a tense breath, as if preparing for something difficult.

He took her hand and pulled her to her feet. "Come with me outside and I'll show you."

Solemnly, he led her to the backyard. " Don't be afraid. I'm not going to hurt you."

The wind lifted strands of her blond hair, tousling it into pretty disarray. Her eyes glimmered in the low light, but he didn't see fear or sense fear. Not yet.

He stripped off his clothes. "Stay with me, please. There's more." The night air prickled his skin. He breathed fully of its crispness, closed his eyes, and shimmered. His thoughts calmed, accepting the decision of his lifetime.

On four feet, he jogged in circles around her, then stopped in front of her a few feet away and sat on his haunches. Watching Michelle.

Immediately her hands flew to cover her mouth. He didn't know if she would scream or faint.

But she didn't run. And she didn't scream. She dropped her hands to her side and stood in front of him, staring.

He chuffed. Once. Twice.

His insides screaming for her to accept him, he strolled close, shaking his head. "Casey?"

He nodded his head.

She blinked, over and over, fast. "It's you? How could this be?"

He slanted his head to the left, then the right, then nodded. Did he dare rub across her legs? How does one not explode into a million pieces upon standing face to face with a strange new reality? How could Michelle?

She reached out tentatively to touch his fur. "You're beautiful. It was you. It was you I saw in the field and outside my kitchen window. It was you who made me feel safe and amazed. I can sense it now. It feels the same as it did those nights and as it has just being around you, non-lynx you."

Casey's limbs quaked. His heart beat out joy and gratitude. His heart and soul expanded to contain it all. A gleeful yowl escaped his throat.

Michelle bent on one knee and looked him directly in his eyes. "Your eyes. These are your eyes." Excitement burbled up unrestrained. He could see it in her eyes. "You're a lynx. And a man." She gave him a quizzical look that drove what could only be called a combination purr and chuckle up from deep in his chest.

He didn't know he could do that. Purr, yes, of course. But laugh? *Maybe I've never had a reason to laugh like this.*

She slowly walked all the way around him, surveying his body. "I'm speechless. No I'm not. I want you to talk to me. Can you switch back to human form? Can I watch?"

So he shimmered.

Again her hands went to her mouth. Her eyes were wide and blinking as though her mind was finding it difficult to take it all in. Not him. The truth.

"What do you say to all that, huh?" Exhilaration filled him once again as the brisk temperature hit his skin and Michelle's reaction came a far cry less than screaming in terror. He picked up his clothes from the ground and dressed.

He took in her awestruck expression and sober eyes and tried to deduce her thoughts. His entire body screamed silently, desperately, to take it all back. After all, secrecy and distance were important tenets of his kind. They'd been strictly enforced, drilled into his head from an early age.

And now he'd broken those rules. The training he'd undergone flooded his mind and body with cascading dire results of his actions. He gritted his teeth, trying to allow the old thoughts but not get swept away.

He'd broken the rules, but it didn't mean it was wrong. *Everything evolves*, he thought to himself.

What had seemed like nanoseconds had probably become a drawn-out, awkward silence. Casey eyed Michelle, still wondering about her.

"You okay?"

Michelle held his gaze.

"You're shivering. All right with you if we go inside?" He tentatively reached around her shoulders, hoping she wouldn't flinch. He breathed out slowly when she leaned into him.

* * *

THE WORLD as she'd always known it had just disintegrated all around her, leaving her to stand on new ground. Very unfamiliar and unexplored ground. She chuckled to herself and peered up at Casey from beneath his warm arm. "Boy, when you share a secret, you really go wide. Or would it be go long? I'm looking for a football metaphor here and I should just stop."

Unease mixed with relief swirled from Casey. She wanted to reassure him she wasn't going to go crazy and call animal control.

They sat together on the couch, an awkward silence stretching between them. She dove in.

"I have so many questions." She stared up into his hazel eyes and tried to get a glimpse of his wild side. What she saw was the same Casey, who'd always carried a bit of wildness.

"I'm sure you do. I'll explain everything." His voice was soft, vulnerable. He caught her gaze and peered close. "First, I have one. Did I just lose any hope of being with you?"

"No. I'm not afraid of you."

He dropped his head against the back of the couch and stared up at the ceiling. "How can that be? I've just revealed to you a part of myself that only my kind know about. I'm a were-cat. I turn into a lynx. How can that possibly fit into your world view?" He turned an angst-filled expression on her and her heart dipped.

"You forget I'm psychic, sensitive. I see and feel things most people don't and most people scoff at my abilities. If you're looking for a girl who is most likely to fall for a half-human, half-lynx species, you found the right one." She took his hand in hers and brushed a gentle kiss to it. "I want to know everything. Maybe something in your explanation will tell me you and I don't make a good fit. But right now, I see you, Casey, furry and beautiful and wild-natured. While everything has changed, nothing has."

Casey laughed heartily, melting the awkward between them. "You talk Yogi-speak. I like it."

"Most people would call that flaky talk." Michelle flipped her hair. "You know, blond and flaky."

He grabbed her close and pulled her up to stand with him—her feet inches off the ground. "I like flaky talk, too."

His lips, inches from hers, beckoned for closeness. He loosened his grip around her and she slid down his body, sparking imaginatively delicious thoughts. He placed a soft kiss on her lush lips, and stayed, not lifting, but pressing harder.

She wrapped her hands around his head and demanded a long exploration of his tongue, his mouth. Compelling urges swept up and down her body as she languished on his lips and licked at the tip of his tongue. Through hazy eyes and slitted lids, she saw a reflection on his face to match her desires. Her breathing came in long pulls, and her beating heart pounded wildly against his chest.

He stroked her soft cheek and she allowed the desire and tension to bloom.

"Casey, don't leave," Michelle pleaded. She felt his knowing. He knew full well what she meant. She was asking him to stay present in this moment, not raise his reserve and pull away.

She'd laid her vulnerability out there for him to match, or not. His tender heart and tremendous strength only drove her to want to be closer to him. The risks be damned.

He picked her up, a low growl rumbling in his chest, and carried her to her bedroom. He stood her on the carpeted floor, his gaze never drifting from her eyes, and removed her clothing, one piece at a time, until she stood naked in the darkness.

She reached to pull off his shirt, but he ripped it off first, then his pants, and lastly his boxers, all landing in a pool at his feet.

"Casey, your skin is so exquisite." Michelle ran a hand across his muscled chest.

Her touch raised goose bumps on his skin, but the pure admiration in his eyes fed her soul like nothing else had before.

He took her hand and led her to the bathroom across the room. Quickly, he turned on the water. She was grateful it didn't take more than seconds for warm water to spill from the rain showerhead.

He stepped into the shower, leading her close behind, and gently shoved her under the spray. He stepped up, naked skin to naked skin, as the water spilled over them. "I thought you had questions," he teased.

Michelle glared at him through strands of damp hair that fell across her face. "Not now."

He chuckled, a carefree laughter that delighted her senses.

He kissed her right shoulder, then her left, then brushed soft kisses one by one, getting closer to her full breasts. "My god, Michelle, you're gorgeous."

A moan rolled out from her throat, and she arched her head, taking in every atom of his kisses.

He dropped kiss after kiss on her breasts, then licked each taut tip, catching droplets as they gathered on her nipples.

She opened her eyes and ran both hands over his shoulders and down his body, grabbing his behind and rubbing it. "You have an amazing ass."

She knelt on her knees, taking his hardness in her hands and caressing. She never wanted to stop. She dipped her head to catch water droplets that drizzled down his body from the shower. He dropped his head back and slammed his hands against the stall wall behind her. He gasped as she took him into her mouth. She allowed herself the intimacy of licking and sucking on him, as he stroked her head and moaned.

Suddenly he pulled on her shoulders and she stood, gliding up his body to meet his lips, fierceness to fierceness.

As Casey reached around her to turn off the water, he grabbed a large towel from the rack on the wall and wrapped it around her. He grabbed a matching one for himself, then took her hand, pulling her to the bed and opening the blankets for her. While she climbed in, he toweled off quickly, then slid in beside her.

The feel of his skin against her incited a powerful inclination to bring him inside of her.

But patience, excruciating patience, directed her. He looked down at her, his eyes glistening, and dipped his head to kiss her, hard.

Screw patience.

When they each pulled back to breathe, Casey's eyes gleamed with passion. Her heart beat fast and spirited at the unabashed desire he shared. Sure, she'd had sex before, before she'd turned inside herself and away from passion. But this absolute senseless and driving thing with Casey was not merely sex. It was waves crashing on cliffs, drenching rain on pavement, brilliant sunlight sparkling on Lake Michigan.

She felt his restraint and tried to match it.

"I want to savor every nanosecond of this closeness with you," he said, his voice dusky.

Slowly he moved down to worship each part of her with his kisses. Her shoulders, the swell of her breasts, her nipples, her abs.

She squirmed, frantic. "Casey, I, I—" He silenced her with a deep kiss.

On a sudden urge, she shoved him on his back and lay on top of him, nuzzling his neck and running her fingers through his hair. Her eyes slitted, she traced the muscles of his body, winding down his chest, his abdomen, to his groin.

He flipped her on her back, his muscles flexing exquisitely. "Casey!" Her voice came out raw, eager. How much longer could she wait?

Gently, he moved her legs open and she complied without any hesitation. He kissed her femininity, waves of pleasure rippling from him.

She grabbed his head and pulled his face to her lips, exclaiming, "Casey, I'm going insane." Her voice sounded throaty, breathless, but she was past trying to restrain herself. And she knew she wanted nothing more than to be with him, no holding back. She wanted him inside her.

He took a second for protection, then returned to her as though no time passed. A powerful shudder shook his body as he pressed against her, exploring her feminine parts with his male counterparts. She wriggled unabashedly. A growl grumbled up from his chest. A glimpse of his raw nature echoed through her sensually. He pressed again, tantalizing her as she thrashed and whimpered.

The vigor of his desire drove her as she sensed him reaching the moment they both wanted. He entered her slowly, methodically.

"I want to make it last," he whispered in her ear.

A smile lit in her heart. "You're driving me to the point of no return," she managed to whisper back. "You feel so good."

He pulled back and thrust harder. Michelle arched her back and trembled. "Casey," she whispered hoarsely.

He thrust again. "Michelle." He thrust deep, his eyes closed. His climax mirrored hers, like two beating hearts, they trembled and hollered together.

Casey brushed Michelle's lips with a delicate kiss. "You okay?" he whispered.

Michelle smiled, her eyes still closed. "Yes."

Spent, content, she rolled from underneath him and snuggled under his arm. He tucked the sheet around her and kissed the top of her head.

He rolled sleepy eyes at her and smiled. "It's too early for bed." His lids dropped.

"I'll make us dinner," Michelle offered but didn't move. She wanted to hold this

moment in her heart forever. Yes, it was sex and she was completely satisfied. But it was more. Casey had been himself with her. The intimate connection they'd introduced had blossomed. The special gift he'd given her bathed her in something she never wanted to go away.

She reached for him and kissed him gently, reverently. He lingered a moment, but restlessness stirred in him.

"I love you."

She smiled, wondering. "Are you leaving?" She could ask him to stay as he'd promised. But the urgency hammering from him let her know he needed to take care of things.

"I'm sorry. I'll arrange for someone else to keep watch." He pulled on his clothes and stared down at her. "There are things only I can do."

She sat up in bed and pulled her knees up to her chest. "I understand. Take care of yourself."

He bent to kiss her, igniting a glow inside her once again. "You, too. I'll answer all your questions soon."

She watched him walk down the hall, pausing to rub the willing heads of several of her cats. "You're about to have company," he called to her.

CHAPTER 9

Casey changed into tight-fitting dark clothes and waited in his car until he saw Asher drive his car down the road into the field next to Michelle's house. He climbed out, knowing leaving his car here and jogging to his next destination made the most sense.

Asher walked toward him, so he waited, tapping his fingers against the roof of the car. "You need me to take care of your girlfriend, huh? Happy to, Case." Asher laced his words with innuendo. His charm came naturally, but left a bad taste in Casey's mouth.

"I'm not talking about a visit or some kind of Asher-designed interaction," he growled. "This is business. I expect you to watch without being detected and take action only if harm shows up."

"Sure. I know. All business tonight. But don't think it escaped me that you didn't deny Michelle is your girlfriend."

Casey stared at him, silently. The bobcat could slither and slink with the best of them.

His golden yellow eyes were keen, of course, and he had uncanny agility. His intellect was equally keen, an attribute that was useful in his line of work as a sportswriter and made him an asset to the colony. As a pure, Asher was prone to giving Casey a hard time. It was an arrogance that made Asher a pure pain in the butt.

But Asher knew when to submit to his leader. "Sure. I understand."

Casey slung his small bag of tools over his shoulder and took off for the building next door. As a were-cat, Casey could take the two blocks stretch on foot to the building in minutes. In his dark clothing and on foot, he could slip through the darkness without detection.

As he reached the line of trees that protected the large building from prying eyes, he crouched low and sped across the lawn, keeping an eye on the surveillance cameras placed at various corners. When he reached the building, he crawled between the brick walls and the low bushes that lined the building.

But walls were no obstacle for him. He squinted and opened his sight to what there was to see behind the walls. Clinging close to the exterior of the building, he scanned while walking the perimeter.

The brisk autumn breeze whispered across his face and he raised his nose to pick up all the scents he could. The more intel he gathered the sicker he felt in his gut. He had to get inside to be sure, but he already had a pretty comprehensive picture of what this building was about. He felt dirty just being near it, but he had to get inside.

He placed his tool bag on the ground, unzipped it, and pulled out his glass cutter. Earlier, he'd hacked into the building's security system and knew he was up against a pretty stringent system. Quietly and swiftly, he picked a window he could unlock from the inside and would give him a large enough opening to drop inside. He went to work, silently cutting a circle, then removing it with a suction tool, and carefully moved his hand inside to unlock the window, then pushed it open.

No time to waste, he had to disengage the alarm from the mainframe computer. With that done, he crept to the room he'd seen from outside.

Down the hall, to the left, then a right. The whole building fuzzied his mind. It stunk of ill intentions and evil. He reached the door he wanted, pulled in a deep gulp of air, and let it out slowly.

He heard feet coming his way and saw behind the corner wall two people in lab coats. He cracked open the door and crept inside, searching around for a place to hide. His senses screaming, he ignored everything around him but the door he knew opened to a closet. He quickly pulled it open, stepped inside, then pulled the door closed behind him.

He breathed a sigh when he saw through the closet door that he'd just made it into hiding before the two lab coats entered the big room. The room was lined with cages and filled with cats.

As the coats walked from cage to cage, they filled water and food dishes. From his hiding place Casey counted twenty cats. All ages, all breeds. He could sense free floating confusion and anger from the cats. When the cage door on one young cat was opened he hissed and growled and hit the coat who'd tried to pick him up.

"Come on. They're fed and watered. Let's weigh them and get this over with," one coat said to the other.

"Go ahead, you try with this one. He's always the tough one."

"Grab him by the back of the neck and weigh him," the other coat gritted out. "Tomorrow it gets serious here and some of these cats are going to be really angry tomorrow night."

"The drug works that fast?"

"They're upping the dose. Something about moving faster because of the deaths. Something went wrong."

"What's gone wrong?"

"I don't know. No one tells me anything. It's safer that way, anyway. Keep that in mind," said the coat who seemed to be in charge. "You'll live longer."

The two men turned off the lights as they walked out the door. Casey listened as their feet walked away, went through a door, and took some stairs to another door. He didn't hear them after that door closed, but he waited in the closet.

From the room came small cat vocals. Little meows from kittens. Low, throaty meows from adult cats. Distress sounds, to his ears. Anger swept through him, raising his pulse, gritting his teeth. He balled both fists, controlling his fierce reaction to the plight of these innocent cats. If he had his way he'd sweep them all, all twenty of them, up in his arms and take them away from this hostile atmosphere.

His fingers twitched. He could open all the doors and let the cats run free. *That would throw a wrench into things, I bet.*

But first he had to find out more specifically about this place and its goings on, especially about the deaths the coats discussed. Didn't that take precedence?

Instinctively, he put his hand to his heart and bowed his head, thinking. The coats had referred to something happening tomorrow that would affect the cats. How could he step into the room and look into the cats' faces and leave them behind?

He pulled in a deep breath and let it out heavily. He had to leave them behind. This was not a rescue mission, it was a mission to learn more about William Carter's plans for the cats and Michelle's property.

Casey gathered his emotions and slipped out of the closet. *It sure would be great to be telepathic right now, like Asia. Being of like species will have to do.*

Quietly, he walked the rows of cages, whispering hope and encouragement to the little captive creatures.

"I'll be back to get you out, very soon." He held the truth of his words strong and steady until the room quieted.

The floor he sought next was up three flights of stairs. He took them swiftly, then quietly crept to another room that held fewer cats and a line of computers. He strode immediately to the cages, planning to assure them he'd protect them. But two steps toward them he stopped. He almost doubled over with nausea, hitting his stomach hard. *I have to do better than this. Man up, Casey!*

He stepped closer to the cages. Two held adult cats that hissed and spit at him. He stared into their eyes and couldn't find their personalities, souls, anything that made them who they had once been. They were more than just angry feral cats. Their amber eyes burned with hatred. And they could barely stand on deformed legs. And enormously long claws curled menacingly from their feet.

Looking at the two twisted and deformed cats made Casey's gut ache.

He turned his attention to the other two caged cats and caught his breath. "Madeline." The furry gray cat crouched low in the cage and peered up at him with sleepy eyes. *Drugged.* As a feral, Madeline would typically be too afraid to act subdued on her own while he stood so close. The cat sitting in the cage next to her looked equally sedated.

Casey knew he had little time to gather enough information to bring a light on the research being conducted here, so he settled for a cursory search into cupboards, along counter tops, and inside drawers. He snapped photos of as many things as he could, then shoved his cell phone back into his pocket.

His brain jammed with images of vials of blood and curious liquids, meters and machines, and more, he turned back to Michelle's feral cat. "Change of plans, Madeline." His eyes on the other three cats, he spoke softly. "I'll be back."

He pulled Madeline carefully from the cage and gently placed her in his tool bag, then zipped it almost completely closed. A quick scan of outside the room told him the coats weren't around, so he threaded through the hallways and stairs until he reached the first floor room where he'd entered the building. Hoping against hope that Madeline would remain still, he reached through the window and set her on the ground, then climbed through it himself.

Sprinting toward his car, the sense of foreboding lifted incrementally with each step that took him farther from the Carter building.

He peeked inside the bag as he reached his car and saw Madeline sleeping. While that made things easier for him, it twisted around in his gut, cutting like barbed wire. It was unnatural behavior for Madeline. She needed immediate attention.

He drove into the main street, and punched in Lara's phone number.

* * *

MICHELLE LOCKED HER BACK DOOR, dumped her purse and bag into the passenger seat in her car, and slipped behind the wheel and headed to work.

Even though Carter's threat sent chills racing throughout her body, damned if she'd let it deter her from living her life.

A lazy yawn stretched across her face. Memories of lovemaking with Casey last night fluttered sweetly in her heart. His mixture of tenderness and ferocity sent her to a place of unbelievable ecstasy. The thought of it even now made her heart skip erratically.

Soberness settled over her remembering him standing in front of her, sharing his secret self, the beautiful body of a lynx. It'd made a whopper of a surprise, and prompted questions about what else she didn't know about life. The wonder of what life could be welled inside her and lightened her steps as she walked into Aegar Investigations.

She checked the clock and smiled. She'd actually made it to work early.

A few minutes later, with the coffee brewing, Michelle looked up from her desk as Sterling and Lacey walked in.

Sterling lowered her head a bit and peered at her. "Michelle?"

Lacey giggled. "That clock must be wrong, my dear." Then she sniffed the air. "Coffee? You sweet child." Lacey grabbed a mug and filled it, then held it to her nose. "Mmmm."

Michelle chuckled. "Maybe I'll start a new trend. Be early to work and have coffee already made when you arrive." She smiled.

"You know we're just teasing you, right?" Sterling slanted her head and smiled at Michelle. "You're the best office manager slash cat rescue owner I've ever known."

Michelle beamed. "Thank you."

Lacey looked over the rim of her mug at Michelle, sipping coffee. Michelle let another smile escape.

"You're very happy this morning." Lacey studied her. "Do you have good news about your property?"

Michelle frowned. "No. It's worse. While you two were out of town William Carter stopped by and made some threats."

Sterling's mouth dropped open. "Threats? What did he say?"

Michelle summarized the encounter and included Casey's promise to help. "Casey believes the whole mess is William Carter's doing and that ultimately his plan to take my house will fall through."

"That son of a bitch. This time Carter has gone too far." Lacey remained quietly staring at Michelle, while Sterling pounded her fist on the desk. "There's got to be something big in Carter's plans. You know we're here for you."

Michelle wriggled under Lacey's scrutiny. She couldn't share her secrets, but it was hard to ignore them bubbling up and threatening to escape her lips.

"It's great that Casey is investigating." Lacey grinned. "He's skilled at it. Right?"

Michelle whacked her palm to her forehead. "I can't keep anything from you. I am happy today, despite my dire circumstances. Casey and I … we've, well … "

"Hooked up." Lacey finished her sentence, beaming.

Sterling's eyes widened. "How did I miss that?" She wrapped her arms around Michelle. "So he's watching over you?" Sterling winked.

"He is." Michelle dropped her gaze, unable to suppress a smile. "And you're okay with that, sweetie?" Lacey lifted an eyebrow.

Sterling opened her arms wide and glared at her sister. "Lacey, I'd say she's more than okay with Casey's closeness. She's practically glowing."

"Yes, she is. I'm happy for you. You deserve happiness and love with someone wonderful—Casey."

Michelle breathed in a deep breath, then released it slowly. She wrapped a lock of hair around a finger and pursed her lips. "He is wonderful. I've known that for some time. The problem has been me. But so far I'm able to be close with him and not freak out. Maybe he's even good for me. Maybe I'll fully get my life back."

"You've worked hard at reclaiming it. You know what they say, what goes around comes around. You've worked on your issues and lived a caring life; the good is coming around for you." Lacey patted her on her shoulder.

Her kind words and support sifted through the darkness and the fears like soft snowflakes on a cold ground. "Once I get past this stupid William Carter problem, I might actually believe you."

The phone rang and Michelle answered while Sterling and Lacey walked into their private office. It was a potential client. Michelle took down the man's information, then put him on hold to pass it on to the sisters.

Fortunately, the business had survived a slump during the past six months and now the sisters' schedule kept them very busy and the company in the black. Michelle's heart warmed just thinking of her good fortune to work for two strong, kind women.

With monthly reports to generate, Michelle had plenty to do, too. She set aside the sticky business with Carter and opened the Excel spreadsheet she needed to begin. Numbers and formulas were her "thing," and it was easy for her to become engrossed in cells, rows, and numbers. It felt concrete, productive, and structurally sound compared to much of the rest of her life.

She glanced up at the clock and realized, in between phone calls, she'd been working on reports for almost two hours. She turned toward the window overlooking the downtown streets and let herself linger on unprovoked thoughts of Casey. Casey, the delicious man who could change into a lynx. She'd seen him shift and it had seemed so easy and smooth. So second nature. What actually was second nature to him, she wondered. There were all those questions left unanswered last night. Delicious sensations of kissing his lips, caressing his skin, and losing control in his arms shimmied through her. These were sensations she would like more of. A smile from inside landed on her face.

From on top of her desk came the sound of her cell phone vibrating. "Hi, Casey." Michelle couldn't keep the smile out of her voice.

"Hey, beautiful. Sorry I had to leave last night, but I had work to do."

"I understand." *Geez, I'm practically cooing.* "Thanks for the note."

Silence on the other end filled the space between them. Finally, Casey spoke. "You didn't stay home."

"No, you told me to go to work, take care of Cats Alive. Besides, I … last night … I've got to live my life." Her heart raced as she searched for the right words.

More silence. More holding her breath. "I know. I did say that. I guess I really want you protected. Sorry. I'm just trying to keep you safe until everything falls into place."

She heard his teeth grind and she could envision his sober face. It somehow comforted her. "I appreciate your help—"

"I know," he interrupted her. "Well, I have to talk to you. Can you get away for a while or would tonight be better?" He stumbled awkwardly over his words, which was very unlike Casey. Worry spread like icy fingers in her chest. "I feel like we left so many things up in the air last night. I'm eager to see you. But if you're busy, it can wait." He cleared his throat.

"I could meet you over my lunch hour. And if it takes longer I'm sure Sterling and Lacey won't mind. Would that work?"

The muffled sounds from the street below kept her grounded, but fear hung so close, as though it sat just inside her peripheral vision, letting her know all was not well.

"Yes, that would be perfect." She heard concern lace his voice, but also a bright lift that soothed her.

"I'll pick you up outside your office, then. What time?"

"Just a second." She put him on hold and hollered to the sisters, asking if she could take an early lunch and maybe a long lunch.

"Of course," they chimed in together. "Do what you have to do."

"Casey, I'm ready to go now."

CHAPTER 10

After leaving Madeline with Lara, Casey had called a meeting of his colony, Lara included. Since it was mid-morning and most of the cats worked, he'd decided to have lunch at his house. It would be the second meeting he'd called about Michelle. Last night they'd met at Lara's house to let everyone know about Michelle. It wasn't a discussion. He'd tried to make it clear that as the leader, he aimed to guide the colony into a sustainable future, one that would possibly have new rules and new ways of doing things. He'd announced that he was getting emotionally close to a human, Michelle. That announcement met with some disdain and some tentative acceptance. Today he was taking things a step further.

Pulling up to the curb where Michelle stood, a lump formed in his throat. She stood there, all bright and shiny and perfect, not knowing what was ahead of her. Longing to protect her and not scare her away filled every cell of his body.

She waved and climbed in the car. Before she had time to speak, Casey pulled her close to him, as close as the console would let him, and held her tight. "I missed you, sweetheart."

Her embrace felt like coming home. He breathed in the scent of her hair, all warm and flowery, and let his muscles relax.

She pulled back and studied him. "I missed you, too. You okay?"

He turned back to the wheel as she relaxed against the seat. "I'm just happy to see you." It was true. It also was only part of the truth. Nerves were jangling loudly in his ears. He wasn't afraid, but he knew full well how ominous things were right now. Not the least, introducing Michelle to his colony.

"Where are we going?" Michelle rested her hand on his leg and warmth pushed his pulse higher.

"My house. You haven't been there, have you?" He took in her profile as they drove along. Her nose, a nose that turned up just enough to be cute. Her lips, full and tempting. Her hair, flowing in the breeze from the open windows, dancing like gossamer.

"No." She ran her fingers through his dreads, tempting his senses. "Hmm … I wonder why I haven't. Not even before when we were dating."

He ducked his head, his eyes on the road. "I think it will all make sense to you very soon."

"Ooh, that sounds mysterious."

Tension fired between them and as much as he wanted to tell her everything, he now wanted much more to take her to bed for the day. He licked his lips at the thought.

"Yesterday was really nice." She dropped her gaze to the floor. "I know I've been difficult. Thank you for understanding."

"We've both had our personal issues. Thank you for not running away and screaming when you saw me as a lynx." He covered her hand with his, and she looked up and smiled. The air felt thick with emotion—real, honest emotion.

He pulled into his driveway and hit the garage door opener. As soon as he stopped Michelle was out of the car and out in the yard.

"This is gorgeous. I guess I've always thought of you as a city boy." She turned to flash a grin at him. "Your house is definitely country, rural, whatever you call it."

"I can manage in the city just fine, but put me in the middle of forest or field and I'm happy." He walked up behind her and dropped his arm around her shoulders. He sniffed the damp air. "I love this lush natural setting for my home."

"I do, too." She studied him silently for what seemed like minutes at a time. Her hands against his chest stirred emotions inside him that comforted him. "I can see now that this fits you well."

She started walking to the front door and he stopped her. Excitement tinged with reservation slithered around his gut. "I want you to know all about me, Michelle. No holding back. But what I've exposed you to already is only the tip of the iceberg. Life is not what you believe it to be. There's so much more."

She squeezed her eyes, sending him a quizzical expression. "I know that, Casey. I'm fine with that."

"If at any point in this lunch time you feel overwhelmed, let me know. I'll take you right out of here." The wind through the trees whispered seductively of things unknown and mysterious.

"Okay," she mumbled. "I'm sure I'll be fine."

He wanted to hold her, somehow ensure he wouldn't lose her when she learned it all, but just then other cars drove down the lane to his house and turned in his driveway and the side of the lane to park.

"Let's go inside," he said in her ear, and led her through the front door. "Look around if you want, but since it's your lunch time I'm going to get started on a plate of deli meat and cheeses, breads, and other foods." He left her in the entry as he stepped into the kitchen.

She peeked into the kitchen and gasped. "This is a nice kitchen." He watched her survey the room. "It's so spacious. I see you have commercial grade appliances. Nice. I love the slate flooring and countertops. I like the large windows and the skylight is a great touch."

"It works for me." He smirked and ducked his head into the bottom of the refrigerator to retrieve a selection of cheeses, then placed them on the island in the middle of the room. "Have a seat?" He pointed to the tall chairs that sat around the island.

Michelle was already picking her way through the adjoining family room, clearly admiring the comfy looking upholstered furniture. "I love your stone fireplace and the floor to ceiling bookshelves.

"Hey, Case! What's for lunch?" called a young man from the foyer.

"Whatever you make for yourself, Asher."

Michelle stepped into the kitchen just in time to hear another person ask about Lara. "Is Lara coming?"

Casey winked at Michelle just to assure her. "Lara is on her way."

At Casey's wink, the blond woman turned to her. "Oh, hi Michelle."

Everyone, all six strangers, turned toward her. "Hi. Do I know you?" She nodded her head toward the young woman.

Without missing a beat, the woman extended her hand and grabbed Michelle's, shaking it in a strong grip. "I'm Elizabeth, Elizabeth Sands. But everyone calls me Tizzy."

"Nice to meet you. It seems you already know my name." Michelle smiled up at Tizzy. "Your eyes are so unique, they remind of the color of cognac."

Casey stepped up beside Michelle and spoke close to her ear. "Remember what I said. No holding back." He wanted to make this easy for her. The only way he knew to do that was to stay by her side.

"So, Lara is coming? I'm guessing there are things going on here I don't know about." Casey squeezed her hand. "Everyone, this is Michelle Slade."

A group welcome went up, and she accepted it graciously. She looked from face to face, eyes to eyes. "No way. It couldn't be possible. Your eyes are all different but they share the same beautiful clarity I first saw in Casey's golden eyes. Are all of you lynxes?"

Casey cleared his throat. "Yes, they are. Everyone here knows you because I told them about our relationship. They have been a part of the investigation into why cats are missing." He stopped and assessed the room for impact.

"I don't know what to say. I guess I simply wonder why? Why you all have been so kind as to care about the missing cats?" Michelle wrapped a lock of hair around her finger and tweaked at it.

All eyes turned on Casey.

"Michelle, rather than tell you, we're going to show you who we are and why we care." He squeezed her arm and left his hand lying there as he smiled down at her.

They each disappeared out of sight. As the man Casey had called Asher turned to leave, he nodded at Michelle, then grinned at Casey. "Casey, make sure she doesn't pop. This is a lot to take in."

"Go." Casey glared at the man, then turned to Michelle. "I'm not the only were-cat, sweetheart. I know this is big, but I don't want to keep secrets from you anymore."

"I know. No holding back. That's how I feel, too." She leaned against his chest and he wrapped an arm around her. "I'm not afraid."

Then the mini parade began. She pulled back from Casey and watched lynxes stroll into the kitchen from the hallway and from the family room behind her. She squeezed Casey's hand.

"You're all so beautiful," she breathed. "Different, but all striking."

"We are larger than regular lynx, but other than that we share many characteristics," Tiz said.

Suddenly a bobcat ran through the kitchen and jumped onto a couch in the other room. It startled Michelle, and she let out a short burst.

Casey suppressed a chuckle. "Like the lynxes in the room, the bobcat has a ruff of facial fur, pointed ears tipped in black, and a short tail. His fur is a yellowish brown with dark bars and spots." Casey felt like a tour guide in a zoo.

The bobcat briskly pounded his tail against the couch and chuffed.

"That's enough, Asher." Casey slanted his head at Michelle. "Bobcats belong to the same genus as lynxes. This one is too playful for his own good."

Asher turned yellow eyes on Michelle and chuffed again.

Casey frowned, noticing goose bumps dotting Michelle's arms. He rolled his eyes when Asher jumped off the couch and stood feet away from her. He arched his back and let loose a snarling growl. It rumbled deep in his throat and ended with a full-bodied roar. It nearly blew Michelle off her feet as she stood in the ferocious authority of his growl.

Casey lunged at the bobcat and hollered. "Enough!" His

commanding voice was unmistakable. Asher dropped his head, his eyes down.

Michelle turned her delicate blue eyes on Casey. "So, you're in charge?"

He nodded. "Yes, this is our colony of were-cats and I am the leader." Casey wrapped his arms across his chest, inches from Asher. "I apologize for his actions. That was uncalled for." Then he rubbed a playful hand atop Asher's large head.

Behind him, Asher shimmered into his human self. Michelle stood stoic.

* * *

THE FRONT DOOR opened and closed and Michelle stopped breathing. Lara, her former roommate and good friend, walked into the kitchen.

Casey gave her a quick hug, while Michelle stared. "Things okay at the clinic?" He said it so low that Michelle wasn't sure she got it right.

Lara nodded, then hugged Michelle. It felt good to see a familiar face, but the implications thundered through her. "You're a lynx, too?

"I see Asher has been performing for you."

"Is that what this is?"

Casey turned around, then swatted naked Asher's head. "Pants on, you nut. You trying to scare Michelle?"

"Oh, Casey, it could have been worse, I guess." Lara patted Casey's arm. "Sorry, Michelle. You've never met my little brother. That was on purpose. He's a wild card." She laughed heartily.

"I had no idea about you, Lara. You're a lynx."

"I am. I'm sorry to keep that part of me secret from you. According to the were-lynx rules, it would have been wrong not to."

Michelle's brain stuttered, trying to process everything she was learning. "Um … yeah, Casey told me. Secrecy and privacy help safeguard your kind." Suddenly a premonition popped up, grabbing Michelle's attention. She saw Lara treating a cat that appeared to suffer from severe disfigurement. Her breath froze in her lungs. The premonition stopped but the sick feeling in her gut continued.

Casey spoke up quietly. "Did you just have a premonition, Michelle? Like all of us," he said, directing his words to the were-cats, "Michelle has special gifts. She is highly sensitive and experiences premonitions."

She felt a blush creep up her neck and redden her face. "I'm sorry. Sometimes I get caught up in a premonition. You know about me, Lara." Lara nodded, and Michelle pointed to her. "You found out cats are being stolen. That's how Casey and your colony got involved."

Casey's eyes pinned her. "Yes. Some of Lara's clients reported that their cats, roamers, had gone missing. We went into action. Do you want to share your premonition?"

Michelle checked in with her gut to find the sick feeling easing up a bit. "I saw Lara treating a cat. Its legs and feet were badly deformed."

"That's another piece of the puzzle. Thank you, sweetheart." He pulled her close and she relaxed against his wall of a chest. It soothed her. "We can talk more later about that situation. Right now let's eat and relax a bit." He turned concerned eyes on Michelle.

She looked around, taking in the laid back feel of the room. "Things are pretty easygoing among you all, right? I know you don't eat humans, so I can relax, too."

"Right. We're not natural enemies and I hope you can relax." Casey squeezed her arm again and elicited tiny quakes of gratitude inside her.

"Right now I'm pretty much in awe. I ... I ... "

"Yeah, what do you say to all this, huh?" He pursed his lips, then touched the tip of her nose. "Lara will be back in a second. She slipped out to shimmer. That way you'll know what we all look like in both forms. Because we have to be naked to shimmer, we're all accustomed to our nakedness showing up occasionally. But it's just a part of how we work. You're not going to be subjected to male or female nudeness all the time."

She was listening, but only sort of. Awe and curiosity had filled her completely. It would be a while before she would be able to recognize who was who as a lynx. But already she saw differences. Their fur and their telltale lynx markings were there, but each one had a variation of colors and their eyes looked distinctive.

When Lara joined the group, her difference was obvious. She wore the same markings as Asher, as she, too, was a bobcat. Her smooth brown fur and black colorations blended with her nut-brown eyes to present a beautiful were-cat.

Lara walked right up to her and rubbed her leg. Her fur was smooth and made Michelle's skin prickle. "You're amazing, Lara."

Lara chuffed and nodded her large head. Michelle laughed. "Oh, you agree. Sweet."

Asher waltzed back in and headed to the kitchen counter. "Didn't someone say something about lunch?"

"Just give Michelle a little more time. You can make a sandwich if you can't wait." Casey's voice was firm but kind.

"I've seen you before." She pointed to a russet lynx lounging on the carpet in the living room. "I saw you at my house a few nights ago. What were you doing there?"

Casey pulled her close under one arm. "That's Quinn. It was his turn to take watch over you and your property. You weren't supposed to see him." He frowned at Quinn and shook his head.

Quinn's matching russet-colored eyes flashed at Casey in such a way Michelle thought she could read his meaning. Get off my back, or something akin to that. He rose and padded out toward another room.

Casey sighed heavily in his wake. Then one by one, he pointed to each lynx and named them for Michelle and shared their occupation and special talents. Asia, a reporter, could communicate telepathically with animals. Lara had healing powers. Conrad worked as an investment banker and had superior strength. Tizzy was a teacher and had the ability to leap really high. Quinn, a construction contractor, had superior spatial ability. Asher worked as a sports reporter and had an ability to charm others. Booker, a physician, also had the power to heal.

She didn't think she would ever forget this moment. Something she'd never known about the world has just opened up before her and brought her into a new reality. The implications swelled inside to a point she couldn't contain. Possibilities were endless.

Her eyes met Casey's and saw something new there. He emanated a mixture of confidence, openness, and reserve. Probably the perfect traits for the leader of a group made up of part human, part paranormal creatures living in a world of humans. At least she thought that was what she lived in.

As the members of Casey's colony shifted back into their human forms, Michelle stood apart, watching them sit down to lunch. Something seemed to constrain their conversation. They talked, but it felt strained.

Casey set a plate with a sandwich and fruit in front of her. She couldn't make herself take a bite of the sandwich. She popped a grape in her mouth and struggled to chew, but her mouth was so dry. Every time she looked up she caught Lara staring at her. She was a guest here, among private people. The last thing she wanted to do was behave rudely. But it was obvious. Something else brought them together today. Something more than a meet and greet with her.

Sitting next to her around the counter slash table, Casey rubbed her arm. His skin warmed her concerns. But she still wanted to know more.

"She's ready, Casey. Quit dragging this out." Lara kicked him under the table. "Yeah. I need to get back to work." Hazel eyes that glimmered with green glints

turned in her direction. It was Asia.

"Yes. Good idea." Casey set his glass of water aside. "Michelle, I told you you'd never be alone until this mess with William Carter gets straightened out."

Michelle nodded her head but kept quiet.

"The colony has helped out, taking turns watching your property and keeping you in a line of sight when you've left your house, because I can't always be at your side."

Michelle held up a hand in protest. "I don't expect that of you. Or any of your friends."

Tizzy chuckled. "It's okay, Michelle. We got your back. We live a quiet life and keep to ourselves, as Casey has probably told you. But when danger occurs, our unique abilities allow us to set things straight. With you, it's a little more personal. Casey has become attached to you. And the problems swirling around you appear to connect to a larger problem."

Michelle rubbed her chin, her thoughts whirling. "Is the bigger problem related to my house? Or do you mean the missing cats?"

Booker's topaz eyes gave away his identity. "We've collected enough information to know there's a bigger problem, but we don't know what."

Casey directed his gaze at Lara. "And there is still much more we don't know, but we're working on it. In fact, I learned some pivotal information last night." He turned sad eyes on Michelle. "This is going to sting a lot, sweetheart. I penetrated the building down the street from your house. I needed to know more about the research project. I had to piece it with other things I've learned. It turns out, William Carter Enterprises is responsible for the missing ferals and roamers."

Fear froze Michelle's drooping heart. "What do you mean responsible for?"

"I found caged cats in that building that belongs to Carter. I don't know all that's going on there. We're working on the pieces still. But it's not good."

Michelle felt something ragged and shadowy roll off Casey. It sent slivers of fear piercing her veins. "Tell me."

Lara sighed heavily. "Michelle. It appears Carter is doing tests on the cats. Some of the cats have suffered deformities. You saw that in your premonition. I don't know why, yet."

"This is terrible. What is he after?"

"We don't know." Lara studied her, then continued. "He had Madeline in one of the cages."

Michelle clenched her teeth. She couldn't scream. It wouldn't do any good. The helpless feeling she was so accustomed to carrying around threatened to weaken her muscles. Her heart raced in her ears and she wanted to … do what?

Casey's arm encircled her. He held her, steadied her. "When I saw her she was sedated. Something big is happening tomorrow and it's killing me that I don't know what it is. But it won't happen to Madeline. I took her to Lara's clinic and she is being cared for."

Michelle shook her head. The air around her thinned and she struggled to keep her grip on the present. "Thank you, Casey, Lara. All of you for your help. It means so much to me." Tears blurred her sight, and she heard her voice get quiet. "What can I do? Those other cats need help. What have I done to prompt such malicious action?" It all poured over her, like a bucket of cold water dumped on her head, drenching her. The rape, the trial, the potential loss of her house, and now the cats' disappearances, all tied to her.

"No, Michelle. This evil is not your doing." Casey cradled her in his arms. "William Carter is the darkness that infiltrates this town, irrationally but significantly."

He caressed her hair as she rested against him. His voice, reverberating in his chest so solidly, offered promise to make things right.

Asia spoke up. Her voice was laced with a low grumble that got Michelle's attention, pulling her back to the present. "I can communicate telepathically with animals, Michelle. I've read Madeline and she's better. Her trauma at the Carter facility has left her troubled and fearful. But she's going to recuperate just fine. You had something to do with that, not the research on cats."

Michelle studied each person sitting at the table and gathered her determination. "What's next?"

The room gave a collective sigh and the others sent out vibes of getting down to serious business. She soaked in it, pulled strength from it.

Casey directed a soft gaze at her, wrapping her in a cloud of love. "Maybe you've had enough of a shock for today."

"Shock? You mean learning about you and your colony?" She shook her head. She had to make him understand. "I've seen something wonderful. It's been a gift to discover the truth about you and your friends. I'm privileged to be one whom you trust. I won't let you down. And right now, I'm drawing from your strength. Shocked? Maybe. But in a good, eye-opening, amazing way."

Casey nodded his head, soberly. "There is a lot more to share, about ourselves, I mean. But right now the most compelling thing to attend to is what next what Carter has planned."

The members sitting around the table all nodded. Booker spoke up first. "Have you formed a plan? I have patients this afternoon at the hospital, but tonight I'm all yours."

"Actually, right now all I need is for you all to do your turn watching Michelle." Casey's angry expression chilled the air in the room. "And Lara, give us a schedule for watching the facility. I don't want anyone going inside, but keep us abreast of who and what comes and goes. I suspect things are escalating. But we're going to introduce a change of plans for Carter."

CHAPTER 11

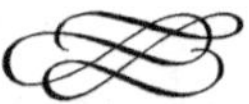

Casey walked with Michelle up to her office, arm in arm. "Come in. Say hi to the sisters." Unease still stirred in her gut, but Casey's presence calmed her.

They walked through the door and immediately Sterling and Lacey walked into the outer office. Casey exchanged a look with Michelle. "Hi, you two," he said.

Michelle hung her coat on the hook and watched them try to constrain their exuberance from Casey.

It didn't work. "What's up?" he asked, studying them.

Sterling held up a disk. "We have footage!" She shoved it into Michelle's computer and waited. "What you're about to see is a gathering at a restaurant of various businessmen and women. It's pretty fuzzy, but you can make out some faces."

Casey peered closely, stroking his stubbly beard. Michelle watched the footage, too, squinting her eyes, hoping it would help clear the picture.

Pointing to one face, Casey blurted out, "That is William Carter. What is this, a board meeting?"

Lacey shook her head, contemplative. "No. Not of Carter Enterprises. Keep looking."

Impatience drove through Michelle like hot peppers. "I don't recognize anyone but him. What's so exciting about this grainy footage at a restaurant?"

Casey exchanged glances with Lacey, then Sterling. "I recognize a few other faces. For one, my dad, right there."

Michelle squinted again, trying to make out the man's face Casey pointed to. "Your dad, eating with William Carter? I don't understand."

Casey stared unblinking at the frames.

Michelle gasped, pointing to another man's face. "No, no. That's Bruce Dobosky." Her heart pumped hard in her chest.

Casey's arms wrapped around her, instantly warming the cold drifting through her.

"I'm sorry, Michelle. I didn't recognize the son of a bitch or I wouldn't have sprung this on you." Sterling dove to stop the images from filling the screen.

"No. Don't. I'm okay. What is this meeting about? It seems like more than a chance dinner together." Michelle pursed her lips and grounded herself to the floor as the footage resumed.

Between the three of them, Casey, Sterling, and Lacey identified nine men and women from Laurelwood. Each one held a reputation for being a powerful politician, judge, businessperson, banker, scientist, or developer.

"We've been able to piece together information that points to an organization made up of these people. They fly completely under the radar locally, probably because of their connections." Sterling ejected the disk and continued. "They seem to share interests in influencing business, finance, and politics. They call themselves The Nexus Group."

Lacey propped herself up on Michelle's desk and rolled her eyes. "They meet in secrecy. That's all we know."

Casey's gaze scanned the room, but his eyes were distant. "That's a lot. Do you know how long they've been in existence?"

"For nine years," Lacey said. "I did a search on the number nine and didn't come up with much, except in numerology nine stands for taking over."

"Nine people. Nine years." Casey stared at the floor. "I wonder how the nine is significant for this group."

"Yeah, like this ninth year is part of a timeline, or something." Michelle's brain whirred in circles, trying to pull something useful out of the air. "Has anything happened in the past, say, when they first organized?"

Sterling punched in a link and brought up a news article reporting the beating of a teenage boy, the son of one of the members. "The article says that the boy was mugged and beaten by a group of athletes from the Laurelwood High School. The boy had been hooded, so he had no way to identify the young men, but he did recognize who he thought was the team quarterback."

Casey read out loud from the article that the boy survived, but soon after the quarterback disappeared. His body was found later in a farmer's field in a nearby rural area.

Michelle squirmed uncomfortable in her seat. "Vigilante group?"

Sterling troubled her lower lip. "I don't think we have enough information to predict what the group's goals are. But we'll keep looking."

"This whole situation with my house and the missing cats is growing. My brain needs a break. I'll finish up these reports this afternoon, then I'm going to go home to spend some time with my cats. I've also got some stuff to attend to with Cats Alive."

"I've got things calling for my attention, too." Casey tweaked her cheek, smiling softly at Michelle.

"I'll walk you out," she offered.

"As far as the hallway. I don't want you alone for even a minute."

While Sterling and Lacey beamed at her, Michelle walked with Casey to the hall outside the office. "Thank you for today, Casey. It means a lot to me that you've shared all about yourself with me."

He pulled her close, tilting her lips to meet his. A delicate kiss to her lips flipped her heart. "I've been alone and lonely for so long, it's a gift to me from you to allow me to share the truth. I've had nightmares of it turning out completely different. Thank you."

She answered with a kiss. "So is there anything else I need to know about you?"

"Oh, probably a thing or two. Nothing you need to know right now." He took her hands in his and dropped his gaze to look at them. "I've got some things to do. I might not see you tonight or tomorrow. But whatever happens, please don't turn me away."

The elevator door opened and two people talking walked out and down the hall. When she was sure they were out of earshot, she responded. "I know I've pushed you away before. I don't plan to do it again."

She pivoted to return to the office, but stopped to toss a grin over her shoulder. "If you don't fuck up."

* * *

Urgency pushed Casey's pulse. There wasn't much time. He could feel it all around him. Something was perched on the edge of dropping. But he had to talk to Jackson. He pulled his car into his work parking space and leaped out. And stopped just as quickly. "Agent Callahan."

"Mr. Mitchell. Walk with me." Dressed in a gray suit and gray dress shirt, the agent put his dark sunglasses back on and walked toward the end of the parking lot, where his black SUV sat. He opened the passenger side for Casey and motioned him inside.

As he slipped into the driver's seat, he eyed Casey. "It's been a few days since we talked. What do you have for me?"

Casey drummed his fingers on the door handle. He was not about to share what he'd learned with this agent. Not when he knew only enough to cause havoc with Michelle's life. "I don't know anything. Carter is surrounded by privacy measures. I've been unable to penetrate them yet."

"Really." His dry voice made Casey's skin crawl. "Do you not understand the assignment? There is no wiggle room. I need information from you ASAP."

"If you know lives are at risk, you know more than me." Casey scrambled inside, trying to keep his temper quiet. "Look, I'm willing to help. But I need more time."

The silent man in the back seat got out and opened the door for Callahan. "I'll give you a week."

The other man slammed the door closed and climbed back in. As Casey walked toward the Carter, Inc. office building, he watched the SUV drive away.

He swept away any thoughts about the meeting with Agent Callahan. He had actual important business to deal with and he didn't need nonsense cluttering up his mind.

He grabbed some documents from his office. He took the steps up to Jackson's office two by two. "Hi, Julie, is Jackson available?" Without waiting, he knocked on the door and opened it enough to peek in. Of course, he could see through the walls that Jackson was in his office, but he had to keep up a pretense with the normals.

"Come on in, Case."

Casey gave him a stilted grin. "Mind if I close the door?"

"Go ahead. Have a seat." Jackson peered at him, his eyes locking on Casey's. "Spill."

Casey eased back in the chair and realized he'd been tight, held in, all day. He let a sigh escape, gathered his thoughts, and told Jackson about the recent developments with The Nexus Group and reminded him he was going undercover.

Jackson took it all in, his face grim. "I'm so sorry you've found your dad is a part of something destructive with my father. But you know he has no limits. He'll pressure people, pull them in to something they don't understand, and create an illusion to suit his needs."

"I know. I hate that my dad seems to be involved in whatever this group is too. I can only hope he's unaware of what exactly he's gotten himself into. But I promise you this: if my dad is dirty, I'll make him pay." His words sounded harsh and unloving. He didn't want that kind of obstacle between them, but he wasn't going to tolerate deceit.

His mind tracking multiple thoughts, Casey walked to his own office on autopilot. The stuff he'd picked up at Carter's research facility and learned at Aegar Investigations earlier reminded him of a comic book storyline or something from a summer blockbuster. Not something out of real life. Of course, some people would see him, a were-cat, as something from a fantasy.

His first thoughts were all Michelle. *What is she doing, where is she, is she safe, can I avoid hurting her with my next move?*

The noises coming from other offices and the break room disrupted his thoughts of her. It grated on him that he didn't know much about Carter's plans. The Pretid device figured into them, clearly, but instinctively Casey saw that quite possibly the device testing was a way to gather personal information on participants and somehow use the device to administer a drug, one that was already in animal studies at the research facility near Michelle's home.

He walked to the windows and scanned the nature area that made a courtyard outside the Carter, Inc. building. The trees swayed, carefree, going with the direction of the fall breeze. Autumn leaves drifted to the ground, covering it in dark rust and deep purple.

He turned back to his desk and inside his gut, something shifted. He knew his next steps.

A quick call to Michelle came first. It rang once and he heard her voice on the other end. He melted.

"Hi, Casey. Miss me?"

"I do miss you. But I have a favor to ask you." When she didn't say anything, he continued. "No matter what you see or hear in the next few days, don't give up on me."

"Casey, you sound so serious. You're scaring me."

"I know, I know. It sounds ominous. It's something I have to do and I wish I could tell you more but I can't. Just promise me you'll—"

"I'll be here."

He heard her breath, her voice, and he believed her. "Thank you. I know you can take care of yourself, Michelle, but we can't underestimate William Carter. The colony will be watching over you. You won't be able to reach me, but if you need something, don't hesitate to call Lara."

"Okay. I don't understand, but don't worry about me."

"I'll be thinking of running my hands down your back, to your behind." The thoughts of her naked skin raised pressure in his groin.

"Stop. You're making me miss you more."

"I'll be in touch soon. Good bye, Michelle."

He set down his phone, shifting gears. His inside growled with demands. Casey wanted to march to his dad's office and insist on an explanation.

But his brain knew better. If he did that he'd surely raise suspicions with Carter and his merry men and women. No, he had to be patient and smart. That meant making an appointment with the devil himself.

After a brief conversation with Carter's secretary, during which he'd poured on his charm, he had his appointment. Admittedly, suspicion gurgled in his stomach when he was able to schedule it for that evening. *Hell, I'm not one to question destiny. William Carter doesn't know it yet, but his destiny lies with me.*

He flexed his fingers, feeling the gathering tension. He needed a run. He had a few hours before his meeting with William Carter. The more he thought about it the more he felt the stirring in his skin and body to shimmer. He gathered up the paperwork he'd been studying for days, shoved it in his briefcase, and shrugged on his jacket.

He eased his Prius around traffic, trying to remain calm and patient. He'd never experienced an information overload before. The things he knew about Carter—his research facility, his property takeover—spun in his head, trying to land in a coherent picture. Clearly, too much information wasn't the problem. It was a lack of important pieces. That's why he had no choice but to talk to Carter.

Casey nailed his car horn when another vehicle swerved in front of him, too close, and he had to slam on the brakes.

His impatience churned just under his skin. Finally, he took a left turn that led him out of the city and toward his home.

When he arrived, it took him no time at all to step inside, strip, then finally shimmer.

He shoved open his back door, a door specially made to open with a foot pedal, and strode out into the early evening. He grabbed big swigs of air and the spinning in his head calmed. His nose lifted to gather the musky, sweet scents of the forest around him. His ears perked as birds chittered while squirrels chattered and small animals scurried beneath brush and logs.

He shook out his muscles, beginning with his head and ending with his tail. He settled into a slow trot, feeling each foot connect with the ground beneath him. He sped up, sprinting through the trees and letting himself almost disappear in the sanctuary that was this forest. Swerving around one tree, then another, Casey reveled in the release of tension and the refilling of his soul.

He ran until his breath came fast and full and his heart pounded out a strong, rapid beat. He could run like this forever.

But it would be running away, and really, he didn't want any such thing. He knew that with all that he was.

He headed back his house, slowing his pace for a cool down. At the border between wild forest and field and his backyard, he plopped down into the brown and drying grasses. *Breathe, in and out, in and out.* Emptied of tension and frantic thoughts, Casey felt ready to go face-to-face with William Carter.

CHAPTER 12

*M*ichelle lifted the phone off the receiver for what felt like the hundredth time that day. New clients, return clients, regular clients, all clamoring for help … right now, of course.

Between dealing with phone calls and finishing up monthly reports, Michelle hadn't had time to think much, not even about Casey's strange phone call.

This second time around with him had brought him to her at the moment she really needed him. The transparency and intimacy gave her strength and, most of all, hope. She wished that his strange request wouldn't trigger old stuff in her. She could promise to believe in him but if the situation brought up her defenses, she didn't know if she would let them have the car keys—could she trust him enough to relinquish control?

Michelle tossed a stray lock of hair out of her face. *Damn it! The rape changed me, but I'm not going to let it define me anymore.*

Her queasy insides told her it wasn't as simple as making a declaration. There would be challenges, but she had enough determination to fill a fountain.

Simultaneous thoughts of Madeline and Lara popped into her

head. The sisters were gone for the day, and it was past five o'clock, time to switch gears.

She punched in Lara's cell phone number and waited. "Hi, Lara. Busy?"

"Actually, just finishing up."

"Could you come over for pizza at my house, my infamous house?"

Lara laughed. The sound tinkled in Michelle's ears, urging her to grab on to it and believe the best. "Infamous house?"

"Yeah, the one stalked by lynxes and William Carter, not that there are any similarities in the two."

"I'll do you one better. I'll bring the pizza and Madeline." Michelle's gasped. "I would love to see her."

"It's a deal then. I'm just leaving the office in a few."

"I'm on my way out the door. Thank you, Lara."

* * *

THE GARAGE DOOR at Michelle's house glided open at an annoyingly slow pace. "C'mon, slow poke." She parked, closed the door, and pulled her things from the passenger seat. Unlocking the back door, she sensed movement behind her. Her heart in her throat, she slowly reached inside her purse and wrapped her hand around her pepper spray. From the corner of her eye she saw the passage door to the backyard was slanted open. *That's supposed to be locked.*

She pivoted, pointing her pepper spray at whatever she found. A masked figure, dressed all in dark clothing, reached out toward her face, muttering, "Get out of this house."

She screamed and pressed the pepper spray button, aiming the burning spray at his face. He ripped at his mask and turned toward the back door.

Outside in the backyard a fearsome yowl erupted. The man stumbled out into the dusk, just in time to be slammed by a fury of golden fur and claws—Conrad.

Michelle's hands drew to her mouth. Conrad shouldn't expose himself to this man.

She stood there, watching, and realized Conrad was doing very little actual damage to the man's body. He sat on his haunches, chuffing, after scaring the man into racing through the yard and out toward the street. As the man disappeared, Conrad nodded at Michelle. She wasn't sure what to do, go to him or leave him to his business. When she heard a car pull into her driveway, her heartbeat picked up its pace. Conrad nodded her to go inside, where she peered through the closed blinds in the living room windows and saw Lara coming toward the door, juggling pizza and a cat carrier.

"Come in. Here, let me take the pizza." A crisp breeze flew in the door, bringing chills to her skin. Michelle's anxiety still raced through her veins, pumping her heartbeat higher. "You just missed the excitement."

Jojo, Munchie, Tiger, and Izabelle all ran toward Michelle. "Hungry? Let's feed you guys, too."

Lara stopped mid-step and pierced Michelle with a long look. "What excitement?"

"Here, let me take Madeline to the back room where she can chill. How is she doing? I want to know all about it." Michelle's words tumbled out at high speed, but she couldn't help it. Fear mixed with relief and happiness to create unstoppable chatter. She hurried to the back bedroom and placed Madeline, already covered by a cloth over the carrier, on the floor. She lifted up a corner of the cloth and took a tiny peek. As expected, Madeline let loose a low growl, but she looked like herself. Her face said back off, but her cuteness pulled at Michelle's heart. How terrible that she'd undergone an ordeal at Carter's research facility. Michelle laid the cloth back down over the cage.

She quietly walked out of the room, closing the door behind her. Back in the kitchen she pulled plates and glasses from the cupboards and set them on the table, ready to enjoy pizza with Lara. *At least pretend to enjoy.* Circumstances unsettled her nerves. Adrenaline trembled her fingers.

"Hey, Lara. I didn't know you'd be here." It was a fully-clothed and human-looking Conrad, walking in from the garage passage door.

Lara sat emphatically at the table. "What. Is. Going. On? Aren't you supposed to be outside, discreetly watching the property, Conrad? And Michelle, why so jittery?" She grabbed a slice of pizza and took a bite, waiting.

Michelle exchanged a glance with Conrad. He nodded to her. She turned to Lara, her heart rate finally slowing. "I came home a few minutes ago and was surprised by an intruder. Conrad scared him off."

"Did you get a good look at him, either of you?" Lara studied them both, pinning them with her eyes.

"He wore a mask. He told me to get out of the house. I shot him with pepper spray and he ran outside." Michelle took a slice of pizza and set it on her plate. Veggie. Her favorite. She couldn't gather enough saliva in her mouth to think about taking a bite.

"What about you, Conrad?" asked Lara.

"I attempted to remove his mask, but he was so frightened by my appearance and vocalizations that he was a scrambling ball of arms and fists. Do you mind?" he asked, reaching toward the pizza.

"No, help yourself." Lara handed him a slice. "So we have no description." She frowned. "But we probably know he was dispatched by William Carter and we know he was trying to scare you, Michelle. Sure he wants you out of the house, but this was most likely a fun prank for him. Make you afraid to be in your own home." Izabelle purred appreciatively as Conrad bent down to rub her head. He threw another slice down his throat, then shoved back his chair to leave. "Back on duty. Thank you for the pizza." He placed a hand on Michelle's shoulder. "Carter can try to scare you but as long as we were-cats are around, which is every moment of every day, you'll be safe."

Michelle thanked him and watched him saunter outside, where she expected he would shimmer. The danger surrounding her and her home was getting to her. "It's not right that you and Conrad and the other members of your colony should be inconvenienced and put in danger because of me." She dropped her head to her arms resting on the table.

Lara shoved at her head. "Don't be silly. You don't understand how our colony works yet. We willingly take care of our own. Now you're one of us, simply because you know about us and you haven't freaked out."

Michelle lifted her head, her eyes growing heavy. "That sounds heroic of you." She tilted her head, thinking. "Casey has been heroic for me. He's helped me reclaim my life. That's a big deal."

Lara ducked her head sheepishly. "I don't know if it's heroic to watch over my best friend." She placed her hand on Michelle's and Michelle took comfort from it. "Especially a friend who is caught in William Carter's crosshairs. It's nothing we can't handle."

"Have you taken on similar projects in the past?" The wind outside blew through the trees, releasing more leaves in the darkness to dance in front of the kitchen window. It made her long for simplicity in her life.

"We have helped rescue injured animals, helped children enjoy nature, things like that." She rolled her eyes. "We keep to ourselves. It's safer for everyone that way. But there are times when it's right to step up and help others in need. That's what the colony has done since Casey took leadership."

The wind blustered outside, sending shivers up and down Michelle's spine. "Would you like to spend the night?" Her voice sounded faint to her ears. "I guess I'm still unsettled from the intruder. But if you can't, I—"

"It sounds like a good plan," Lara interrupted. "Life minus my former roommate is lonely. Plus, that way we both can keep an eye on Madeline."

"She's all right. I checked her through the carrier." Michelle cleared the table and led Lara into the living room. Lara flounced into the upholstered chair and Michelle took the couch. The cats followed, settling in around them both.

"Well, she's still very feral. But there's been no attempt to tame her. When Casey brought her to me he was pretty shaken up. She'd appeared to have been drugged, but it wasn't anything harmful, I guess, just a sedative. Probably to keep her manageable."

"No serious ailments?"

"She had apparent deformities that other cats caged in the facility displayed; severe deformities, evidence they'd been given something. But she responded to muscle relaxant I gave her. I need a sample of that before I can say more about what its purpose is." Lara shivered. "It scares me to think about it. I don't want to speculate what Carter has planned for the cats. I just want to stop him."

Michelle sat across from Lara in silence for a few minutes. The conversation was sobering. Mindboggling. But what about Casey? "You mentioned things changed when Casey became the colony leader. Can you explain more about that? How long has he been the leader? Is it something you all vote on?"

Lara propped up her feet on the ottoman. "He's been the leader for about a year. He took over after his dad's tenure. Before that, the colony leaders have followed the ancient rules."

"Ancient?"

Lara laughed. "Yes, ancient. Records of were-cats date back centuries. We've always been secretive, protected our own, and followed the old rules. There's lots of them, but in the case of leadership, the rules required that a colony leader be a pure."

"A pure what?" Michelle's muscles started to loosen and she sank comfortably into the cushions, interested to learn everything about this species.

"Original were-cats carried the genetic trait, hence, pures. Moggies are were-cats who come from one were-cat parent and one normal. Or a cat who's become a were-cat by being bitten. Originals, pures, took great pride in being direct genetic offspring. They felt moggies were less sophisticated, untrustworthy because of their mixture of genes. But as Casey is fond of saying, everything evolves. Even were-cats."

"Interesting. He's probably right."

"While in the past leadership was passed down generations of pures, Casey decided it was time for change. Everyone agreed, or at least most of us did. But it's very important that Casey rule nearly perfectly, because the pures are always waiting for him to mess up so they can replace him. Not all of us. I'm pure and I'm behind him all the way. I think there are four pures in our present group."

"It sounds like a tough job." Michelle heard a tiny meow from Madeline and ran to the bedroom to check on her. "Are you okay, sweetie?"

Lara walked up behind her. "She's been having nightmares."

"How do you know?

"She told Asia. Asia can communicate telepathically with animals, remember?"

"Oh, yeah. That's amazing. You're all making me jealous with all your power and keen hearing and eyesight and special abilities."

They walked back to the living room and slumped into their same seats. "You're perfect the way you are. Don't hate on the were-cats," Lara teased.

"Never. Thank you for sharing all this."

"I'm sorry I couldn't before. But you understand, right?"

"I do. I think things happen when it's the right timing. If you'd told me years ago, I might have failed miserably to be a good friend."

"I doubt it. You've always been open minded and able to appreciate that life is full of surprises."

Silence fell again and Michelle tapped her fingers on the couch, contemplating. "Are there any other rules I should know about?"

"If there are, you'll find out. I'm really happy about you and Casey. He's a gem. You didn't know him in his younger years, though. A little more on the wild side, then."

"There's a lot of that in him still. How old is he?"

Lara pursed her lips and slanted her head to her left, then her right. "He's thirty-five years old. I'm thirty-two."

"I did some searches on lynxes and learned they don't typically live in colonies. They're loners. And this area is not your natural habitat. What's up with that?"

"Aren't you the smartypants?" Lara tossed a couch pillow and hit Michelle's head playfully. "All true. But as I said, everything evolves. Our colony has adapted to this area. There's no reason we have to live in the mountains. We're part human, just like you. We can live in a city or out in the forest. It's up to us, not instinct or survival."

Michelle heard a noise in the backyard and flinched. "Did you hear that?"

"Of course. I have the keen hearing of a lynx, remember?" Lara walked with her to the kitchen window.

Peering through the darkness, Michelle smiled. She heard chuffing and saw a beige-white lynx sitting in the yard. "It's Tizzy." She waved and the lynx nodded, then trotted off toward the bushes.

"The next shift arrives. Hopefully we'll do better than we did earlier." She rolled her eyes. "Conrad is good. I don't know how he could have missed that man in your garage."

"Sneaky, I guess. Which is different than stealthy, like Casey."

Lara's laughter bubbled up out of her throat like a song. "Thanks for being here tonight," Michelle said. "Please make yourself at home. I've got to make contact with some people about Cats Alive."

It was still early evening, early enough to make calls and respond to emails. Several emails were simply reports from foster parents about the process of socializing the cats and kittens with them. One parent complained about the former owners of two cats, who had handed them over to Cats Alive because the cats were leaving too much hair on the furniture.

Exasperated, Michelle paced the kitchen floor on that one. She rehearsed giving the former owners a piece of her mind. How could they abandon the two cats when they'd been a part of the family for four years? *Ever heard of brushing?!* The foster parent said the cats were doing owner searching. It made Michelle's heart dip, imagining the furtive pacing and meowing as the cats waited for owners who would not come back for them.

She knew in time the cats would accept their new circumstances, but it still made her blood boil at the heartless treatment. *Why don't people understand that cats are not a piece of old luggage or a worn out lamp to toss away?*

A big sigh and she was back in her seat, responding to the emails. One grabbed her attention instantly. An owner of a roamer asked for help finding her cat. By the look of the cat in the photo attached, it was light gray with dark stripes. "Aww, you're so cute."

Michelle read on and learned that the cat was chipped and always returned home after spending some time outside. She made a call to the owner to get a description and summary of the cat's habits and personality.

"Her name is Graysan? You think she's about two years old and she's spayed. She's friendly? That will help. I've got your address, so I'll set some humane traps around your neighborhood and hope to catch her quickly."

Before Michelle hung up, she gave her mini-lecture about allowing cats to roam. She tried to pound it home that cats who roam are more likely to die young, suffer with ticks and fleas, get hit by a car, or become diseased. "Once they become acclimated to a solely indoor life, they do much better. It's what responsible owners do."

She heard Lara finish her shower and check on Madeline before walking into the kitchen.

"How is she?" Michelle asked, without turning away from her laptop. She was just finishing posting the missing Graysan on the Cats Alive website and sending the link to other cat rescues.

"She ate and used her litter box, so that's good." Lara walked into the living room and looked through the on-screen TV guide, flipping rather quickly. "It's still early. Feel like a movie?"

"Sure. My head is spinning. A little vegging would be good. Nothing intense. I don't feel like crying or getting scared."

"Coming up." Lara selected the movie, a romantic comedy, and they sat back to enjoy.

Part way into the movie, Michelle turned her ear toward the backyard. A sound had drawn her attention, but as she waited, everything seemed quiet.

Lara stopped the movie and turned to her. "I hear something, too," she whispered. "Are we just jumpy?"

Lara's eyes flew wide open. At the same moment, Michelle noticed a red dot floating on Lara's chest. "Get down!" she screamed, and dove for the floor herself. Michelle's four cats scrambled down the hall, out of sight.

Crashing from the back door sent Michelle's nerves almost over the edge. With no time to think or prepare, suddenly she faced men with guns pressing her to the ground, her face into the carpet. She saw boots and dark pants tucked into them. There were no words, only the sound of heavy breaths, as the two pairs of boots put plastic ties on her hands and feet. Trying to turn her head to see Lara, she got a boot pressing hard on her back. "Don't move."

Lara screamed, but it muffled in the carpet and brought a punch to her head. Michelle fought the waves of fear that pounded in her head and sent trembles through her arms and legs.

A voice muffled, she thought behind a mask but she couldn't see, spoke gruffly. "This is for you, blondie. We're not going to use the guns tonight. But you've been warned to leave this property. It doesn't belong to you anymore. Pack your things while you can and move out or we'll be back, and if that happens you won't be leaving with anything."

The only thing Michelle could hear was her heart pounding in her ears. She couldn't think, couldn't breathe. Terror froze her body flat on the floor.

Lara! And Tizzy! She rolled up on her side and saw Lara was still unconscious. The men might still be around, but priority now was to get out of these zip ties and help Lara.

Thoughts of what she'd learned in the personal safety class she'd taken after the rape had surfaced through the panic that ripped through her when the "boots" first charged in. It was almost second nature, as the class had promised. Funny that boots hadn't noticed, but she'd clenched her fists and held them side by side while he pulled the zip tie tight. Now, she relaxed her muscles and turned her fists sideways and tugged her hands through the loop.

She sat up and used a fingernail to lift the locking bar from the ratchet mechanism on the tie binding her feet, and pulled the tie open.

Relief flooded her, but she wasn't done yet. She gently shook Lara. "Lara, wake up, sweetie. I'm going to get you out of the handcuffs."

Lara moaned, lighting up Michelle's hopes. She checked her breathing and her pulse, so she knew Lara wasn't dead, but still, the sound she'd made was a good sign of life.

She made quick work of lifting the locking bar first on the tie around Lara's hands, then her feet. By then, Lara was rubbing her head and trying to sit up.

"Take it slow. You've been unconscious. I'll be right back. Just lie still."

The back door stood open. It was a sight that chilled her blood, but she had to check on Tizzy. Cautiously, she stepped onto her porch, carrying her flashlight. It was a huge, metal one with a long, bright beam. Michelle stepped into the yard making a mental note to thank her dad a hundred times for impressing on her the importance of such a thing. It lit the yard and would serve as her backup weapon, if need be.

Clouds hid the moon and stars in the sky and Michelle felt the darkness on her skin like a cotton sheet. Even with her flashlight, out beyond the beam was the unknown. Her nerves urged her to run.

But there was nowhere to run to. No place where she could escape from William Carter's reach. Running and hiding was not the answer for her anymore.

She trudged to the hedge and slipped through to the field. *So far no men in sight.* But where was Tizzy?

She jogged through the field to places she'd seen Casey and Quinn in lynx form. No Tizzy.

Had she left when her shift ended and no one replaced her?

Her beam found Tizzy's car parked in a group of trees, barely visible. She rushed to it, running around the driver's side, and found a naked Tizzy slumped to the ground.

CHAPTER 13

"Tizzy! Wake up!" Michelle checked for a heartbeat and found a faint one. She stood in the dark field, fear biting at her heels, trying to rouse Tizzy. There was no blood anywhere, so she'd probably been hit over the head. Thank God she wasn't shot.

Michelle stood and peered back toward her house. The distance was too far to … do what? Drag her? Carry her?

Everything in her longed to call Casey. But he'd told her he'd be unavailable and to call Lara if something happened. Well, Lara needed her help, not the other way around. Ruefully, she slammed a palm to her forehead. "Think, Michelle. Think fast."

She couldn't leave Tizzy lying on the ground. She wouldn't. The car keys dangled from the ignition. If she could get her in the car, she could get her back to the house.

She grabbed her shoulders and bit by bit, pulled Tizzy up into the back seat. She was slender and probably didn't weigh very much. But she was muscled. Michelle's back screamed in protest and her arms ached, but she got her completely in, slammed the door shut, and slipped behind the wheel.

Her foot shoved the gas pedal to the floor, and swiftly spun out the tires in the dew-wet grasses and dirt. Michelle pulled in three deep breaths, then slowly pressed again and this time moved through the rough field and onto the lane.

Sweat beaded above her lip. She kept intense focus on getting back to her house. Once there, she raced up the front porch steps and banged hard on the door, hoping Lara was doing better.

She kept banging until the door opened and a sleepy-eyed Lara stood in front of her. "Where did you go? I—"

"I've got Tizzy in the back seat of her car. She's out. Is there any way you could help me get her inside?"

Lara rubbed her head and pointed behind Michelle. "We don't have to. Lynx physiology wins."

Michelle jumped as a hand touched her shoulder and she saw a fully dressed Tizzy standing behind her, shivering.

Spontaneously, she wrapped her arms around her and squeezed. "Thank God! You're all right? Here, take my sweater. That tank top makes me shiver." She led the others back inside and shoved them each in to chairs. "Lynx physiology?"

"We have an ability to heal quickly." Lara continued to rub her head. "What happened to you, Tizzy? You have a concussion, too? Oh, wait. Is that a prick there on your shoulder?"

Tizzy pulled on the sweater. "Yes. I heard you scream and came tearing out of the brush to see what was up. I arrived in time to see two men run out of the house and run down the street in the direction of the Carter building."

"But not before they darted you, right?" Lara shook her head. "This is crazy stuff going on."

"Yes. The dart fell out, so it didn't deliver the full dosage of the sedative. I made it to my car, but just barely. Thanks Michelle, for bringing me here. Smart thinking."

"Well done you," Michelle countered. "Metabolizing the drug quickly. And you as well, Lara, healing from a concussion. Would that dart gun have a laser sight?" Michelle asked, piecing together small slices of the story.

"I'd say so." Lara nodded slowly. "That would explain the red circle on your shirt just before the big intrusion."

"I saw one on your sweater, too. Seeing it probably saved us from being drugged. But why drug us?" Michelle ran her fingers through her hair. She didn't wait for an answer as she remembered her terrified cats.

Each one located a few minutes later, she left them to get relaxed.

"I think it's a campaign of intimidation. Sending you a message that nothing can stop William Carter's plans from going forward. It's scare tactics." Lara picked up the first cat to make his way out of hiding. "Hi, Tiger." She put him on her lap and he nestled in close.

Tizzy pursed her lips and frowned. "It's really important to him to get what he wants. For some reason, he is enjoying intimidating you. He wants the final word on this house. His project, too, is important to him. We know he's had setbacks with it and he's not willing to give up."

"It seems like a lot of effort and a lot of imposition on my part to remain in my own house." Michelle choked back sobs in her throat. "I'm sorry you've suffered because of me."

Lara tossed a pillow at Michelle's head. "Will you please stop apologizing? We wouldn't do this if we didn't want to."

"Not even if Casey ordered you to?"

"Don't make me throw another pillow. That effort hurt my head."

"I'll do it." Tizzy let go of a pillow and a high-pitched laugh.

"Okay, I understand. You're here because it's what you do. Thank you."

Michelle sat with Lara and Tizzy in silence for a few moments. Her thoughts were settling a bit. But one thought kept floating at the front of her brain. "I don't think William Carter knows about your colony. The intruders saw you, Tizzy, running out of the field toward them and they probably panicked. The sedatives were meant for me. Maybe they were warned that you were here, Lara, but a lynx in this area? That scared them."

"He may not know about us, a local colony, but it appears he knows something about the existence of were-lynxes." Tizzy said. "Considering the testing on cats he's doing, it does prompt concerns about any feline species."

"We need to know more. But that's what Casey is working on. We have to be patient. And on guard." Lara stretched and yawned.

"My bosses at Aegar Investigations, Sterling and Lacey, are working on it, too. They've found a group of influential people in Laurelwood who have banded together in secrecy. The purchase of my house is on their agenda."

Tizzy sat forward in her chair. "You mean like the Moose Lodge or, I don't know, some fraternal organization?"

"It's called The Nexus Group. I don't know what their plans are, other than to purchase property around Laurelwood and expand their present research project."

"When did you learn about this?" Tizzy's voice held an edge.

"Just today. Casey stopped into their office after lunch and they shared what they had discovered." Anxiety suddenly throbbed at Michelle's temples as she questioned whether or not she should have shared the information.

"And then Casey disappeared. Great." Tizzy's edge had bloomed to a definite disgust. "Is that what a leader does, Lara? He's going to give moggies a bad name. The pures are going to judge it as a typical, irresponsible move by a moggy."

"Maybe it's something only he can do, Tizzy. I'm sure we can trust him. As for the pures' attitude, I disagree with you." Lara studied her. "Now, why don't you go home and get some rest. Sedatives do rough numbers on a body, yours included. I'm spending the night, so I'll be here if something happens." She turned to Michelle. "Unless you're ready to give up. Then I'll go home and I'll let you explain your decision to Casey."

Michelle focused on her gut, and let herself try out giving up and staying to see how each felt. She closed her eyes and let her body provide information. When she opened them again, she knew. "No, I'm not giving up. This house is rightfully mine. Carter is a bully and I'm not going to be bullied."

"Good decision." Lara nodded her head and Tizzy smiled.

As Tizzy closed the front door behind her, Michelle turned her attention on Lara. "Are you in touch with Casey? Did he tell you what he's doing?"

"No. When he can, he'll check in with me for an update." Lara gave her a warm look. "Feeling abandoned? Truly, it's a good thing he doesn't know about what happened here today. He would declare war on Carter Enterprises. He's struggled with his feelings for you, Michelle, but there's no question he's in love with you. When he can surface, he will. You can trust him."

"Trust is not easy for me, but I'm learning."

* * *

CASEY CHECKED his face in the rearview mirror and put on his best bad boy face. He climbed out of his car and walked toward the William Carter Enterprises main building.

The wind tossed the treetops about and the sky was absent of stars and moon. He pressed a buzzer at the main door and a voice came over the speaker.

"William Carter Enterprises is closed for the day." The night guard's voice sounded bored but brusque.

"I know, but I have an appointment at nine o'clock with Mr. Carter."

"Name?"

Too bored to form sentences, fella? "Casey Mitchell."

Thanks to his keen hearing, he heard footsteps approach before he saw the guard. The man in uniform punched in a code on a pad on the inside not far from the door, then inserted a key and opened the door for Casey.

"I apologize for keeping you waiting. Mr. Carter will see you now."

Casey nodded and fell in step behind the guard. He could have found his way back to Carter's office, no problem. But he didn't feel like sharing that bit of information.

They took the elevator to the top floor and the guard continued leading until they reached first the reception area, then the door to

Carter's office. He knocked twice, then cracked open the door. "Sir, Mr. Mitchell."

Without acknowledging the guard, Carter stood and greeted Casey. "I must say this is a surprise. Have a seat, Mr. Mitchell."

Casey did as instructed. The leather chair was deeply cushioned and he sank a bit. He'd read about executives who purposefully provide chairs that make visitors feel small and at a disadvantage. Totally something Carter would do.

Carter sat in his large and luxurious chair and eyed Casey. "Is there something wrong with the chair, Mr. Mitchell?"

"No, nothing at all. One thing, though. You can call me Casey. If you use my title and last name, I'm going to look around for my father." He pasted on a merry smile aimed at Carter.

"You're your own man, I understand." Carter gave him a Cheshire cat grin with too- white teeth.

Casey cleared his throat. He wanted to appear just a little nervous, but he didn't feel it. This meeting was a complete charade, one he hoped would give him the information he needed to shut down Carter for good. "Thank you for seeing me on such short notice. Since it's late, I'll get right to the point."

Carter's fake smile never fell, but his eyes, the empty grey eyes of the heartless man, shuttered for a nanosecond, then simply looked cold.

"I have been working for your son for eight months. His agency is top notch, and I'm proud to be associated with him." He stopped for effect, letting the corners of his mouth dip. "But honor and high ideals in my work are not what I'm seeking."

Carter studied him, his smile gone. "Why is this of interest to me? You've known Jackson most of your life. You know his morals. Why is that suddenly an issue for you?"

Casey leaned forward, adopting an earnest expression. "I'm sick of being prohibited from doing whatever it takes to serve clients who appreciate that kind of dedication."

"You're not a do-gooder? I find that hard to believe." Carter chuckled, a gravelly laughter that turned into a cough that lasted a full minute.

"I understand. A man can change. Or maybe I've just come to a better understanding of who I am. Let's not kid one another. You know I've done my share of breaking the law."

"You're referring to your thievery? That was years ago."

"I know. But it's in my blood and I'm tired of pretending it's not. I don't care about the same things Jackson does. And if I could be so bold, I think I have skills that would benefit your company."

"You're asking me for a job?" Carter laughed heartily, tears coming to his eyes. "Never thought I'd see this day."

"Like I said, I've come back to my senses, to who I really am."

Carter stood. "What about Jackson? You're not concerned about losing his friendship? And what about Michelle Slade? You two have gotten close."

Casey watched the tall man stride from one wall to another, and then come back to his chair. He noticed there were no windows; only dark mahogany wood paneling lined the walls. Pictures of William Carter with dignitaries and heads of state and celebrities hung on the walls and sat on shelves. There were no pictures of his family.

"I am enjoying Michelle's company, such as it is. She's a woman and she has her purposes." He winked at Carter, feeling like a slime-bag. There was no truth to anything he said. "As for losing my friend-ship with Jake, I don't expect that. He's kind and accepting. Were I to find a more lucrative position, he'd probably congratulate me." Casey smirked, adding attitude to his lies.

Carter rocked in his chair, rubbing his chin and all the while staring at Casey. "So what are these skills you mentioned that could help my company?"

"I'm experienced in guiding companies through drug and medical device trials. I'm familiar with ways of ensuring expeditious approval by the FDA."

"I have people who do that. What can you do for me?"

"I could do it successfully." Casey didn't miss the slight twitch in

Carter's cheek at his reference to problems with drug trials in the past.

"It happens I'm working on something right now that could use some higher level expertise." Carter's eyes narrowed. "It requires discretion."

Casey guffawed. "Yes, you do need someone better on the Pretid trial. You're using the device in an insulin pump trial but your staff's tactics are clumsy. You've had trial participants who've suffered insulin shock." He sat forward for emphasis and to present an aggressive, fearless position. "And the funny thing is, you don't care about how effectively the pump delivers insulin, you just need the device to access information that will give you the participants you want. Those who may offer the genetic predisposition you want."

Carter's fingers tapped a staccato beat on his desk and leaned in. "You've been messing in my business."

"If by messing you mean learning more about you and what you're doing, then yes. It's very doable. Despite your need for discretion and your layers of secrecy and security, information is out there. I found it."

"You're saying you could get my project to its conclusion quickly and successfully meet my goal. And I'm supposed to trust you?"

"C'mon. You've got a file on me. You've done a background on me. I know you have. You know all about me. The thing you're forgetting is that I'm already a criminal. I'm eager to do what needs to be done."

Carter stood. *Apparently the meeting is over,* Casey mused.

"Meet me for breakfast. Be here at seven-thirty tomorrow morning and we'll hash out the details over coffee and waffles."

CHAPTER 14

Coffee couldn't brew fast enough. Michelle stood at the coffeemaker, wringing her hands and tapping her foot. Sterling and Lacey were at work in their office. The whole place rang with deafening silence. It was driving her nerves into constant movement, constant, swirling thoughts.

Sleep eluded her last night. All the commotion and death-defying moments aroused her survival instinct into perpetual vigilance. She left for the office by six-thirty, after putting out bagels and cream cheese for Lara.

Now, at eight o'clock, she'd reached a breaking point.

New things, new beliefs, new experiences threatened to spill out of her like blood and cover the floor. And that was weird, because she was open to *new*. She was a person who was willing to embrace the full spectrum of reality, even to welcome it. Her experiences in life had subtly hinted and not so subtly informed her that reality included so much she didn't know about.

But two of her best friends sat feet away, not knowing. Longing to share the good and bad things that had happened to her in the last few days pressed outward, demanding to come out into the light.

I can do better. Coffee in hand, back at her desk, breathing deeply, she heightened her awareness of her feet, solidly planted on the floor. A few seconds of conscious grounding settled her nerves and slowed her thoughts. She'd promised Casey she wouldn't reveal anything about the lynx colony and she would keep that promise.

Her cell phone rang, sending her heart flipping, but it wasn't Casey. Still, it was almost as good news. A woman looking for cats, plural, had checked the Cats Alive website and had selected two potential candidates. Michelle made arrangements to meet the woman and her two children at one of her longest active foster moms', Evelyn Duro. Evelyn had taken in foster cats from the inception of the cat rescue. In her retirement years, Evelyn was patient and kind and a genuine cat lover.

There was always a steady stream of homeless cats needing homes, but fortunately, some days some cats got lucky.

Michelle gathered her purse and told the sisters she had an appointment to give two cats a home.

"Yeah!" Lacey raised a hand in the air, celebrating. "Have a happy adoption."

"See, that's part of the fun of working with you," Sterling said, smiling. "I get to learn about good people doing good things. Go, thank the adopters for me."

Despite all the terrible circumstances hovering around her, Michelle ran down the stairs to the main floor practically gleeful. She looked at her cell phone for the hundredth time and decided on a quick stop to pick up a breakfast sandwich at the diner down the street. If she hurried, she'd have time to grab it and eat on the way to Evelyn's.

The diner was simple and the food was straightforward. That's what made it popular. It always gave her a good feeling to walk through the door and sink into the ambiance. It felt all homey and basic goodness. She smiled to herself as she strolled briskly down the sidewalk, amused by her ability to pick up sensations that enriched her experience, even at a simple, old-fashioned diner.

She pulled open the door and walked straight to the line at the counter to place her order. Instantly, heaviness and bleakness slammed into her. Surprised, her nerves flustered as she ordered. Her happiness turned slimy and gooey.

Her order was passed to her and she paid, deeply troubled. Michelle walked slowly toward the door, scanning the room. The bag with her sandwich inside nearly slipped from her fingers as she saw Casey at a table, surrounded by six or eight people. One of them was William Carter. He slapped Casey on the back and let out a gravelly laugh.

She froze, her steps stuck in molasses. Casey sat between William Carter and Darrel Dobosky. His was a face that had plagued her for years after the rape, but she hadn't seen him in person or as a phantom in months. His facial features were caught in time in her mind—a surly looking young college senior with brown hair and dimples—but in person she saw he'd gained weight and he didn't wear his twenty-seven years well. At least that's what he looked like to her. Slimy, sweaty, and fat. His just desserts for spewing what her Jewish friend would term a mishegoss of malicious deeds into the lives of good people. Her.

What, why? Casey sitting with that bunch didn't compute. He looked comfortable, happy, joking it up with them. Confusion fogged her brain as she stood staring. Self respect and defensiveness bloomed all at once, spurting up to clear her head. In that moment he locked gazes with her, frowning. Then he turned back to the conversation at the table.

Her feet now moved fast, as she couldn't get out of the room soon enough. Outside, she measured her steps to the parking garage, repressing the impulse to run, and slipped behind the wheel of her Jeep.

It hurt. It hurt so much. Her gut twisted painfully. She couldn't breathe. "Oh my God!" she cried, more as prayer than exclamation. What had she done to deserve this betrayal, this pain?

She'd done everything right all her life. Followed a path she believed to be truthful and grounded and kind. Why had she been singled out that night, that dreadful night that Darrel tore her heart and soul wide open and left her with darkness and fear?

That night had nearly killed her. She should have seen it coming or run faster or screamed louder, maybe dressed differently.

She'd lain there on the ground, crumpling inwardly. Alone. And only darkness inside her. And now, weighing if Casey was a part of that darkness, that same crumpling that stifled her breath and stabbed at her heart. Tears throbbed beneath her eyelids. It hurt so much.

But things were different now, she reminded herself. She wasn't weak and unskilled. She could take care of herself and navigate difficult emotions. And she had genuine friends to turn to when she needed help. She'd done nothing wrong. In fact, she'd been amazing. She retained her love for life and for living a good path. She didn't cower from taking action when circumstances called for it. She was fucking brave. She was sensitive and she cried and got angry, but that wasn't weakness, it was being real. The good may die young, but another way to frame that was the good die of an old life of fear and darkness and inhibitions.

Her muscles took to her thoughts, relaxing and feeling confident. The crumpling expanded out to become resiliency and insight.

Michelle swiped at her eyes and turned the key in the ignition. Still emotionally shaky, she felt gratitude. She'd survived that night and every night since. She was out of darkness. Now she had a dual adoption to take care of.

* * *

"WELCOME ABOARD. I'll see you at the research facility as soon as you can get there." William Carter reached out a hand to Casey.

Casey took his hand and accepted his limp shake. "Thank you. I'll be there soon."

The man walked with his other people into William Carter Enterprises and Casey drove away, stunned. He had done his homework and felt confident that he could waggle himself into a job with Carter, but he wasn't sure who got the best end of the deal.

The sneaky bastard never missed an opportunity to express his authority. Carter had set Casey up. He couldn't have known for sure that Michelle would be at that restaurant, but it was not a wild chance, either. He'd probably had one of his goons keeping an eye on her and learned she regularly got coffee there for all three of them—herself, Sterling, and Lacey.

Carter had played him and intentionally set out to hurt Michelle.

The thought of it knotted his stomach and he indulged in a low, rumbling growl.

He could still see the shock and pain in Michelle's beautiful face. He couldn't prevent it. There was nothing he could do to save her from that moment, and it killed him inside.

Even now, he couldn't make it better. He couldn't chance discovery by calling her or going to her at her home or her office, anywhere. Everything inside him leaned toward her, pulling him to her side to comfort her and declare his love and devotion.

It would have to wait. He'd asked her to trust him and all he could do was hope she would, somehow. He slammed his fist against the steering wheel, imagining the intense pain she'd suffered on seeing her rapist at the same table as him. Carter was diabolical. And tonight would be the beginning of his undoing.

As he drove by Michelle's house on his way to the research facility, he couldn't stop himself from turning down the lane and driving to the field beside her house. He knew he was taking a risk but he took it, nonetheless.

Booker's car was parked in the grove of trees, so Casey pulled up beside it and got out. He whistled short bursts of sound, and Booker came trotting up to his own vehicle. He shimmered into his human form and slipped on his pants, then walked up next to Casey.

"You found me." Booker's laid-back demeanor belied an intense drive to protect and heal. A physician, he had healing powers, which came in handy in his profession.

"I whistled. You found me." Casey rapped him on his back and felt the easy camaraderie flow between them. It soothed his aching heart. "Anything going on here?"

"Asia monitored the building down the street last night and said it seemed like they unloaded a special delivery. It was a caged animal.

She got a scent. No doubt it was a lynx, an unfamiliar individual but definitely a lynx."

His heart clenched. "She saw it?"

"Yeah. Probably drugged, though."

Before Casey had a chance to react to this devastating news, Booker continued.

"Did you hear about what happened here yesterday?" he asked.

Casey slanted his head at Booker and pinned his gaze. "Happened here? What happened here?"

He listened to Booker's retelling of the intrusion and the darting, all the while tensing his muscles, tighter and tighter. He dropped his head into his hands and tried to tune out the crashing in his ears. *I should have been with her. Oh my God, she could have ...* Thoughts of various scenarios stabbed at his brain.

Booker put a hand to his shoulder. "Casey, you can't be everywhere or be prepared for every possible little thing. This Carter has an army of goons working for him. Nothing gets by and nothing is beneath him. It's not your fault."

"The question is, what do I do now?"

"No," Booker corrected. "The question is what do *we* do now?"

"I go to work. I'm working for Carter undercover. I'm heading to the research facility now. You think you can get in, be stealthy?"

"You're going inside? Does anyone know about this? It's dangerous, Casey."

"Jackson knows. But you're the only one in the colony. Lara is my contact. I don't want it to get around that I'm inside. But we need to end this mess. I could use your help if you can get in undetected."

Booker's topaz eyes glistened, thoughts almost visibly churning behind them. He shot a grin at Casey. "You got it. I'll figure it out."

"Maybe around the receiving docks area. You know where they are?" Booker shoved a fist into Casey's shoulder. "Go. You'll be late for work."

Casey briskly walked up to the security guard shack at the Carter facility and knocked. The man in uniform spoke through the intercom, confirming Casey's employment status, then pushed under the window a lanyard with a security badge attached, buzzed the front door, and motioned Casey toward inside. "You have to go first to personnel. You'll be expected." With a stern expression, the guard turned away.

Personnel gave him his orientation quickly. The young woman in HR probably spoke too freely, but that was okay with Casey. He learned he was getting the short and fast version of orientation because William Carter wanted him in the lab ASAP.

The brunette with the coquettish green eyes seemed innocent, too sweet to be involved with the destruction that was William Carter. It was a new thought. He'd lumped all Carter Enterprises associates with the man. Could many of them simply be working at a company that paid reasonably well and offered good benefits? It was a significant consideration, but right now he couldn't let any extraneous thoughts interfere with his mission.

Ms. Green Eyes had instructed him to follow the red line to get to the lab. Around corners and down to the basement level. When he reached the lab door, again he had to check in with a guard.

He stepped into the lab, his pulse pounding. This lab looked very similar to the one he'd broken into the other day, except there were people working and much activity going on.

A man in a blue lab coat walked up to him and reached out his hand. "You must be Casey Mitchell. I'm Walker Anderson. I know you're not going to work here in our labs, you'll be at corporate headquarters, but Mr. Carter wanted me to show you around."

The tour began and ended in labs. Each lab held lines of caged cats. Casey had to steel his emotions, as he heard every sound, every cry, every hiss, and whimper. It all added up to fury inside him.

"There's just one more place to show you and then your dull morning is over," Walker said. He showed the two guards at the door his security badge and nodded at Casey to do the same.

The guard opened the door and Casey's nostrils filled with the scent of an animal, not a cat. Another lynx. A were-lynx.

Walker let him into an adjoining room. "This is our latest subject. He's been in the study for about two months. He was shipped here from Alaska. He's a special case and you won't be involved with him."

"Walker, I'm not going to be directly involved with any subjects, but I do need to know all the details of this study. Are you going to be able to give me the details or do I need to talk to your boss?"

Walker clasped his arms across his chest and glared. "I can give you any details you're authorized to get."

"Well, then I'll just give the main boss a call." His gaze swept the room. "Do you get good reception down here?"

"I do. But that won't be necessary. Let's go into my office." He led Casey to his office, and motioned toward a chair at a small round table. "As I'm sure Mr. Carter has shared with you, the research we're doing here is a bit unorthodox. How much experience do you have with animal testing?"

Casey laid his forearms across the table and leaned close, close enough for Walker to be able to catch a glimpse of his wild nature in his eyes. "I'll ask the questions."

Walker swallowed hard and looked down. "What do you want to know?" "Primarily the answer to one question. What is the goal of this animal research?"

"We're doing different studies."

Casey glowered and let a very low growl rumble in his throat, just enough to get Walker's attention. "Okay, let's try it this way. Are the drugs you're testing on domestic cats the same as you're testing on the lynx?"

"You could say that. The tests on the cats have resolved some issues—"

"Narrowing down specific drug type and dosage? Any losses?"

"Yes. That happens, as you must know. Some subjects couldn't tolerate the drug at all after we raised the dosage twice."

"I know you've been having problems with the data from the electronic diary associated with the insulin pump." Casey tapped his fingers on the table. "Got those smoothed out?"

"We think so."

Casey nodded his head, reading Walker's body language. "Did anyone report those issues to the IRB?"

Walker stiffened. "I'm sure someone did."

The guy was lying, Casey could tell. He knew someone had reported, he just wanted to find out if this guy had. And Walker had delivered all the telltale signs. "What is the end application? Why is this so hard, Walker?"

The young man wiggled in his seat and looked away. Seconds passed. Finally, he turned a fresh look on Casey. "Mr. Carter wants the lab to produce a particular drug that has the capability to enhance certain attributes."

"In cats? What attributes?"

It appeared that Walker was now resolved to go all in. Now words tumbled out like a confession. "Not cats. Cats were the first animals we experimented on. It took a while for us to come up with the appropriate drug. The drug enhances innate feline characteristics, such as claws, teeth, and musculature."

"So bigger and more ferocious than your average house cat." "Precisely. We're moving on to a larger feline now."

Casey nodded his head. "The lynx. Do you have any more lynx in the study?"

"No, just the one." Walker rolled his head around his shoulders. "But we received a new shipment yesterday, a female. She'll be integrated into the study soon. We started the protocol a week ago for the one you saw. First we had to get it squared away with the cats. Already the male is showing signs of the drug working."

"So the insulin pump. You're using that as a delivery system. You don't care anything about insulin, right?"

"Right."

"The insulin pump study is a cover for your real goals, using the digital diary to locate study subjects who carry specific genes and creating angry cats. Why a lynx?"

Again, Walker looked down at his feet.

Casey lunged across the table and grabbed Walker by the neck, just beneath his chin so that he could put pressure on his windpipe. "There's more you're not telling me. Spill!"

Struggling for air, Walker put up his hands and stammered. "I'll show you. Just let me breathe."

Casey dropped his hand, but pulled at Walker's arm, dragging him to his feet. "Show me."

CHAPTER 15

Casey marched with Walker into the portion of the lab where the lynx was held, separated from the larger room. He could smell its fear. He looked into the lynx's glassy eyes and saw pain. A yowl threatened to escape his throat, loud and ferocious. He swiveled his head to stare at Walker. "Why a lynx?" he asked again.

"The natural abilities of a lynx, a feline, make it a good candidate for Mr. Carter's plans." Again, Walker looked down, fidgeting with his fingers.

"Such as?" Casey's patience burned at the low end, nearly running out.

"Lynx are stealthy, powerful, and intelligent. They have keen hearing and eyesight.

They're good hunters."

"Of course, they're wild animals. You still haven't told me the end goal. Is Carter progressing his drug to use in humans?"

Walker stared at the floor.

Casey reined in his anger and surveyed his impressions of the lab area. All very organized and clean. He landed his gaze on Walker, who was fidgety and still hadn't answered his question. "You take pride in your work, don't you Walker?"

Walker perked up. "I do. Or, at least I have."

"But not so much now, with this particular study."

Walker turned panicked eyes on Casey, and shook his head.

"Are you new here at this lab, Carter's labs? I'm guessing you love your work, but this work," Casey motioned to the lynx and the room filled with cats, "is not something you have the heart for."

"I have obligations to Mr. Carter. And to these animals." His face dropped.

"I get it. You're worried about the animals and you feel your 'obligations' to Carter are lifelong and unbreakable. You didn't know that when you got the job. You were new in the field and this job with its pay and benefits fit your needs, so you took it."

Suddenly Walker got antsy. "What is your interest in me? Aren't you just a lawyer, hired to supervise the legal work for this study?"

"You still think your study is legal? But yes, I'm here to help Carter meet his goal under the facade of a legal drug trial."

"When the drug is finalized, Carter's plans for production begin. At least that is the plan, once the property down the street is secured and construction of the manufacturing and containment center is completed."

"Containment of the poor souls who are transformed into who knows what by the drug?" Casey shook his head slowly, the idea of Carter's ambition striking a sour note in his gut. "He's out of his mind."

"You've got to see the bigger picture to truly understand," Walker said.

Casey suspected that Walker was feeding him information that could possibly thwart Carter. He studied Walker. "Tell me about the bigger picture. I know Carter is no humanitarian. So what does he want with ferocious half-humans, half-were-cats?"

"I'm not privy to all information. But ... " Walker drew in a deep breath, then let it out in one puff. "He's building an army."

As crazy as it sounded it didn't surprise Casey. "The timetable for moving into production and containment depends on the extra space.

I see." Casey shared a gaze with the other lynx. It appeared Walker didn't know this was a were-cat. *I wish Asia were here right now.*

Change of plans.

"Thank you for providing information about this study, Walker." He clapped a hand to Walker's shoulder. "If there is anything more, don't hesitate to contact me. Let's exchange cell phone numbers, just in case."

They walked into the outer lab, and Casey determined to be back soon.

"Just a minute," Walker said, heading toward his office. When he came back out seconds later, he handed Casey a file folder. "Since you're managing this trial from the legal end of it, you should have this. You know, to read later." He dropped his voice to a whisper. "You're right. I'm very concerned about the process and the possible outcome of the study. I … I … I did report the problems. I would like to be a part of interrupting it, but I don't know how to avoid getting killed."

"I thought so. Thank you." Casey glanced around, keeping his voice low. "You can be my inside contact. I'll be in touch soon. I can find my way out."

Casey headed out on the scenic route of the lower level. Guards walked the halls everywhere or sat at locked doors. Finally, he saw a sign for the loading dock and tuned in his senses for Booker. With so many guards and locked doors and video surveillance, he might not have gotten inside the building, and all things considered, that would be fine.

Rounding a corner to yet another hall, Casey caught a whiff of were-cat. Which meant Booker had also detected him. Casey looked up for cameras, but not one was in sight. How odd. He hadn't seen cameras in any of the labs he'd been in so far. Carter probably didn't want any footage that could be used against him. Scary thought.

Booker stepped out from behind an opened door and walked toward Casey. He was wearing a blue lab coat. "Where have you been?" he asked.

"Investigating. I guess you got into the building without a problem. No alarms set off or anything?"

"It was tricky business. There's a lot of activity in the receiving area and guards are everywhere. I grabbed this lab coat from a bunch lying in a laundry cart." He stood silent for a second, sniffing and listening.

"Thanks for sneaking in. But plans are changed. I probably didn't think things through well enough. I just reacted to the plight of these animals, who are suffering. We need an organized, multi-person approach. Right now, we need to get you out before you're detected and set off red flags for Carter. I'm going to leave out the front door. Any suggestions for your departure?"

Booker grinned, lopsided. "The same way I got in. Don't think about it."

Casey hid the folder Walker had given him inside his suit coat, tucked into his pants, and made his way upstairs. He had initially intended to visit with Carter, but Walker had given him enough information that he decided to hold off on that visit until he had no other options. Carter's sparring tactics drained him. Better to avoid the bastard if he could.

He walked to his car, gathering strength from the breeze that ruffled his hair and the sun's rays on his face. A longing to talk with Michelle, ease her mind and bring her up to speed fired in his belly. Did he dare chance it?

He drove to the nearest coffee shop and parked. He couldn't chance it. Casey had no doubts that Carter's spies were watching and listening to both him and Michelle.

He sat inside the shop, a small mom and pop he felt offered safety in its anonymity, and ordered coffee. He waited until the waitress set it down in front of him along with a smile and friendly greeting, before he pulled out the contents of the file Walker had given him.

It was a mission statement, specifically outlining Carter Enterprises' role in influencing local money, law enforcement, resources, and politics as a member of The Nexus Group. Casey's heart froze as he read Carter's chilling aspirations. Apart from the group goals of property acquisition, Carter's specific intentions outlined retribution, payback, from Michelle for accusing her rapist.

Casey nearly doubled over with anger and disgust. A ridiculous and insane manifesto, yes. But certainly something the mind of William Carter could produce. He'd even enjoy the whole siege.

It wasn't a fair fight—Carter Enterprises and The Nexus Group against Michelle. Casey gathered up his papers and shoved them into the file, resolve surging through his body. It was time to gather his resources and end this before it got beyond stopping.

* * *

WHATEVER CASEY HAD MEANT to her, Michelle realized she couldn't rely on him to help her anymore. In fact, why had she trusted him in the first place? Why had she put her future in his hands? It was her problem, her life, and it was time to take responsibility for her own difficulties. It was time, past time, if she were honest with herself.

Exhilaration from the morning's two cat adoptions empowered her. She'd passed through hell, and by God she'd survived. Time to triumph, she vowed.

On her way back to the Aegar Investigations office, she called Sterling and asked for help from Ben, Sterling's cop husband. So when she walked into the office she wasn't surprised to see Ben in the sisters' private office. Dressed in his homicide detective suit and tie, Ben looked ready for business.

Both Sterling and Lacey were talking with him when Michelle walked into their office and said hello.

"Two cats on their way to a forever home, Michelle?" Lacey asked. Michelle took a seat and shot them a small smile. "You bet."

Ben chirped up. "You don't sound very happy about it. What's up?"

"No, I am happy … about the adoptions. So happy." A frown took over and she dropped her gaze to stare at the wooden floor. "I saw Casey with William Carter this morning. They were having breakfast together and he looked like he was having fun."

Lacey released a heavy sigh. "That can't be. I'm sure there's an explanation. You know him better than that, Michelle."

Michelle lifted her eyes and shook her head. "Do I? There's more. Darrel Dobosky sat right next to him."

"Michelle, I know Casey very well and those are not his kind of people. You should reserve judgment until you can talk to him." Ben perched on the edge of Lacey's desk, his brow furrowed.

"Well, at any rate, I'm not waiting around for his help anymore. I need to step up to the plate and deal with Carter. He's threatening me, not Casey."

Sterling nodded. "So what do you plan to do?"

"I was thinking of hiring a good detective I know, one I can truly trust, to help me get an order of protection. I guess with Casey help-ing, and his friends, I thought it would prevent problems with the police, who I expect are smelly with the Carter stink. But not you, of course, Ben."

"Smart move. I'll go with you to the courthouse and you can apply for a temporary order of protection. The judge will schedule a hearing for another date. But he'll have the order served to Carter."

Lacey shook her head. "I'm not sure. Carter isn't going to abide by the order, and I'm afraid it will stir up things into something worse."

Michelle jumped to her feet. "I know. But I'm tired of sitting around waiting for him to make a move, crash into my house, kill my cats, whatever he wants to do. I'm not weak. I want to take action."

"Okay, let's go to the courthouse," Ben said.

"Yes, go ahead." Sterling waved her toward the door. "We'll manage without you."

"Thank you." Michelle nodded to both sisters, then followed Ben to the door. He opened it for her, but Michelle stopped short when she saw Casey, his tall and muscled frame filling the doorway.

"Michelle, could I talk to you, privately?" His expression tried for hopeful, but his trepidation went spiraling throughout her limbs.

She lifted her chin. "Ben and I were just leaving to apply for an order of protection. I don't have time to talk right now." Mixtures of sorrow and longing weighed heavily in her gut, but she could be strong, she told herself.

"An order of protection?" Casey yelled. "You're going to poke the hornet's nest, Michelle." He leaned against the doorframe, shaking his head.

"Carter's already going after me. While you've been enjoying his company, Carter has been busy, intruding in my life, hurting my friends. I'm going to show him I'm no pushover after all." Michelle's breaths came fast and furious.

"I asked you to trust me." His voice dropped low and flat. He stared at the floor for what seemed like endless, tortured moments.

And she let him.

Finally, he raised his head and straightened his stance. "Okay. I understand. But please, before you go, let me inform you and Ben and Sterling and Lacey about what I've learned. If you still want to go, I won't get in your way." He rubbed his hand across his mouth, his eyes troubled.

"Fine." Michelle stepped aside and let Casey enter the office, while Ben and the sisters gathered in their private office.

Casey made a phone call to Jackson that lasted two seconds. When he set down his cell phone, his pensive expression made Michelle's heart pound. Whatever he had to share, it was serious.

"I asked Jackson to pop over. He needs to be brought up to speed. He has a vested interest through his business regarding his father's endeavors." Casey paced across the office, back and forth, waiting for Jackson to arrive. Michelle watched him, uneasiness growing in intensity with each of his steps.

When Jackson walked in, he went to Lacey and kissed her. "What's up, Casey? You sounded scary sober on the phone."

Casey laid it all on the table, literally and figuratively. Each one ruffled through the papers, having their individual reaction of shock and anger. Except for Michelle. She gave no outer indication of how the news hit her.

From orchestration of the acquittal of Michelle's rapist, to the creation of the manifesto, the organization of The Nexus Group, to the consistent land acquisition that locked Michelle's home inside a group of Carter's properties, to his drug studies with the cats, to his goal for achieving ultimate local power, Casey spelled it all out.

"He sounds outright demonic." Ben put his arm around Lacey, flexing his biceps.

"More like insane." Jackson said the word as though realization had just pierced his mind that his father's malicious and criminal activities came from a very sick mind, collapsing any hope of goodness in him.

"He's definitely off the charts when it comes to lack of boundaries," Lacey added. "I'm sorry, Jackson. I mean, he's your father. But there is nothing he won't do to get what he wants."

Casey eyed each of them, landing a soulful gaze on Michelle. She was speechless. Her pattern had popped up, just as it had in the past, and she got lost in it. She'd formed her opinion about Casey's activities with Carter based on fear.

"There is one more thing. From talking with the lab guy this morning and reading the papers he gave me, I see that Carter's drug research on the cats was always leading to something bigger." He stubbed his shoe on the wooden floor and looked as though he was measuring his words. "Heck with it. I'll just say it. He plans to produce a drug that will enhance feline traits in humans."

"What?" Jackson was the first to respond, but each one wore the same shocked expression. "That can be done?"

"The lab guy said they have perfected the drug with cats. Now they've moved on to larger felines. They're already experimenting on a lynx."

"Well, I'll ask it. Why?" Ben flashed wide eyes at the idea.

"His drug, according to the papers, prompts a rapid onset of clinical paranoia and aggression. It also enhances muscle mass and provokes the growth of longer claws and teeth."

"I missed that in reading the papers," Ben said. "What is Carter going to do with the drug?"

"And what does this have to do with Pretid's electronic diary?" Jackson fisted his hands.

Casey sighed. "Pretid's device uploads data to a program that stores everything about a study subject. That information tells Carter who carries a recessive gene for were-animalism. That fits into his larger scheme. The insulin pump is being tested as a delivery system for subjects chosen for the project. He's engineering warriors. I don't know why."

"Wait a minute. Were-animals? What are we talking about, something like a werewolf?" Jackson looked stunned. "They don't exist. Do they?" He exchanged glances with Lacey and Lacey looked at Sterling, and Sterling's look landed on Ben.

"They do." Casey nodded his head. "Hang in here with me. I know it's unimaginable, but the truth is, I'm a were-lynx. Michelle can attest to that."

Michelle swallowed. "It's true."

"And I am the leader of a colony of other were-lynxes." Casey slanted his head. "I don't know about werewolves. But I do know about were-lynxes." Jackson stared at Casey. "Want proof?"

Jackson rubbed his chin and smiled a half-smile. "No. I believe you, Casey. You're my friend and you have no reason I know of to concoct such a story." Jackson slapped him on the back. "Did you know Lacey's first husband lived with her as an embodied spirit after his death? Accepting that took a stretch of the mind, too. "

"We know things about life are way more complicated than typically believed," Ben said. "Thank you for telling us."

"So back to why Carter would want to create half-mad were-lynxes," Lacey prompted.

"He doesn't need a reason," Sterling said. "But he probably has one and it's something that needs to be stopped. ASAP, no doubt. I'm sorry, Michelle. I agree with Casey about the order of protection. I certainly understand your need for one. I admire your willingness to thwart Carter's intention to ruin your life. But there is something huge lifting its ugly head. You need more than just your own feet to trample it."

"Friends who investigate, remember?" Lacey said. "We're here for you."

All the encouragement and advice penetrated Michelle's impulse to throw caution to the wind and address Carter herself, alone. "Thank you." Michelle dared a glance at Casey. "I'm sorry." She dropped her gaze to the floor. Before he could speak she continued, quietly. "It was too easy to fall back into my fears. When I saw you sitting with those people, I shut down. The last thing I want to do is turn you away. Thank you for finding out more useful information to stop Carter.

Casey closed the space between them and pulled her close. "I thought I'd lost you." He nuzzled her hair, his breaths caressing her cheek. "I understand, sweetie. I'm sorry for what happened to you and that I wasn't there for you." Casey's eyes glistened, full of sincerity.

"You were doing the right thing. Carter needs to be stopped."

He dipped his head to bring her back to life with a warm kiss. "So we're good?"

"Very." Relief swelled in her heart. This was one time she was happy she'd been wrong.

"Okay, everybody is good." Ben flashed an unsteady smile. "Now what?"

"So I can introduce everyone and if you're willing to help, you can help with the rescue of the animals at Carter's lab," Casey said. "Meet me at my house in an hour. I'll text you the address."

CHAPTER 16

The hour everyone at the Aegar office agreed on gave Casey time to meet with his colony before the others arrived. He told his fellow were-cats all the details he'd gathered in his investigation, including the latest—Carter had captured a were-cat and was planning to make him something unnatural and fierce, then produce more of his kind.

Instinctively, lynx who live in the wild respond to threats by displaying their power and by hiding. But as part of the evolving human population, were-cats had evolved out of the hiding tendency. They tackled problems head on. Rarely did that call for violence. Until now, that is.

Ideas floated around as they all brainstormed for a final solution to Carter's plans. One in which they all survived and didn't become hyped up jungle cats.

It stacked up pretty simply. Step one, one group would get inside, using Jackson's security badge and the help of Walker, who was more than willing to help with a rescue, just as Casey had suspected. A second group would follow Booker's way in, slipping unnoticed through a passage door at the receiving docks. His lock-picking skills would help and Casey would shut down the alarm system. Step three, begin removing cats and securing them in vehicles. Thankfully, Quinn and Asher owned pickups, so with everyone pitching in his or her vehicle, there would be enough room to rescue all the cats. Step four, release the lynxes, the one Casey had seen and the one Walker said had just been brought into the facility. Step five, confront William.

But first, Casey had to introduce his colony to Ben and Sterling and Jackson and Lacey.

"Are you sure you can trust them?" Asia flipped her silky brown hair behind her shoulder and arched her brows. "This is not our way, to share our existence with humans. You know the stories from the past. When humans have learned about were-anything, they have responded with violence, feeling threatened."

"I agree with Casey," Asher said. "We can't sit by and let Carter change the world. It's unnatural and just wrong." He walked to the refrigerator and pulled out a bottle of chilled water, twisted off the cap, and downed it in seconds.

Around the room Booker, Lara, Tizzy, Conrad, Quinn, and Asia added pros and cons to revealing themselves to four more humans, but ultimately the decision was made just as a knock sounded at the front door.

The five walked to the family room behind Casey, Michelle by his side, their arms brushing. It felt good, more than good. His body's response to her was so swift. She glanced at him and his heart melted. He'd do anything to protect her. But the Carter problem reached beyond Michelle.

He motioned Ben, Sterling, Lacey, Jackson, and Michelle to chairs and couches.

This is a very nice home you have," Sterling exclaimed. "Nice property, too. You have a couple acres?"

"I own one hundred acres. I need a lot of space." Casey cracked a smile, hoping to ease the tension in the room. Lara gave him an empathic expression, then nodded.

"Yes, it comes in handy to have this kind of seclusion and undeveloped land," Lara added.

"Handy for what?" Ben looked puzzled and turned to Casey.

Casey cleared his throat and proceeded to tell the humans in the room about their true identities. Names, job titles, and true nature.

The four sat silent, taking furtive looks of the members of his colony. Studying them himself, pride swelled in his chest. His were-lynxes were good individuals. And they'd been open to extending the small circle of humans who knew of their existence. They'd remain cautious but to him, willingness to accept good humans meant they felt secure.

"Any questions?" Casey asked.

Ben burst out with a hearty chuckle. "What do you eat? I don't mean to be rude, but I was just wondering."

"It's a good question." Lara nodded her head. "We eat what humans eat. We're part human, remember."

Sterling's brows knitted. "You said Booker is married to a human, so … that's possible? No problems with interspecies whatever?" She glanced at Michelle and grinned a tiny grin.

Booker shook his head. "No. We're every compatible. When we're ready we'll have children and those children will inherit the were-cat genes. Our lifestyle is pretty normal, with added aspects that don't impinge on our relationship."

"I know it's a lot to contain," said Michelle, "but it's just one of those things in life you've never encountered before. It may be hard to accept as natural, but it is."

Lacey and Sterling chuckled. "I agree. We have to be open to other possibilities." Lacey shared a look with Sterling.

"Want to share with the group about your extraordinary experience that makes this easier to take in?" Michelle arched an eyebrow at the group.

"Nicholas, my first husband, was killed on duty as a policeman. He returned to me as an embodied spirit. Only I could see him. So, yes, we believe in things most people don't."

While the group fired questions at Lacey, Casey left the room. Moments later, he strolled back into the room, fully lynxified. Shouts ensued, while Michelle smiled to herself.

"He's actually harmless," she said. "He's a were-cat, a human who can shimmer into a lynx and back again to human. He can hear you if you want to talk to him, but his lynx vocal cords don't work like his human cords do."

Lacey reached a tentative hand toward Casey and he trotted closer to her, close enough to rub her leg. "Casey, you can hear me? You can understand me?"

Casey nodded emphatically, twice. He chuffed quietly and sat on his haunches, surveying all four of them.

"This is too much, man." Jackson rubbed his head and stared into Casey's eyes. "Why didn't you tell me before?"

Asia explained the need for privacy and the socialization of were-cats in her colony. "Lynx, not were-lynx, live alone most of the time. But it's better for us, with human abilities and human needs, to live peacefully in a group of our own kind. Other than that, we keep our lynx-selves hidden."

While Asia was talking, the other members of the colony left the room and Casey slipped away, too. When he returned he was in human form and was followed by the other were-cats.

"You're all so beautiful, but scary," exclaimed Sterling, and Ben and Jackson nodded.

Casey sat alone on the couch watching while the others mingled with the human guests. His life-long companion, loneliness, thrummed throughout him in great contrast to the warmth of possibilities, and the danger of sharing with Michelle and the others sat quietly in his mind. He wanted guarantees that nothing would turn bad, but now was not the time to get stuck behind that road block.

Now was the time to put the group's plan into action.

"If I could please have everyone's attention I'll go over the plan for tonight." He stood in front of his colony and his friends and knew he was asking them to put themselves in danger. Grave danger that could end their lives. "I appreciate everyone's willingness to take action. It's important that we do this. But if anyone would rather not participate, don't feel obligated. Just say so and you can leave."

Casey surveyed the faces around the room and found determination in each one.

He nodded, knowing everyone had a stake in the outcome of their plan and a willingness to do the right thing. "Okay. We each have our assignments. We enter, we put cats in carriers, and secure them in the vehicles."

"You can bring them all to my house for now," Michelle said. "I've got the room."

Her eyes were wide, but she looked unruffled. Eager. Casey breathed in deeply, appreciating her courage. Of course, it had been there all along. She'd been doing what needed to be done for stray cats for years. That took diligence and skill.

"So let's head out. Park as close to the receiving docks as you can without getting caught," Casey directed. "Give me and Asia time to get in and set off the gas canisters and shut off the alarm system, then we all head to the labs. Let's make this clean and quick."

They each went to their cars, and Casey gave a quick squeeze to Michelle's shoulders and brushed a kiss to her lips before she quietly slipped behind the wheel of her Jeep and followed the others down the lane.

Watching her leave made his gut squeeze. She wasn't going to be alone, but he wouldn't be with her, protecting her. He drew in a sharp breath, then sped to the main road, gathering his determination and fury to put to good use.

* * *

MICHELLE PULLED her Jeep into the lineup, under the cloak of a dark, cloudy night. Adrenaline pushed her blood through her veins, setting her muscles on edge, ready for action. But her heart ached with knowledge that Casey and all his friends and her friends were in harm's way because of her.

She shook her head, her long ponytail slapping her shoulders, trying to clear her mind. This was no time for indecision. Nothing could distract her from the job she was about to do. Penetrate the William Carter hellhole, rescue the cats, and pray that everyone got out unharmed and alive.

She checked her cell phone for the time. Standing in the chilly night air, she wrapped her arms around her chest and tapped her foot on the ground impatiently. She imagined Casey and Asia gaining admittance with the help of his ID badge and Walker, then acting quickly to spread the gas canisters Ben brought throughout the hallways, quickly putting the guards to sleep.

Ben and the others climbed out of his vehicle and walked up to her, all business, except for the gentle touch of his hand on her arm. "It will take them a few minutes to get through the building. I'm sure everything is going according to plan."

"It's awfully quiet." Her teeth chattered, but not just from the cold.

"That's a good sign. If things fall apart, we'll hear all about it." Ben's eyes twinkled, clearly used to this kind of activity.

Just then, Jackson's cell phone vibrated in his pocket. "Yeah. Thanks. We'll be right there." He hung up the phone. He raised his voice just enough for everyone to hear. "Casey said the guards are down, so we can head for the lab via the loading dock area. He's unlocked it by swiping his ID card at a main terminal."

Michelle's heart pounded in her throat as she crept toward the building with the others. *Calm down. It's just another cat rescue.* But she knew better. The risks were much higher and they would get only this one chance to interfere with Carter's dreadful plans.

They climbed up on one dock and cracked open a passage door. Nightlights glowed inside and a faint odor remained. Casey had warned them to expect the stuffiness of the gassed halls, but assured them the gas would have already done its job on the guards and would have significantly dissipated, so they would be safe from its effects.

They followed Casey's directions to the labs. As promised, Walker had left them unlocked, so the team broke up into four groups of three. Three groups ran to different labs and the remaining group took stations spaced down the halls to expedite removing the cats and transferring them to the vehicles.

Walking with Ben and Lacey into a lab, Michelle gasped. Twenty cats in captivity, all sending out signs of distress, caught her off guard.

The pain and confusion pierced her heart and she had to grab hold of a countertop to steady herself.

She glanced at Lacey, who also was highly sensitive, and saw the effects of the free- floating angst on her. Her fingers trembled and she stood still, sucking in deep breaths.

"Are you all right, Lacey?" Michelle called. "It's pretty thick in here."

"I'm fine. Let's get these cats out of here." Her eyes widened as she perused the room. Ben grabbed Michelle's arm. "You steady?"

"I am. It looks like the lynx has been moved," she said, peering into the room Casey had described. "So how about Lacey and I transfer the cats to carriers and you run them to the hallway crew?" An image suddenly grabbed Michelle's attention and Ben stopped. "I'm okay."

He nodded and grabbed the first two cats in their carriers and ran through the doorway.

In front of her eyes Michelle saw a large lynx, huddled in a cage. She focused deeply, trying to squeeze everything out of the premonition. Chills made her shake. The room was dark and the lynx rolled into a ball. Then the premonition stopped, and frustration knotted her stomach. *What did it mean?* She bit her lower lip, begging for more information, while she opened a cage and removed a little black cat to slide into a carrier.

Ben was gone for only minutes, but by then Michelle and Lacey had more than half of the cats in carriers and ready for him to transfer.

"Well, this may have been a bad idea," Michelle said, watching the carriers stack up when the goal was to get them out of the building. "I'll help carry them out." She passed Jackson on the way to the hallway crew. His eyes shone intensely and sweat beaded his brow. "It's harder than it looks, huh?" she said. "There are so many cats."

Without stopping he called back over his shoulder. "We're more than half done. We'll just keep at it."

She passed two cats to Quinn, who promptly handed them to Booker to load into a vehicle.

Michelle's breathing was coming in big drags. The cats were heavy and every moment weighed on her. All the cats needed to be removed before the guards started coming around.

She reentered the lab and almost ran into Lacey. She had her hands full with two large carriers of cats, but she didn't pause for help.

Inside, Ben was loading up the last two cats. "There's a few carriers over in the corner," he said, breathless.

Michelle picked them up, her back screaming, and carried them to Asher. His breath heaving, he grabbed them and took off, just as Ben followed up behind Michelle. Quinn reached around her and took the cats from Ben.

"That's all the cats from that lab." Ben bent over and rested his hands on his knees, breathing heavily.

"These are the last of them from our lab." Sterling, Tizzy, and Conrad came to a breathless stop beside Michelle. "Let's get out of here," Tizzy said.

"Have you seen Casey and Asia, or this Walker guy?" Fear raised its tentacles again, twisting Michelle's stomach tightly.

"No, not yet. Maybe something's wrong," Tizzy said. "All the more reason to finish up here and move the cats out of this vicinity and get them to Michelle's."

Jackson pursed his lips, then shook his head. "No, we can't leave them here alone. I'm going in search of them. Maybe I'll find both the lynxes, too."

"I'm going with you," Michelle spoke up. "Don't any one of you give me any trouble over this. I'm going."

Michelle jumped, startled by a low moan coming from one the guards lying farther down the hallway. She knew that if she could hear, so could they.

"We don't have time to stand here and debate it." Ben's statement was more of a declaration. "I'll go, too."

"Ben, I think you should go with the others," Lara said. "They'll need help unloading the carriers. Asia will be very helpful with the captive lynxes because of her telepathy. I'm going to Michelle's house, too. I imagine my healing ability will be useful."

"Oh, right. You can handle it, Jackson?" Michelle asked.

"I'm used to dealing with my father's messes. Yes, I can handle it."

Ben turned to the remaining members of the group and pointed toward the way out. "We'll see you guys at Michelle's."

Michelle handed him the key to her house, then watched them walk away. "Let's get moving," Ben said. "We have very little time left."

Sticking together, Jackson and Michelle walked through the halls and found another stairway partially hidden by curtains. A creepiness slithered throughout her body.

Jackson turned the doorknob and it gave way. He cracked open the door and started down the stairs. Dim lights lit the way as Michelle followed behind him.

The chill in her premonition came up the stairs. "I think this is where the lynx is. I had a premonition." She didn't know for sure what they'd find at the bottom of the stairs and she was half afraid to see. She heard soft voices inside another room.

"We mean you no harm," Asia whispered.

Slowly, Jackson and Michelle walked closer, then peeked inside the doorway. Michelle's heart leaped into her throat when she saw Casey, maybe not safe, but definitely sound.

Confusion and grogginess drifted into Michelle's senses. She walked quietly with Jackson to stand out of sight of the animals in the cages, but within Asia's and Casey's peripheral vision.

Asia peered into the glassy eyes of a male lynx and held his gaze. Its appearance was the same as the lynx in her premonition. Michelle held her breath, hoping the telepathy would give Asia good rapport with the poor animal. Minutes dragged by and the air was thick, emotions dripping as Asia held an invisible space for all that he'd endured to be acknowledged.

She turned around and all Michelle could see was Asia's expression, her heart, torn open by what she'd learned.

"He is a were-lynx," she whispered. "He's been in captivity for two months. The drugs are causing havoc with his mind."

Casey put his hand on Asia's bent shoulders. "Is he safe to come out?"

Asia nodded her head. "He hasn't shimmered during captivity. He's aching all over."

Michelle stood in close. "Have you had a chance to communicate with the female lynx? She's been pacing this whole time."

"Yes. She's a few years younger than us. She's also a were-lynx. And she's pissed."

Casey snickered. "I don't blame her. How long has she been in captivity?"

Asia rolled her head around her shoulders. "That is unclear. Anyway, she's safe to let out."

Casey broke the lock on the male's cage and opened the door, offering a hand to help him climb out. The lynx staggered out, barely able to stand upright on all four legs. "Take your time. If need be we'll carry you out of here."

In the corner, the female yowled, twice, and scratched at the wire cage.

"In case you didn't get that, that means let her out." Asia's smile lit her tired face.

Casey broke off the lock and both of them assisted the female out of the cage. Instantly, she shimmered into her human form.

"Oh my God that feels good." Her voice was raspy and she didn't appear at all bashful. She resumed her pacing, but this time on two legs. "Who are you guys? What took you so long?"

Questions tumbled out of her as her eyes darted around the room. Michelle threw her coat to her and the young woman quickly shrugged into it. It covered her body to her knees.

"Thank you. I'm Kennedy. Any of you familiar with were-cats?"

"I am a were-cat and so is he," Asia said, pointing at Casey.

The other were-cat still struggled to walk on his four legs.

"Can you shimmer?" Casey stood next to him, steadying him. "I don't think the people who worked with you knew your true identity."

The were-lynx attempted a shimmer and managed to produce human hands and arms. Long, thick claws appeared on his hands. His arms were so muscled and enormous they probably wouldn't completely bend.

Michelle gasped, then instantly wished she could take it back. The were-lynx yowled in what sounded like agony when he saw his hands and arms. He flexed his fingers and his biceps. A frightful glare filled his eyes.

Asia put a hand to his hunched shoulders. "Remember, I told you we wouldn't know what would happen until we tried. It's okay. We'll help you." Her voice was nothing but soothing and assuring, convincing that she would keep her promise.

Suddenly William Carter came crashing down the stairs, dragging Walker with him. "Isn't this special. My son and his friends taking an interest in my work."

"You left out a word, Father," Jackson said. "You meant to say diabolical work."

Carter ignored Jackson and turned to Casey. "Son, you don't understand what's going on here." His nostrils flared and he pointed to Michelle. "Probably because this young woman has poisoned your mind."

Casey slitted his eyes and pinned Carter. "I'm not your son."

He turned his back on Carter and gave Michelle a wry grin. She knew he was telling her to let it pass for now. The clock was ticking and they needed to get out of the building. She read all that and he'd made it very clear. She'd have to talk about that with him sometime.

Carter's raucous laughter echoed maniacally around the room. "You're right. But your father is just as much a part of this project as I am. It's a family affair." He pointed to Kennedy. "Casey, meet your little sister."

"What?" Kennedy's deep brown eyes went wide. "I don't have siblings. My parents are dead, killed in a car crash."

Casey whirled around to face Carter. "Don't listen to him, Kennedy." He pointed a finger at Carter. "He's full of lies. And Carter, I know about my dad. Just shut up."

He turned back around to help Asia with the pained were-lynx.

Asia continued to talk softly to the distraught were-lynx. More and more of his human self appeared as she talked him through successive shimmers.

Jackson stepped up to distract William. "Dad, why are you saying these things? Why are you conducting this research? I'm not going to let you continue with it."

Carter shoved his fingers through his thin, gray hair, a muscle in his cheek twitching. "You're not going to *let* me continue?"

His voice was eerily calm. It sent shivers through Michelle, because he was verging on rage, not calm. She saw Walker lying on the floor, dazed and beaten, heard the anguish from the male were-cat, the anger from the female were-cat, and saw Casey's somber face as he reeled from the harm Carter dealt in and she tried to keep a lid on her fuming emotions.

Certain things had to happen for this rescue to be a success. Containment popped up first. All the cats had been removed and were now safe in her house. But what happened right now in this room could make or break their efforts to stop Carter's plans.

While Jackson kept Carter's attention on the far side of the room, Michelle sidled to the door at the top of the stairs and twisted the deadbolt knob to lock it. No one else would be able to crash this party, she thought to herself. She knew no one had brought a gun. They couldn't do much to threaten Carter into submission, so getting him tied up was probably not going to happen.

Her entire body craved to just get out of there, with the two former lab subjects, and get them to safety. Lara would be able to address their health issues.

Jackson's voice grabbed her attention. While the father and son yelled at each other, Walker had scooted toward Lara and Casey, so at least he was out of range of more beating from Carter. What could she do to progress the escape?

Then Carter's words permeated her thoughts.

"You're listening to the wrong people, Jake." Carter's eyes flashed anger and contempt. "And so is your friend. That woman is destructive. Do you know how much that boy has suffered since the trial?"

Jackson planted his hands on his hips, eyes wide. "It's unthinkable to me that you side with a rapist, then to make matters worse, attempt to steal Michelle's house, all because that boy, as you call him, is the son of your friend."

Nausea threatened to shut down Michelle's heart. The words coming from Carter's mouth stabbed her gut, and her mind started treadmilling, an inner dialogue that assessed her part in creating pain for Darrel.

That can't be, she thought. *He hurt me. He got acquitted.* "What kind of suffering are you talking about?" she yelled.

Jackson and William stopped fighting and all the air in the room got sucked out.

William didn't miss a beat. He pointed a long, thin finger at her, accusingly. "Darrel has been depressed, unable to work, hardly able to leave his home. All because you seduced him into having sex and then cried rape. I told you I'd make you pay," he raged. "I'll take everything from you, just as you stole everything from Darrel."

Michelle stared at him, speechless. His soul was so corrupted he didn't even realize the truth. But a niggling thought in the corner of brain wondered. Had William Carter done something harmful, though perhaps not meaning to, and suffered shame too overwhelming to tolerate? Was that the bedrock of his destructive ways?

"So you think Darrel is misunderstood? That he didn't mean to hurt me?" It took all her remaining strength to offer his messed up mind a tiny bit of understanding.

Instantly ill at ease, Carter ran his hand through his hair and clenched his fist. "Don't psychoanalyze me!"

She studied him for one nanosecond, realization seeping through her that many years ago a young Carter had felt hurt, betrayed, and misunderstood. And he'd closed his heart.

"You can steal my house. You can make a wedge between Casey and me. It won't work. Darrel has made his own suffering." He might take everything from her, but he couldn't touch her peace or sense of herself unless she let him.

The thought hit Carter's face, and the truth registered for a moment, then dropped to the floor. "Shut up!" he howled.

"No, you shut up." Jackson leaned close to his father's face. "Michelle is not going to lose her home or anything else that is important to her. Work is in progress right now to charge the mortgage broker and title company you used to cause a problem with her ownership."

Michelle's heart skipped in her chest. This was news to her.

William screwed up his face and stared at Jackson. "What are you talking about?"

Jackson chuckled, a cryptic, sad sound. "People care about injustice and they care about Michelle. She's not losing her property. You've accomplished nothing. And this drug trial, that could put a bad mark on my company, is going to be sorted out. You're not going to get what you want."

Carter's face contorted, as the reality of Jackson's words pierced his ego. Michelle screamed, as William reached for Jackson's neck.

"No, he's your son!" she hollered.

A flash of half-man, half-lynx screeched by her and grabbed William in his massive arms. His face, now human, bore long fangs and was blotted with patches of fur. His human legs were bent and deformed and ended with enormous paws with deadly claws.

"You did this to me!" The man's voice came out raspy and filled with rage.

William screamed. Asia grabbed the man's arm and pleaded with him to release Carter, but he batted her away like a gnat.

Jackson and Casey yanked at Carter, trying to pull him from the man's grip. Kennedy stood screaming, and Michelle wasn't quite sure if she sided with the were-cat or was simply screaming in shock.

Chaos and vengeance and fear filled the room like thick smog. Michelle ached for all parties involved in the mess Carter had unleashed with his projects. She didn't have the heart to try to hurt the were-cat, but she couldn't stand by and watch Carter's death, either.

"Stop! You don't want to do this!" Her eyes trained on the were-cat. He took one glance at her and in his eyes she saw his sorrow at his inability to resist the raw and raging animal inside him that William had made him into.

While William stared wide-eyed, the man turned back to him, pulled back his claws above his own head, then ripped out William's throat.

"Dad!" Jackson grabbed his father and eased him to the floor. Blood gurgling out of his mouth and the ragged tear at his throat, William looked into Jackson's face, pleading.

"I love you, too, Dad." Jackson's tears slipped down his face, while the life in his father's body left.

CHAPTER 17

The room was silent, except for the sobs coming from the were-man. All strength ebbed from his body. Asia went to him, lowering him to the floor.

"I'm so sorry this happened to you." She seemed to know something Michelle didn't. "His name is Adrian. He is twenty-six years old. He is a social worker. Adrian, these are your friends."

Adrian coughed convulsively, as Michelle, Jackson, and Casey greeted him.

Michelle's heart nearly stopped. She felt Adrian's essence weaken down to a small dot, a light inside him just bright enough to glimmer behind his brown eyes. The drugs and the captivity had taken a toll and he wouldn't survive.

Weakly, Walker crawled to him. "I'm so sorry, Adrian." He spoke the name reverently. "I didn't know you. But what I did was wrong. I'm so sorry." He hung his head and put his hand on Adrian's.

"I could tell you didn't like what you were doing," Adrian whispered. "Thank you for helping me get out of here."

Michelle gritted her teeth to dam her tears. "Yes, let's get him out of here." She put her arm around Kennedy's shoulder. The young woman flinched, still in shock.

Casey and Ben lifted Adrian and carried him to the stairs as Michelle led Kennedy up and unlocked the door. Walker leaned on Asia and followed the line through the halls, up the stairs, and out the front door to Casey and Asia's cars. None of the guards did anything but stare at them, obviously still dazed and confused.

She'd overheard Jackson call Ben. He would take over the investigation, but first off, he'd see to William Carter.

Everything in Michelle wanted to get Adrian out of this death space and back among good people. Since the others had taken her Jeep, she rode in Asia's car, Adrian lying in the back, moaning and coughing.

"Hang on, Adrian, please hang on," she begged.

Minutes later their two-car caravan pulled up into Michelle's drive. She climbed out of the car, knowing there wasn't much time left.

While Jackson and Casey carried Adrian to the backyard and laid him down, Asia gathered the others. Michelle kneeled beside him, putting her hand to his. "Look up, Adrian. You can see the moon and the stars."

He drew in a sharp breath. The moaning stopped. His eyes glistened in the light from the sky.

"It's so beautiful." His voice came in raspy determination.

Michelle turned over his deformed hand. "Feel the grass, breathe the autumn scents in the air."

A very soft, rumbling purr came in spurts from his throat.

"Look around." The other were-cats strolled up to circle him with his own kind. Behind them stood Ben and Sterling, Jackson and Lacey, and Walker and Kennedy.

Asia, her brown eyes glimmering from her furry brown face, stretched out beside him.

She chuffed and rubbed her head against his arm.

The silence of the night wrapped them in a rarefied moment that would be his last.

Adrian closed his eyes. "Thank you. Thank you all," he whispered. "I'm at peace."

Michelle's heart throbbed as she watched Adrian's body sink against the ground. The peace he emanated soothed her sorrow and the love the others gifted him with in his final moments sent chills through her body. This sad end to Carter's experiments came with gifts of love and peace she couldn't ignore. These beautiful beings, lynx and human, were the kind of creatures she wanted to be with.

* * *

LARA WANTED to do an autopsy on Adrian's body, so Ben arranged for an EMT he worked with to transport him to the vet clinic, with promises to keep quiet. He was a good buddy, so Ben trusted him. Walker welcomed the opportunity to share what he knew about the research. Soon, Adrian would be buried in the field beside Michelle's house. After they'd all tended to the cats, they gathered in Michelle's living room and relaxed after the emotional and physical ordeal.

But Casey had something to deal with before he could relax. He slipped into the bathroom and closed the door, leaning against the wall. Resolved, he punched in the phone number for Agent Callahan, already prepared to do his job as colony leader.

"Casey, good morning." Callahan's voice on the other end of the call elicited cringes in Casey's body. "You've got news?"

"I'm sure you've heard about William Carter's death."

"An accident. Is that true? What do have for me?"

"It was an accident. I think the police think they have their candidate. They think Walker is responsible for leaving the cage door open. Negligent homicide." Casey tapped his finger on the bathroom wall.

"What do you know? I know you got inside. I've been watching you."

"I did. But I can't tell you anything about Carter's death. Carter actually played me. I didn't learn anything I can share with you."

"Don't know anything or won't share?" Callahan's voice rose an octave. "I'll have you behind bars faster than you can spit if you're holding out on me."

"I don't have any solid proof, but I can tell you that I got rumblings of other plans. I doubt they'll close down because Carter is dead."

"Other plans?"

"I told you, Carter played me, so I don't have anything further to share with the FBI." Casey didn't like lying but in this case, he had to withhold any information that would reveal the were-cat population to the government. "Look, I did what you requested. You have nothing on me."

"I'll be watching you, Mitchell."

As Casey hung up, his mind was already on other things. How to lead the colony from here and, most of all, a possible relationship.

He walked into the room the others had gathered in, and picked up the conversation. "I'm very sorry about your father, Jackson."

Michelle's voice sounded sincere and Casey's heart lurched for her. Her kindness and empathy were extraordinary. "I appreciate you sticking up for me, too."

Lacey rested her head on Jackson's shoulder and rubbed his arm. "It was an awful thing for you to see, babe. I'm so sorry."

Watching everyone from across the room, Casey struggled with finding adequate words. "We're all sorry, man. You deserve better."

Jackson quirked his head to one side and sighed. "My dad made his own bed. I wish it had been different, but he made choices that hurt a lot of people. It came back to bite him, ironically."

No one laughed. The room roiled, thick with sadness and dismay.

"I am nervous about possible retribution from this gang, The Nexus Group, that he was a part of," Casey added. "And there's the matter of my dad's participation in Nexus operations. We're not superheroes taking on all the bad guys in Laurelwood, but this project has revealed a malevolent factor in town and we've been put in its crosshairs. We have to consider our choices, get in deeper or take our chances and not get involved. But for now, let's call it a night. I don't have to remind you to stay alert, it's second nature to us. But the menace isn't gone. Pay attention."

As everyone headed toward the door, Lara suggested Kennedy stay with her and she would check her health. Casey's nerves jangled trying to process the possible existence of a sister he didn't know he had, but he wasn't about to reject her out of hand, either.

"Look, there are a lot of things to sort out about you, but it's not going to get done tonight." Tentatively, Casey put an arm around Kennedy's shoulders. "If it turns out we're related, well, lucky me. Either way, you belong with us, but I imagine you have people already?"

She shook her head. "I don't want to talk about any of that right now." But she reached up and wrapped her arms around Casey's neck. "Thank you. And thank you for not leaving me in that awful place."

As everyone left, he turned to Michelle. "Can we talk? You've been through so much for so long. I'm not sure it's fair to ask you to trust me. To love me."

She took his hand and pulled him out of the doorway. Her hand on his sparked life into his heart. She reached around him and closed the door, all the while eyeing him.

He stood there, waiting for an indication of what was in her mind. Vulnerability felt like shit in times like this, he thought. His life was in her hands and she didn't even know it.

Michelle sent quakes rumbling through him with her sapphire blue eyes glistening up into his.

"Can we kiss?" she asked. "I should have trusted you. I know I've hurt you but—"

Casey picked her up in his arms, bringing her lips to his. His heart beat so hard he felt certain she could feel it. He pressed a hard, hungry kiss to her soft and welcoming lips. He kissed her, releasing all the longing and fear and loss into the air around them. He kissed her deeply, wanting to dispel any misunderstandings. Liquid joy brimmed his eyes, blurring his vision when he pulled back. He set her back down, too raw to take her scrutiny.

"You don't have to ask. You've already got it." She placed a soft, sweet kiss to his lips. Joy exploded like Fourth of July fireworks inside him. He wrapped his arms around her and pulled her up close to match her kiss with hard, pounding passion. He would never let her go.

"I love you, Michelle. I've waited so long for you. I thought I would always be alone because I'm a were-cat and you're not. There's never been a woman in my life I wanted to engage with, trust, be wholly together. From as young as I can remember, I was told privacy and solitude were the things that kept our species around for centuries and that I was expected to follow in those ways."

"They were wrong in our case," she said. "You've helped me come back into the world. I'm your people, if you want me."

In his gut he knew without question that it was right. They belonged together. He caressed her cheek and brushed his thumb over her lips.

Fire lit her eyes. It spurred his breathing to come fast and furious. She lifted his shirt over his head and threw it to the floor, then began unbuckling his belt and removing his pants. His pulse racing, he kicked off his boxers, then pulled her T-shirt over her head, slipped one bra strap over her left shoulder, then the other one over her right shoulder. He drew his hands down her slim shoulders and reached around to unhook her bra. She let it fall and stood before him, all pink and beautiful.

Her breasts heaving, she took off her yoga pants and underwear. She took his hand and pulled him toward her as she lowered to the carpet.

Urgency swept through him. This wasn't their first time together but this stood out to him as a signpost in their relationship. He wouldn't hold back.

When he crushed her in his embrace, he found she wouldn't be holding back either.

Desire fed every kiss, every caress, every lick and nibble. His nostrils flared, gasping for more air, faster breaths to fuel his efforts to take her in completely.

Atop him, she wriggled and arched her back, unleashed passion clearly rippling through her. She leaned into his face to drive him further with her darting tongue and devouring lips. His hardness smashed against her leg, her soft folds, demanding all of her.

Casey rolled her off and laid eyes on her. "You're so beautiful." His voice sounded guttural to his ears, but he didn't try to rein in his emotions.

She brushed her hands across his chest and nuzzled inside the crook of his neck. "I love your skin. The feel of it, the scent of it."

She looked up at him with glazed eyes. He struggled with his body's demands, wanting to make these moments last. He kissed her nipples, driving them to harden, then brushed kisses across her stomach and down to her femininity. She writhed beneath him, moaning and kneading his back muscles. "Condoms are in my bedroom nightstand," she muttered.

He picked her up in his arms and carried her into her bedroom and laid her on the bed. Protection in place, he climbed in bed, enjoying the look of passion on her: tousled blond hair, steamy eyes, and glistening skin.

Back atop her, he savored the touch of her skin, from head to toe, against his. Instantly, she wrapped her legs around him and pulled him up to kiss his lips, hard and full of want. He stroked her folds, slowly and deliberately.

But she would have none of that. She reached for his hardness and he obliged her with a thrust into her. She moaned and arched to him, her legs still wrapping him in close.

"Please, lie against me," she asked in a soft, raspy voice.

He obliged her again, resting chest to chest on her, while they matched thrust for acceptance, melting together over and over until her heated interior rippled around him.

"Oh, Michelle, you feel so good," he ground out. His own climax came, too, just then, muscles tensing and releasing, over and over, until finally she lay spent beneath him as he collapsed against her.

Time passed, he was sure of it. But lying on top of her nearly asleep with her soft breathing in his ear, Casey would have believed time had stood still. He carefully rolled off her, tucking the sheets close around them both.

"Don't go." Michelle's eyes remained closed as she snuggled close to him.

"You mean stay for the night?" He shoved locks of her disheveled hair from her face and kissed her nose.

She opened sleepy eyes and smiled at him. "Stay forever. I love you, Casey Mitchell."

CHAPTER 18

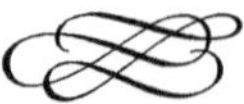

Michelle wanted to let Casey sleep, but she needed to get started on morning feeding. She crept out from under the blankets, smiling at his sleepy face, took a quick shower, and dressed.

The stacks of carriers with cats were coming alive throughout her house. They'd rescued thirty cats, more than they'd expected. The sedatives the cats had been given at the research facility along with the gas they'd taken in during the rescue had made moving them easier. But that was hours ago and they were no longer sedated. Some of them remained calm. Those were most likely the roamers, cats who had homes but were allowed to go outside and roam. The ferals were another story. So feeding time was a chore. Most difficult were the deformed and angry cats. For those, she extended all her love and patience.

Michelle was eager to release the ferals and bring the roamers back home, but each cat needed a thorough exam before that could happen. Until then, they had to be kept separated, too, including separated from Jojo, Izabell, Munchie, and Tiger.

"Good morning, beautiful." Casey's hands on her shoulders startled her, but it passed quickly.

She turned and looked up into his serene eyes. "Good morning." She didn't need anything more than that look from him. He kissed her, one soft, brief touch of his lips, his hands resting on her waist. She stood there with him, his hands on her and her arms around his neck, and simply savored the moment. They were together, hugging and holding, sharing a space of silent awareness of the immense trauma of William Carter and at the same time the powerful joy of their mutual love. It filled her heart completely.

Meows grew louder and Michelle stepped back from Casey. "Hungry cats call. I've fed more than half of them. Once they're all fed I'm going to start shuttling them to Lara's clinic. It will be temporary so she can observe them for negative consequences. Some with the most severe deformities may have to be euthanized. Some will have to be homed as special needs."

"You sound pretty happy. This is a lot of work." Casey crossed his arms over his chest, thinking.

"I'm happy the cats are out of that hellhole. Some of them are going home, and that makes me very happy."

"How can I help?" He surveyed the stacks of carriers and furrowed his brow.

"You already have done so much. I know you have work to do. I can manage." She smiled at him. Yes, she was happy about the cats, but more than that, the change of things with Casey flitted through her like shimmering bubbles. She'd told him last night of her love for him, simply put it out there, no holding back. And so far she'd survived. This was a feeling she could get used to enjoying, one of freedom and spontaneous expression.

"I'll help you load the cats and drive my share to Lara's." He tweaked her nose and grinned. "There is still so much heavy stuff to deal with, but all I want to think about is you."

"I feel the same way, Casey. But we can't stay sequestered here alone. The world and serious issues would pull us back into the mishegoss eventually." Michelle's spirits couldn't be dampened this morning.

"Uh huh." He nuzzled her neck just under her chin.

His warm breath on her skin sent her senses spiraling. "Casey, as marvelous as that feels, work, hungry cats, evil group of people, remember?"

"Fine. It's hard to ignore a good glow." With that he helped finish feeding the remaining cats. Casey by her side, Michelle loaded all thirty carriers into her Jeep and his Prius and delivered them to Lara for inspection and any care that was needed.

Thirty minutes later, Casey drove up the driveway at his parents' house. Michelle reached across the console and put her hand on his. Her nerves jangled, as though ringing a warning bell. Casey's serious demeanor pushed her thoughts into a whirl.

She didn't comment on the beautiful, secluded home sitting amongst large trees and manicured bushes. She knew Casey had thoughts only for confronting his father.

Michelle pulled his hand to her lips and brushed a kiss to his fingers. The scent of his skin soothed her. Would it ever become commonplace?

"Thank you for coming with me, Michelle. You ground me." A frown creased his brow, but his voice implied he was solid and ready to face his father falling off his pedestal.

CASEY GRIPPED Michelle's hand as though she might drift away. He didn't normally knock on the massive wooden front door, but things were not what they'd normally been between him and his parents. The knocking stood as a demarcation between what had been and what was now.

Moments later the door opened and his father stood in the door-way. "Casey, come in, son."

He led them to the living room and Michelle couldn't help herself. "This is an amazing room, Dr. Mitchell. You have a lovely home."

Casey's mother entered the room, sorrow in her eyes. "Casey." She walked up to him and hugged him close, then stepped back to stand with her husband.

"Father, Mother, this is Michelle, but of course you already know who she is." His sarcasm dripped, thick and sour, but he didn't care, couldn't care. His heart was bleeding, had been since he discovered his dad's involvement in The Nexus Group.

Michelle nodded to Camille and extended her hand and Larry took it, shaking it firmly. "It's nice to meet you, Dr. Mitchell, Mrs. Mitchell."

"Please, call me Larry, my wife Camille." He gestured her to have a seat on the couch and Casey sat close beside her.

"I was hoping you and your mother and I could have a private meeting." His father gave Casey a stern glare.

"I can wait in the car," Michelle offered.

He put a hand to her knee as she started to rise. A floral scent wafted to him, and he breathed it in, drawing strength from Michelle. "No, there is nothing to hide from her."

His father shifted in the upholstered chair he sat in, and shifted again, clearly ill at ease. "I feel sorry for Jackson, losing his father. I assume you've heard about William Carter's death. Terrible accident."

"Accident?" Casey fisted his hands.

"Yes, Carter Enterprises was conducting research using a new digital diary and insulin pump. Some of the studies were still in phase one, working with animals. One escaped and attacked him. I guess a lab worker is responsible for leaving a cage open. He's been taken into custody pending charges of negligence."

Casey's composure strained under the weight of so much bullshit. "That's the official story? From Carter Enterprises?"

"I suppose. I just read it in this morning's *Laurelwood Gazette*." His eyes shifted, but he never dropped his gaze from Casey's.

"Hmm." Michelle's muscles tightened against him. He exchanged a look with her and could see fireworks blasting off inside the deep blue of her eyes. He rubbed her arm, soothingly, determined to keep her calm. So much stood between her and the workings of Carter Enterprises and anyone significant associated with the company. He wouldn't blame her if she gave his father a piece of her mind, but it might put her at risk with The Nexus Group.

Casey rubbed his thumb across his chin, contemplating. Several minutes passed and his father sighed a lot. His mother's face was impassive, except for the tears collecting in her eyes.

"Well, anyway, I told you on the phone I had some things to straighten out with you." He cleared his throat. His dispassionate attitude took some doing, but it was the only way he could address his parents right now.

"Yeah, what's on your mind, son?" His father's dark brown eyes, the eyes he'd always trusted in, were blanketed, emotionless. It tore at his gut.

"To the point, how could you, Dad?" *Guess he wasn't going to be able to fake apathy.* His words came out raw and wounded. "I know you're an associate of William Carter. The man whose idea of good business has created a climate of crime and destruction in this town that is escalating."

His father tilted his head. "What do you mean? I work independently, always have, son."

"There's that word again: *son*. Dad, does it mean anything to you? I've spent my lifetime admiring you for the man I believed you to be. Honest, loving, kind, intelligent. But those words are dead to me regarding you."

"Casey, you mean everything to me. Everything I've done has been to provide for you and for your future." Anger and sorrow warred on his face.

"Stop. Stop right there. Do you know how much it hurts to learn you've worked with Carter? You've hurt people. You've killed. You've stolen jobs and made people homeless. You didn't do that for me, Dad. You did it out of greed and ego. You did it to create power and wealth for yourself."

His father crossed his arms over his chest and his right knee over his left knee. "I just don't know what you're talking about."

"Oh my God!" Casey's mind raced. "You're not going to admit anything, are you? Dad, I know what you've been involved in. I know you're lying to me right now."

"Casey." His dad stood tall, innocent eyes shining down on him.

"Keep this focused on just us. No matter what, I love you and I'd do everything to protect our relationship."

Casey stood, his muscles aching to run away and deny the truth of his father, his idol, one of his best friends in a world where he'd had few. "If you can't be straight with me, there is no longer any *us.*"

A sob escaped his mother's throat. "Casey, we love you. When you called and said you had some issues to discuss, you sounded so detached. It hurt. Please, sit down." She turned to her husband. "Tell him."

His father rubbed the top of his head and stared at the floor. Suddenly, his shoulders drooped and his face crumpled. "You deserve to know the truth. To know everything." He shook his head.

Casey stiffened on the couch. Was there any hope he could stomach his dad's confession?

"I was telling you the truth when I said everything I've done has been to protect you and take care of you."

"I heard you. That's about money. Do you think that matters more to me than integrity and compassion?" His heart hammered in his chest, indignant.

His father held up his hand. "No, that's not what I'm talking about." Michelle squeezed his leg and gave him a pointed look.

"Let him speak, Casey." His mother's voice was firm, but gentle. "You asked for the truth, listen."

He settled back into the couch, tension slithering inside his gut.

"When your mother and I first married, times were very tough for us. My parents initially ousted me from the family and the colony. I'd broken a primary rule by marrying your mother. Your mother had finished her degree but I was still in grad school." His father shifted on the couch.

"So, hard times. Everyone has them."

"It's not an excuse. I'm just telling you what you asked to know." His father cleared his throat and looked down again. "Carter approached me. He told me a tiny investment into a group that was going to help Laurelwood prosper would yield not only good things for the community but boost my income."

Casey's mother broke down into sobs. It plucked at his heart but he knew he hadn't heard the whole story yet.

"What I learned later was that Carter was power hungry and he was delving into research projects that would endanger humans and were-cats. I learned that as I got deeper involved with him."

"And the money?" Casey was losing patience.

His father's eyes flashed lividly. "Yes, there was money coming in. But Carter knew about the existence of were-cats. His limited knowledge of were-cats scared me. He'd heard stories about were-cats and went in search to find one. He worked with doctors who belonged to him to get access to medical records. He learned that your mother and I had were-lynx genes. He assumed you had them, too, but I lied to him, telling him you didn't have the genes."

Casey dropped his head into his hands. "Oh my God."

Michelle sniffed. Casey looked down at her to see tears in her eyes, but she gave him a soft smile that assured him.

"So the investment you made paid off? You've lived a good life. I've been safe. End of story? I don't think so."

"No. I didn't invest money. Carter told me my investment would come later, when it was needed." He choked on his words, but struggled to continue. "I could see the effects of Carter's actions and the development of The Nexus Group. When your mother got pregnant, we decided it was time to separate from Carter."

"Let me guess. He wouldn't let you. Threatened you. Is that about it?"

"Casey, he did that and more. But we were determined to start over." He put his arm around his wife and Casey had the feeling they hadn't talked about their life with Carter much. "He told us our baby would be our investment and he had plans to raise the child as a protégé in his company and eventually involve the child in The Nexus Group."

"That's crazy. Why your child?"

"Carter had an idea that the child would surely be a were-cat. Nothing I said penetrated his insane intentions. But your mother went into preterm labor. The doctor told us the baby hadn't survived. It was a terrible time for us. But we had each other and we had you."

Michelle's soft touch on his arm soothed the sizzling anger seething just beneath his skin. He might have been wrong in his conclusions about his father.

"We realized we could never part from Carter. His connections infiltrated all aspects of living in Laurelwood. Doctors, politicians, police administers, judges. We discussed moving out of town but we knew he'd find us. As long as I stayed involved in some capacity, you and your mother would be safe. So yes, I've contributed to the development of horrific crimes, but all the while I was trying to do things that undermined Carter's endeavors."

Tears blurred Casey's vision, but he brushed them away. His mind had no memories of Carter's interaction in his family's early life. He did remember his mother's pregnancy and subsequent loss of the child, but he'd never had reason to question it as anything other than a sad but normal event. "So now it's over? Carter's dead and you're free."

"We haven't had time yet to wrap our brains around this development, his death. There is a lot to consider." His mother dabbed her eyes, then folded her hands.

"And what about The Nexus Group?" Casey's brain whirled. There were still many questions.

His parents exchanged glances. "You've got to understand that we know very little about the inner workings of The Nexus Group. It's a very dangerous organization. Please don't make attempts to investigate it."

"You're afraid of the group. But you're a member?"

"Yes, I'm a member. It's not something I'm proud of or ever wanted. I made some bad choices. And yes, we're afraid what the group might do to us and you if we attempted to separate or report their activities to the authorities, who are probably connected to the group."

Casey rubbed his fingers across his mouth, contemplating. "I want to believe you. I do. But why didn't you come to me, after I grew up, and tell me about the terrible fix you're in? I'm a PI, for god's sake. I could have helped. But no, you chose to keep your secret from me. I can't help but suspect there is more to what's happened than what you've just told me."

"I understand. But I hope in time you'll be able to accept what I've said and forgive me for what I've done. I truly have been trying to keep you safe, son."

Casey pulled Michelle to her feet. She stood close beside him and the warmth of her closeness reminded him he was beginning a new life with new ways. "Dad, Mom, I love you. If what you've said is true, I can understand your actions. But finding out the way I did, second hand and not from you, really rocked my beliefs about you. I need time."

Sorrow pulled at their faces, but Casey could not simply act as though all was well. "Okay, son. Thank you for hearing me out. I respect your need for space, but I hope to see you again soon." His father wrapped an arm around his mother, as Casey led Michelle away. Away from his father, his mother, from the home of his childhood, away from all the corruption.

Casey walked with Michelle to his car and drove away, pain gripping every muscle in his body. That heartsick pain he couldn't get away from.

He heaved a deep sigh. "I've held my father in high esteem. I feel lost now."

"You were right to listen and to take time to consider everything." Michelle gave him a sad smile. "It could be true. And maybe the baby didn't die. It could be Kennedy. Why didn't you say something?"

"We don't know for sure if Carter was telling the truth. I'm not going to build up their hope and take it away if I find out Kennedy is not family." Casey fisted his hands. "I feel so conflicted. My dad should have known better than to get involved with Carter. But if it's true, they've suffered so much."

"The William Carter effect. It's horrific and almost never fails in its intent."

"It really hurts." His body sagged into the car seat.

"The sorrow you're struggling against will sink you, if you let it." Michelle plucked at one of his dreads. "Giving it enough space to expand to its fullest height and breadth and then some more is the only way through to the side where you'll find peace."

"You sound as though you know a thing or two about deep pain." He didn't smile at her, but inside he felt the smile in his heart that was Michelle blooming.

"You're such a good man, Casey. I'm sorry your father has failed you." She caressed his leg and let silence lie between them.

He believed her words, but he couldn't let loose the depth of his loss of beliefs until other matters were resolved. "I called a meeting this morning of my colony. I'd like you to be there, if you're willing." He kept his eyes on the road and waited.

"Of course. I've been smack dab in the middle of all that's been going on in the last few weeks. Is that what the meeting is going to be about?"

"Yes. I'd hoped you would be a part of it." He pulled into his driveway and up to his garage. The others were already inside. He could see they'd made themselves at home in the family room. He wished this gathering were purely social. Last night had been intense and they deserved some down time. However, it wasn't going to happen this afternoon.

In the kitchen, Casey pulled a bottle of water out for himself and passed one to Michelle. They took seats in the circle of chairs and couches in the family room. Casey rolled his shoulders, shifting his morning's confrontation to the back of his mind.

He thanked everyone for their work last night, then continued. "Lara, what do you have to report about the cats? Any troubles with their health?"

"Blood tests show some have a predisposition to respond to the type of drug Carter filled them with. So those with that predisposition exhibit symptoms. Fortunately, we got them out of his project before the enhancements created deformities. Some who don't have the same genetic predisposition have degrees of organ damage. I'm giving them B12 injections to help them get through withdrawals."

"Will they need observation for a while?" Michelle sat on the edge of her seat.

"Yes. Nothing is contagious. They don't have any diseases other than the typical ones homeless cats get." Lara exchanged a pointed look with Casey.

"I know, Lara. We have to work gently with Kennedy. We can't just abandon her nor can we interrogate her. We have to wait to find out her story."

Lara nodded. "Yes, we have to go slowly. She went into shock yesterday and she's recuperating at my house. That's why Asher isn't here. He's keeping an eye on her." She looked out through the expansive windows for a few seconds. "Booker did an exam on her yesterday. She's healthy, but we need more testing."

"That's right. I did just a basic checkup." Booker tapped his fingers on the arm of the couch. "We have no idea at this point what she's been through."

"We're going to have to do a DNA test on her to determine family connection. I need that. I'm sure she will, too," Casey said.

"It makes sense," popped up Booker. "We don't know anything about her. And we surely wouldn't take Carter's words at face value. We can do a sibling test."

"Dr. Booker," quipped Tizzy, using his official title, "how accurate is the sibling DNA test?"

"Typically the test identifies a number of genetic matches between true siblings. For siblings who carry inherited genes not commonly found in the general population, accuracy is better than ninety-nine percent." Booker turned toward Casey. "We wouldn't need your father's cooperation."

"She can stay with me as long as she needs to, but we need a long-term plan, once we know more." Lara pursed her lips. "We could take turns hosting her if that's a better short term solution. We've got to think of what's best for her and the group. We don't have any reason to trust her yet."

Asia nodded. "Yes, we have no concrete proof of her loyalty or state of mind. But I don't feel that means we automatically distrust her."

"That is how we operate and it has kept us safe," Conrad pointed out.

"We seem to have opened our lives to Michelle and her friends without much concern about possible damage." Tizzy tilted her head and arched her brows. The room got suddenly very quiet.

"Different. Casey and I both already knew them. Don't make this about moggy versus pure, Tizzy." Lara shook her head and flashed Tizzy a disgusted look.

"I'm grateful for the trust you've put in me." Michelle's expression and deep blue eyes shined gratitude. "I imagine you relied on your instincts, something you all seem to be skilled at. When you have gathered the information you need about Kennedy, you'll do so again."

"Good point, Michelle." Asia smiled at Michelle, then aimed it at Casey.

"The news is calling Carter's death an accident and Walker is taking the blame for it." Casey glanced down at the floor, trying to control his emotions. A leader of a colony of were-cats does not cry in front of the members, even over the death of another of his kind. Michelle put her hand on his leg and rubbed lightly. "I'll talk with Jackson and probably Sterling and Lacey and take care of Walker. He was involved in the study but he kind of redeemed himself last night."

He glanced around the room and each head nodded in agreement.

"I'll work with Pretid to manage any bad press, just so you know that I'm taking care of that end of the Carter mess." Casey paused, sizing up the feel of the room. "Okay, we've discussed all business. I have one more thing to bring up." He turned his smile to Michelle. "This next agenda item falls under the heading of good news."

"Why are you so smiley?" Michelle asked. She poked him in his arm. "Spill."

"Our resident banker, Conrad, and me, our lawyer, have this to present to you." He stood and pulled Michelle to her feet. She looked up at him, her eyes perplexed. He handed her an envelope. "Open it." He couldn't mask the happiness in voice.

Michelle's eyes widened and her mouth dropped open. The papers in her hands slipped to the floor. "My deed to my house. How did you do that?" Her eyes scanned from Casey to Conrad and back to Casey. She wrapped her arms around his neck and kissed him soundly.

"So, I guess you two are together," quipped Tizzy, a wide smile stretched across her face.

Casey absorbed her joy and peace, so grateful he could get her house back in her hands.

"Hey, do I get a kiss, too?" Conrad sulked. "I did a lot of the work. Turns out Carter's influence doesn't hold up for a judge who's not dirty. I found one of those. The whole mortgage grab and alleged problems with the title search stood on very shaky ground. Without the crooked banker and judge, the whole thing collapsed, as all illegal things should."

"Thank you, Conrad. Thank you, Casey," Michelle said. "Thank you everyone for helping me stand against William Carter. My life will never be the same."

Tears drifted down her cheeks and Casey brushed them away. "Yeah, we make a good team, all of us. You deserve nothing less, sweetheart."

"Aww … aren't they so cute," Tizzy teased. She failed to duck in time to miss the pillow Casey threw at her face.

CHAPTER 19

After the meeting ended and everyone went their separate ways, Casey still had four more people to talk to. Michelle offered to go with him. She sensed exhaustion was taking him over and she wanted to be there for him.

He called Jackson to ask if he and Lacey could stop by. Luckily, since it was Saturday, Ben and Sterling were at Jackson's house, too.

Walking into Jackson's house, Michelle expected to feel a heavy sense of sorrow. It was barely perceptible. Instead, serenity welcomed them in.

"Hi Casey, Michelle. Come on in. It's too chilly to sit in the yard." Lacey motioned them to the couch in the living room. "Jackson will be right here. He's on the phone with his brother."

Ben and Sterling walked in from the kitchen. "You caught us." Sterling licked chocolate frosting off her fingers. "Delicious. Brownies with chocolate icing. Yum."

Michelle listened as Casey chatted about the weather and wrestled with Tyler, Lacey's son, and Joshua, Ben and Sterling's son. The young boys, Tyler eight and Joshua a bit over one, giggled and tried to best Casey.

The homey setting and the truly loving people seemed to lighten Casey's heart.

Michelle smiled to herself, gearing up for a serious talk.

When Jackson walked into the room, Lacey sent her son to play in his room with Joshua.

"Hey, everyone. Sorry about that phone call. Lots of business to take care of with Dad's estate. It's going to be a challenge because there is so much secrecy and protection." He gave a lopsided smile. "It will all work out."

"I'm truly sorry for your loss, Jackson." Michelle's heart dipped.

"Thank you, Michelle." He turned direct, dark brown eyes on her. "I'm sorry for the terrible things my father did to you. I wish I could erase it from ever happening." Jackson turned to walk to a desk across the room and pulled out an envelope. He handed it to her. "You've shared your wishes with your friends and the Cats Alive board for a dream cat rescue facility. From what you've told me, it sounds wonderful. In that envelope is my father's contribution to your new facility."

Michelle's hands trembled as she opened the envelope. The check written for five hundred thousand dollars struck her heart so hard she stopped breathing. "Jackson, I can't take this."

Jackson leaned in close to whisper. "Please. It's the least I can do to pay retribution for my father's terrible acts against you."

"Thank you." For as long as she'd known Jackson, she'd understood how sincere his wishes were to make things right after his father's destruction. "But what's important to me now is that you have support. Your father's death was shockingly brutal and unexpected. A terrible ordeal for you."

"My relationship with my father has always been difficult. When I became aware of who he really was and what he did, our relationship fell apart. I gave him every chance to make different choices and he made his choice. He continued in his illegal ways, rather than clean up his life and be a part of my family. His choices made me sad. Still do. But his death is just the final step in closing our relationship." Jackson rubbed his head and breathed deeply.

"Are the funeral arrangements made?" Casey asked.

"Yes. A private family gathering. I don't want any of the thugs from his company showing up. He's being cremated, so I'll have to decide what to do with his ashes."

Lacey put a hand to his shoulder. "But not today."

Casey nodded. "There are no words to fit the occasion." He drew in a deep breath. "But there are other things to discuss. Don't worry about cleaning up the Pretid study. I'll be able to distance the company and its device from Carter Enterprises. The device will have to start up another study, but it's a good product. There won't be any further problems."

"Unless The Nexus Group gets its hand into things." Jackson frowned.

"Well, there is that possibility. We know so little about them." Casey rolled his shoulders, clearing his head, Michelle suspected.

"Ben, Lacey, and I dropped by the research facility early this morning. Doors wide open, everything cleaned out." Sterling tapped her foot on the carpet. "They wasted no time in clearing out."

"The police didn't find anything. The whole place was wiped clean," Ben added.

"So we just wait and watch?" Lacey asked, her expression troubled.

"We live our lives, waiting and watching, yes." Casey's fingers tapped a slow beat on the couch. "Everything has changed, though. You four know about us, the were-lynxes. We all have had our rugs pulled out from under us in some way. It will take some time to adjust to the changes we've faced."

"Right." Michelle grabbed Casey's hand. "I wouldn't want to go back to not knowing the things I've learned. The bad was very hard, but it brought me into a new awareness and a better life."

"I agree," Lacey said, smiling. "What doesn't kill you makes you stronger."

"What goes around comes around, and in our case, what has come around has brought new friends." Sterling clapped her hand on her knee. "Casey, can you and Michelle stay for dinner?"

Michelle looked up into Casey's glistening eyes and saw an assurance she'd become accustomed to and a sense of adventure, side by side.

"Thanks, but I've got a little more business to attend to tonight."

While the women said their goodbyes at the front door, Jackson walked Ben and Casey outside. From inside, Michelle overheard the conversation. It set her heart singing.

"Casey, just thanks. You're a good friend. Always have been. And thank you, Ben," Jackson said.

Casey wouldn't say anything, but Michelle saw what he saw, the glisten of a tear on Jackson's cheek. He clapped him on the back. "You, too. You too, friend."

Behind the wheel, heading toward Michelle's house, Casey kept quiet. She suspected thoughts churned inside his head, defying being put to rest. So much had happened and so much had been hard. She wondered if they could weather it.

When he pulled into her drive, he turned off the ignition and directed eyes full of questions at her. "Could we just talk here for a bit?"

"Of course."

He dropped his head against the car seat and stared out the window. The evening was young, but the fall nighttime grew dark early as the season progressed. She tried to imagine all the sounds and scents Casey could pick up with his keen, lynx senses.

"Your world must be so amazing." She didn't turn to look at him, but put her hand out to touch his arm.

"It is. Growing up, that was not emphasized at all. Only the danger of living in a world of humans and the need to avoid connections. That's why I've remained reserved with people. It was pounded into me as my duty to keep a distance."

"It makes sense, but it would lead to loneliness, I imagine."

"So lonely. That's what I've been my whole life. But the walls had begun to close in around me. It was so hard to carry deep aloneness around all the time." He continued to stare out into the night, a darkness she knew didn't blind him as it did her. "I had relationships with people, but I saw them doing bad things, things that hurt animals.

Needless destruction to the environment and a general lack of respect for animals and their habitats. I couldn't see my way to find true engagement with such a species."

"That kept you pretty isolated. Your rules and your conflicted emotions." She stared at his silhouette, loving the shape of his broad nose and the cleft in his chin. She didn't know what this was all leading up to, but it was starting to ignite quivers of fear.

He got out of the car and walked around to open her door. He led her to stand in the moonlit night under the stars. Gusts of chilled autumn air lifted her hair and dropped it over her eyes. Gently, Casey brushed the locks aside. He stared down at her with his golden eyes she never tired of, and touched her cheek. "I love you, Michelle. I don't want us to move too fast. I don't want us to miss any steps in forging our relationship. But I mean for it to last a good long lifetime. Would you go steady with me?"

Michelle tried to suppress the laughter bubbling in her throat. She blinked once.

Twice. "What does that mean, go steady with you?"

His fingers in her hair, pulling locks of it up close to breathe it in. "I didn't think I'd get a yes if I asked you to marry me. It's too soon. I opted for going steady. Too silly?"

"No. It sounds perfect. I would love to go steady with you for as long as that's what we want."

She lifted her chin to meet his mouth. His lips came to hers soft and full of promise.

* * *

"Hurry up, bring in those extra chairs. The reception is starting in twenty minutes." Sterling buzzed around the reception hall, making sure everything was in its place and perfect.

"You've done a great job here," said Michelle. "Everything looks lovely."

"It has to. Jackson and Lacey deserve perfect and lovely for their very late wedding reception. I wanted it to be so great it would erase any sadness or regrets that may linger after Jackson's father's death."

"I know it's been two weeks and the reception was already in the works, but you've accomplished what you set out to do, Sterling."

"I had lots of help from these two." Sterling draped her arms around Michelle's parents and beamed. "Two of our favorite friends from way back to Lacey's newspaper reporting days."

"We're happy to be a part of her reception," Norm said, his wife nodding. "She's family."

"Hi, Michelle." Booker walked up to her, hand in hand with a young woman. "I'd like to introduce you to my wife, Shaun."

Michelle reached out a hand and Shaun grabbed it in her own and gave a warm handshake. "It's nice to meet you."

"I'm happy to meet you, too, Michelle. I've been nagging at Booker to introduce us since he told me about you and Casey." The woman's brown eyes glittered to match her pleasant smile.

Michelle nodded. "It's a good day. There's been so much going on I haven't had a chance to get to know you yet, but I look forward to it."

"Me, too." Shaun bubbled with excitement and it dawned on Michelle that the woman could become a good friend.

The couple turned and walked to a table, looking for their nametags.

Michelle smiled to herself. The reception was certainly turning out wonderful.

She turned her attention to her surroundings. The room twinkled with thousands of tiny white lights, draped with swags of ethereal pink fabric around the hall. Centerpieces of silver candelabras draped with pink and white rosebuds and dangling pearl beads decorated the tables. The cake, itself a dazzling centerpiece on the cake table, was six tiers of delicious-looking pink and white frosting covering chocolate and white cake, topped with a bouquet of roses and baby's breath that matched the bouquet Lacey carried on her wedding day at the Justice of the Peace four months ago.

As people began filtering into the hall, Sterling and Michelle directed them to their seats while the orchestra played up on a platform near the dance floor. When it came time to dance after dinner a band would replace the orchestra.

Michelle surveyed the room and the people and took in the wonderful sense of love and celebration that floated around her.

Some minutes later, the emcee announced the couple and toasted to their happiness, then the festivities took off.

The meal was catered by an upscale fine dining restaurant and everyone seemed to enjoy the delicious flavors of stuffed baby artichokes with shrimp for appetizers, a butter lettuce salad with cranberries and Roquefort cheese, and an entrée of herb roasted organic chicken on top of a red bliss potato cake with lemon, blanched garlic, and wilted pea greens.

After the cake was served and guests were settling in their seats to let their meal rest before dancing, Casey shot a strange look at Michelle. He marched to the emcee and took his microphone, then he talked to the band. He walked back to Michelle as the music dropped to a very quiet background sound.

"Ladies and gentlemen, I have something special to say," Casey said. "Don't worry, Jackson and Lacey know all about it and have allowed me to steal the spotlight for just a few moments. I've spoken to your father, too, Michelle."

Michelle's heart raced. She glanced around the room and saw all eyes on her. Casey took her hand and pulled her to stand in front of him. Then he dropped to one knee and set his beautiful eyes on her.

Trembling whispered all through her. Before Casey spoke a word, tears blurred her vision.

"Michelle, I know I said I didn't want to rush into anything. I said I didn't want us to miss any steps in our relationship. But I think the last few weeks we've established something that is working really well. So I asked myself, why wait? I love you more than anything or anyone. I want to spend every day for the rest of our lives with you close. Will you marry me?"

Sobs shaking her shoulders, Michelle pulled him to his feet and whispered for only him. "Why wait indeed?" He stood and looked at her in that way that made her feel as though he saw into her soul. "Yes. I'll marry you."

The room erupted with cheers, but Michelle didn't pay much attention. Casey kissed her and she kissed him back, matching fervor with fervor, and knew her heart couldn't expand any larger than it did in this moment.

"Good job, man." Jackson clapped his hand on Casey's back.

Teary-eyed, Lacey hugged Michelle. "I'm so happy. This is what I've dreamed for you."

Michelle beamed up at Casey. "Me too.

ABOUT THE AUTHOR

After cutting her writing teeth as a feature writer for commercial and trade magazines, a reporter for newspapers and radio, and an executive editor for a communications company, award-winning author Lynn Crandall tuned her voracious appetite for stories to writing contemporary and paranormal romance, women's fiction, and romantic suspense. In her books, she enjoys taking readers on emotional journeys with relatable characters who refuse to back down, and face challenges and tribulations with heart and soul. She believes every love has a story, and hers is with one handsome husband and a large, beautiful circle of family, including her cat Winter. Learn more about her at lynn-crandall.com.

Dancing with Detective Danger
by Lynn Crandall

*E*ven very renowned professional private investigators have a bad day now and then.

At twenty-six-years old, Sterling Aegar knew in her heart that she and her sister qualified as professional PIs and serious career women. Sometimes things simply happen. Not everything can be controlled and unexpected things are bound to occur, she assured herself. Still, she silently surveyed the scene of her latest case and wondered if anything else could go wrong this morning.

The woman's nude body lying submerged in the nearly overflowing tub looked oddly serene. Her eyes seemed almost peaceful and her hair floated like a blond halo around her head.

"Nice doggie," her sister, Lacey Aegar, cooed, but the large German shepherd staring at her continued to growl nastily.

"Look at those teeth!" Though her heart beat emphatically, Sterling barely moved her lips as she spoke under her breath to her sister, not wanting to draw attention from the snarling dog. "Well, sis, what does the private investigator's manual suggest we do at a time like this? I seem to have left mine back at the office."

"As if such a manual exists." Sterling glanced around the marble-floored bathroom, looking for something, anything, to protect herself and her sister from the angry dog. Her gaze paused at the sunken tub adorned with elegant brass fixtures.

Warning flags had gone off inside Sterling's head from the moment she and her sister walked through the opened front door of the pricey condo. Especially attuned to her gut instinct, Sterling always paid attention to its prompting. Sometimes it took time to play out, and following the thread took patience and persistence. Yet a keen awareness and respect for instinct and intuition was something she knew stood her well in many investigations, so she didn't take the uneasy feeling lightly. The warnings this morning seemed to say, *Beware. Something about this new case is not as it seems.* So finding a dead woman in the course of a standard surveillance and infidelity investigation was not only completely unexpected, it confirmed the instinctive suspicion Sterling felt thrumming in her middle.

"Why do these things happen to us?" Sterling spouted softly, bringing her attention back to the threat of the moment—the angry Shepherd standing poised beside the tub.

"Because, sister dear, we are cursed." Lacey appeared quite at ease.

Sterling frowned at her. "Quit teasing. This is serious."

"I'm not teasing. The curse is from Mom's side of the family," she said. "Probably some great-great-great grandfather spit on someone's grave and bingo, generations suffer a curse. Although, the case could be argued today that we're lucky. Mr. Teeth could have attacked us at the front door."

"Lacey!" Sterling hissed. "We've got to do something. We can't stand here all day. That dog is no doubt guarding his beloved mistress, and he doesn't seem to have any sense of humor about us barging in."

"Yeah, poor fella. Do you think he understands that she's dead?"

Sterling rolled her eyes. "Why is it people always feel more compassion for animals than for humans? I mean, the woman is dead, Lacey. And excuse me, I'll wait until later to offer the dog my condolences, if you don't mind."

"Hmm, you've got a good point. Let's just back out of the room."

Sterling swallowed hard, held her breath, and glanced at Lacey. "Okay, now…slowly."

Sterling took one step back simultaneously with Lacey, but the dog leaned menacingly toward them, bared his teeth, and growled a warning.

"Isn't that just like a man," Lacey said. "He doesn't want us to get too close, but he doesn't want us to leave, either."

"Will you quit with the quips?"

"Maybe he doesn't like my outfit."

"Yeah, that's it. He's offended by your clothes," Sterling teased. She rolled her eyes again at Lacey, who was dressed stylishly in a denim micro-mini skirt over black leggings and a simple grey tunic. Several delicate, long silver chains layered under a metallic bohemian scarf completed her look.

"There is nothing wrong with my outfit, little sister," Lacey proclaimed.

"Okay, big sister. It wasn't me who made the suggestion."

"I'm perfectly comfortable with my style of dressing. I'm only thirty years old. I can have fun with my clothes. You should lighten up, too." Lacey slanted her head in Sterling's direction, as though suggesting her sister's clothing choice left something to be desired. "Now, let's concentrate on getting out of here. I'll distract Mr. Teeth and you try to get away."

"Are you nuts? Do you know what teeth like that can do to your skin? I'm not leaving you."

"Right. Well…" Lacey glanced around anxiously. "I'm sure there are plenty of toxic sprays or sharp objects in here somewhere, but I don't hardly dare move, even if I would be willing to hurt him in that way.

"Oh, no, we wouldn't want to hurt the vicious dog. Don't you have something in your purse we could distract him with? Something to eat? You're always munching on something."

"What a brilliant idea!" Slowly, Lacey opened her purse and drew out a bag.

"A sandwich?" Sterling knew she shouldn't be surprised, but the sight of two pieces of bread and some meat coming out of her sister's purse seemed a bit odd even for Lacey. "Okay, you can fling it out the door and down the hall away from us. When he goes after it we'll head out the door. On three, throw it and run."

"On four. You know how I hate odd numbers."

Sterling sighed. "You're such a mess! Okay, on four. One, two, three, four!"

Lacey aimed for the hallway and miraculously, the dog immediately ran after the bait, a limp slowing him a little. Sterling exchanged a quick knowing look with Lacey.

Before the dog had a chance to reconsider, Sterling followed her sister through the front door and down the street to where Lacey's compact car sat parked on the side of the road.

Safely inside the vehicle, Lacey turned to Sterling. "That was fun," she said, a wry smile lifting her lips. "Are you okay?"

"Sure. Are you?"

"As soon as my heart rate slows I'll let you know," Lacey joked.

Sterling's attention landed idly on a robin pecking at blades of new spring grass and she imagined the dog already back beside his owner. Deliberately, she set aside the uneasiness churning in her stomach. She picked up her cellphone from the car seat and punched the numbers for the Laurelwood Police station.

* * *

FROM THE STUCCO-COLORED leather couch and leaded glass coffee table smartly arranged in front of the stone fireplace, to the fine art prints hanging on the walls, the living room of the deceased woman spoke of money -- lots of it. With the insistent barking of the confined German shepherd echoing from another room, Sterling stood watching the plain-clothes officers and detectives working the scene, her thoughts drifting in all directions.

This could have been her life—working a crime scene with fellow police officers. She'd fulfilled her childhood vow to herself to honor her father by following in his footsteps and graduated from the Police Training Institute at the top of her class. With single-minded dedication, she'd picked up the cause: Fighting to keep the city safe from the kind of scum that had killed her father.

Putting in her time as a beat cop on the Laurelwood streets was part of the job, so she'd issued her share of parking tickets and speeding citations. She'd put her all into it right from the start, but always with her sights set on making detective. To some day, as quickly as possible, get knee deep in fighting the bad guys. It was a palpable impatience ramping up her ambition. But it wasn't an ambition solely to make a name for herself or rise through the ranks. Sterling wanted…needed to make a difference in her own way…to ensure innocent people didn't suffer the needless pain that tore at her family after her father's murder. Policing the streets helped calm the inescapable sorrow.

She searched the room for someone who looked in charge and finally landed on one officer. "Excuse me, you've gotten our statement, I'd like to leave."

Pulling up from his scrutiny of an area of the living room, the officer stared for a moment at Sterling, then cleared his throat. "I'm not in charge and we're waiting for the detective who is. He should be arriving soon." The officer turned back to his work, clearly dismissing her.

Back in her corner of the room, Sterling's stomach knotted as her thoughts about her past naturally turned to Ben. Ben Kirby had been a part of all that from the moment they'd met on the job. As an undercover detective on the Drug Task Force, he'd shown her the edge. He didn't merely patrol the city, he prowled it, daring the dealers and runners to make a move. And when they did, he was there to pounce on them without mercy. Ben went after his targets with no thought of a safety net. Get the job done, take down the low-lifes, get them into a cell. Granted, the mid-size, Midwestern town of Laurelwood was not a hotbed of evil, but it did have its share of crime. And Ben didn't give a second thought to laying his life on the line for the sake of justice.

But that was history, she thought with an internal shrug. Sterling drew in a deep breath and checked her wristwatch uneasily as the officers made their way through the evidence collection. Sterling hadn't seen or spoken to Ben in two years, so thoughts of him had no place in her mind, she told herself, letting the hard, familiar ache in her heart bury itself again.

She glanced again at her watch, then over at Lacey who nonchalantly fingered her curly red hair as she stood talking with two of the investigators.

Sterling's agitation was growing, knowing she and her sister had already relayed to the officers the details of finding the dead woman. She felt fidgety, ready to move on, get out of this place. It was prompting thoughts from her past that did no good to rehash.

A detective caught Sterling's eye and walked across the room. "Ms. Aegar, I want to go over this again. You and your sister found the body at eleven a.m., correct?"

Sterling tapped her foot. "Yes, that's correct," she said with forced calm. Patience was not her strong suit, but she didn't care. Pressure inside her was building. The walls were drawing in on her. "Like I said, we're private investigators. We were on an assignment. We rang the doorbell. No one answered." Deliberately, she drew out the words, wondering how many times the simple story needed to be spelled out for this guy.

"So you two just went in anyway."

His tone of voice made her bridle. "I told you, we were on assignment. We rang the doorbell, we knocked, no one answered, and in fact, the door stood slightly ajar. We went in. We looked around. When we walked into the bathroom we found the woman and the dog."

"That's when you saw the body submerged in the bathtub."

"Bingo! I think you're finally getting the picture," Sterling exclaimed. She didn't attempt to hide her impatience.

"You know I could book you on breaking and entering. What kind of an assignment were you working on?"

Sterling squared her shoulders and narrowed her eyes. "You know that's confidential."

"Are you saying you're not willing to cooperate with the police?"

"Is there some point to all of this interrogation?" Sterling hedged, for no other reason than this guy's superior attitude was making her skin crawl. Normally, cooperating with the local law enforcement was SOP, a logical and necessary standard operating procedure. But she was having a bad day and this guy needed to be taken down a notch. "Do you think I'm lying? Maybe you'd like to frisk me to make sure I'm not withholding a murder weapon, or something." She heard footsteps coming up behind her but kept her glare pointed at the officer.

"Don't bluster at the officer, Sterling. He's just doing his job."

The deep voice at her shoulder startled her so intensely her breath froze in her chest, but Sterling squelched her reaction. Deliberately, she turned to face the man. "Hello, Ben. What are you doing here?" She'd forgotten how much taller he stood above her. His dark hair was shorter than two years ago, making his cobalt blue eyes more vivid and his strong jaw more imposing.

"I work investigations now." His smiled reached out effortlessly and grabbed her unwilling heart, but Ben seemed unaware.

"Really? That explains the suit." Sterling turned back to the officer, struggling to keep her voice steady, emotionless, despite the seismic quakes coursing through her body. "Do you have any other questions?"

"Well—"

"We won't be needing you any further right now, Sterling," interrupted Ben, clearly the detective in charge. "But if we need to get in touch with you, where would we find you?"

As if he doesn't know. "Our detective agency's number is in the book." While it was true that Ben hadn't ever actually stepped through her agency's door, if she knew anything at all, she knew he'd kept tabs on her office location if nothing else. That was just the kind of cop he was.

"You and your sister are still in the private investigating business?" Innocence dripped from Ben's richly masculine voice.

"Ben Kirby!" Lacey stepped up and warmly wrapped her arms around him.

"Hi, Lacey."

It was so "Lacey" to walk right up to Ben as though no time had passed and nothing had changed. But Sterling stifled a grin at Ben's obvious discomfort with the display of affection in front of his fellow officers, his arms stiff at his sides. "Ben's working investigations now, Lacey."

"Well, that's good, if it's what you want. It's nice to see you, Ben. It's a wonder we haven't bumped into you before. But, then, Sterling and I don't usually run across dead bodies in the course of our work. Our cases tend to be more like backgrounds and investigating insurance and disability claims and—"

"Ben was just asking about our work," Sterling interrupted. *Leave it to Lacey to lay out all the boring details in the first four seconds.*

"How nice." Lacey shot Sterling a quizzical look.

"And I was just telling him that Aegar Investigating is thriving. So, we better get to the office, Lacey. We have work to do." With one parting look up into Ben's face, Sterling led her sister outside.

"Geez, sis, what was your hurry? Feeling a little uncomfortable? I can see why. Ben looks great. And the electricity between the two of you — wow! It was unmistakable."

Sterling took in a deep breath and slowly let it out, letting her sister ramble on as the two walked to the car. "Don't start with me, Lacey. You know there's nothing between Ben and me."

"Okay, okay. Don't get all edgy. I just think it's interesting that after all this time we run into him." Lacey smiled a whisper of a smile, suggesting she wasn't giving up at all.

"I don't think it's one bit interesting." Sterling climbed into the passenger seat of Lacey's car and deliberately avoided looking at the condo as her sister started the engine. "What is interesting is the fact that we stumbled into a murder scene. It's the first really exciting case we've come across in a long time."

"Work. That's all you want to talk about." Lacey rolled her eyes. "It's in the hands of the police, now."

"I suppose you're right." Sterling sighed. "It doesn't hurt to wish, does it?"

"I know you miss police work. You can't help but resonate with the thrill of the edge. It's in your blood." Lacey eyed Sterling with sisterly understanding.

"I don't miss police work." Sterling was quick to stomp on the suggestion. "I just wish for a little more action at our agency. A little more of righting wrongs. Sometimes it's not a clear line between the good guys and the bad guys with what we often do. I wish—"

"Listen, if you're going to wish for something, make it for something good and definitely doable, like a white chocolate café mocha, Venti. Mmm...I can taste it now."

Sterling shook her head. "You really know how to dream big."

* * *

BEN STOOD behind the richly embroidered slate-colored drapes at the condo's living room window and discreetly watched Sterling walk to the car as he shuffled paperwork through his fingers. Her petite frame, dressed in a slim gray suit, pulled his attention as though he had no control.

That's the way it was with her. He hadn't seen her for two years, but all during that time he'd been unable to will her out of his thoughts for very long. Seeing her up close and feeling her presence stirred up old feelings inside him. During the time they'd been together, the terrible aloneness he'd grown to live with had vanished. It hadn't mattered that before she came along he'd had no one, no family, because she'd completely filled the emptiness in his gut. Then when she left, he'd felt all the more alone for having known but lost her.

Sterling's straight, chestnut-colored hair had grown longer, brushing gently against her slim shoulders. He liked it. And the two years apart had worn beautifully on her fine-boned face. She looked even lovelier than he remembered. In the brief moments he'd stood next to her, he'd taken in everything: her shapely curves; her intense, blue-green eyes; her sensuously curved lips the color of a rich Merlot.

Ben's stomach tightened. It had to happen sooner or later, he thought to himself. Even though Sterling had left his life, it seemed inevitable that they'd run into each other sometime while working a case. He'd like to think it meant their destinies were intimately inter-twined. That even though their paths might occasionally diverge and meander, they were actually headed in the same direction. She'd been emphatic at their breakup that there was no future for the two of them, he just didn't believe it. He believed in possibilities, and though in the interim he'd given Sterling her space, the hope remained strong in him that eventually, along the way they would come together again, perhaps even stronger than before.

Ben watched Sterling drive away and couldn't help himself. Was it too much to hope maybe this time it could be different?

"Ben, you've got to look at this," called one of the officers. "It looks like the PIs who just left have a connection to the deceased.

ALSO BY LYNN CRANDALL

Love in Dunes Bay Series

Then There Was You

Meant To Be You

Could It Be You

Aegar Investigations Series

Dancing with Detective Danger

Always and Forever Love

Fierce Hearts Series

Cravings

Heartfelt

Probabilities

Unstoppable

Finding Finn

Snowbound

Two Days Until Midnight

Captured by Christmas

Nutcracker Sweet

Dark Sides Series

Touch Me

Hear Me

See Me

Writing as Kelynn Storm

Touch of Breeze: The Common Elements Romance Project

Love Between Universes: An Out of this World Christmas